MW01612384

A DIFFERENT SIN

By

Rochelle H. Schwab

Los Hombres Press

A Different Sin

All rights reserved. No part of this book may be reproduced or transmitted in any manner whatsoever without written permission except in the case of brief passages quoted in reviews. For further information, write Los Hombres Press, Box 632729, San Diego, CA 92163-2729.

Cover by Glen Vecchione

Library of Congress Cataloging in Publication Data 92-077821
A Different Sin
ISBN 1-879603-08-X

Printed in the United States of America

Copyright © 1993 by Rochelle H. Schwab

First Edition

1 2 3 4 5 6 7 8 9 10

Los Hombres Press
Box 632729
San Diego, CA 92163-2729

Chapter One - 1854

THE THUD OF THE GAVEL RELEASED THE COURTROOM SPECTATORS from silence. Voices rose in a babble of argument, approbation and anguish: assured, broad-voweled Brahmin accents, loud Irish brogues, the softly slurred tones of blacks who'd found Boston a tenuous refuge and gazed at the manacled defendant with helpless fellow feeling. Not, David thought, that the proceedings could be termed a trial. The Fugitive Slave Law empowered United States commissioners to rule a man a fugitive solely on his alleged owner's affidavit, with no testimony on his own behalf.

From his seat in the third row of newsmen, David Carter stared over the heads in front of him at the parade of witnesses called by the accused fugitive's attorneys to testify that the apprehension of Anthony Burns was a case of mistaken identity: the one possible defense. Burns' volunteer attorney, the renowned Richard Henry Dana, proceeded with an assurance matched by that of Robert Morris, his young colored assistant. David's thoughts strayed from the hearing as he studied the dapper, colored lawyer, admiring his poise in front of the crowded courtroom.

He's a hell of a lot more comfortable up there than I'd be, David admitted to himself. Wonder how the hell he got to be a lawyer? Couldn't have been easy for a Nigra, even up here in Boston. Though Mike managed to become a doctor. Done a damn sight more with his life than I have despite Dad's insistence on putting me through university.

David wrenched his attention back to the efforts of the two attorneys to prove Burns' arrest an error. It seemed damned unlikely

1

they'd succeed. He studied the accused fugitive. Burns' face was an ebony mask, his apprehension betrayed by the drops of sweat beading his forehead, his quick sidelong glances at Colonel Charles Suttle, who'd journeyed from Virginia to claim him as his property. The manacles clanked as he shifted position. Why in hell couldn't Suttle accept a fair price for Burns from the abolitionists, instead of dragging him back to slavery? David wondered. Though he supposed the irate slaveowner wanted to make an example of him. David felt a quick rush of sympathy for the runaway.

There wasn't a damn thing *he* could do though. Anymore than he'd been able to help when Mike, his own half brother, had been carried back to slavery under the provisions of the Fugitive Slave Law three years earlier. David glanced at his scribbled notes, hoping he could make enough sense of them to wire a coherent report. It was as an illustrator he hoped to establish himself, not a reporter. But his costly wire to the editor of his hometown paper had brought him only a request to forward an account of the trial. At least the *Gazette's* return telegram had gained him admittance to the courtroom. He could do a quick sketch or two during the recess. He turned his pad to a clean page and set to work.

He drew the courtroom scene, then did a rough outline of Burns' figure before stopping to massage his cramped fingers. He stood and moved toward the aisle to stretch, muttering apologies as he climbed over the feet of scribbling newsmen.

"It's a long sit in such cramped quarters, isn't it, but not half as long I daresay as for that poor devil chained up there." David turned at the words of the man standing in the aisle beside him. The other man waved his hand in the direction of the manacled fugitive, then offered it to David in a handshake. "I'm Zachary Walker, with the *New York Tribune*. Which paper do you write for?"

"*Alexandria Gazette*. Alexandria, Virginia." No point in explaining further.

Walker withdrew his hand, an expression of apparent distaste crossing his goodhumored face. "Virginia, eh. I suppose it'll be glad to see this poor fellow dragged back into slavery then."

"Hardly, sir," David said. These damn abolitionists were all alike—tarred all Southerners with the same brush. "I have a half brother who's colored, who was taken as a fugitive three years ago. I've some idea what Burns is going through."

Walker's eyebrows rose, two bushy white question marks under a high, ruddy forehead. Dammit, David wondered, what had made him blurt out his family's private affairs? The bailiff's cry ended the recess.

David returned to his seat with relief, thankful to be spared further embarrassment.

Michael peered down the tracks at the approaching train, turned to David. "I wish you'd stay longer. You've hardly been here two weeks."

"Dad'll be with you, though. And I'd like to show these to the editor of the *National Era*." David tapped the portfolio of sketches he'd done: of Burns' hearing and of the contingent of troops that had marched the fugitive to the Virginia-bound revenue cutter the day before. "I'm hoping he'll want to run some of them."

"They're good drawings," Michael assured him. "But it hasn't been much of a visit, has it? I haven't been able to think of anything but trying to rescue Burns—" He raised his voice over the noise of the locomotive. "Don't wait another three years to come back, hear?"

David nodded. He could hardly tell his half brother that his infrequent visits to Boston, undertaken only at his father's urging, made him feel even more inadequate than usual. His own poor showing as a lawyer, too unsuccessful in his halfhearted practice to move from under his father's roof, was galling enough, without seeing Michael's success at overcoming the handicap of color to become a physician. "I won't, Mike," David said, holding out his hand.

He sank into a window seat on the train and slipped a sketch he'd done of Burns from his portfolio. Crossing his legs at the knee, he propped up the drawing, studying it thoughtfully, his pencil held loosely in his fingers.

"Poor devil was scared to death, wasn't he? I see you've caught the way he couldn't take his eyes off his master's face. You do good work."

Startled, David turned toward the man who'd just dropped into the adjacent seat, then winced inwardly as he recognized the *Tribune* reporter who'd accosted him at the hearing. "Thank you, sir," he said.

"Zachary Walker. We spoke at the so-called trial. I never did get your name."

"Yes, I remember. I'm David Carter."

Walker held out his hand once again, enveloped David's fingers in his firm grip. "You piqued my interest with your remark about your colored half brother. I'd like to hear more of the story."

David silently berated himself for shooting off his mouth at the hearing. He studied the reporter a minute. Walker appeared some five years past his own age of forty, though the whiskers wreathing his full face were nearly white, as was his crown of wavy hair. His gaze pinned David with eager interest "There's not that much to tell," David demurred.

Walker's eyebrows rose as they had at the hearing. "I shouldn't think it's an everyday occurrence."

"It's not that uncommon." David flushed, feeling the heat spread downwards. He tugged awkwardly at his stiff collar, loosening his cravat. "My father owned Hetty, that's Mike's mother, and he, well, he bedded her. I understand my mother was an invalid at the time. Mike's a year younger than me."

"You call him your half brother. I gather your father owned up to it then?"

David sighed. "He was far too ashamed to admit he'd fathered Mike, though any of the town gossips could've told you. I know Mike knew. His mother died when he was a boy, but I'm certain she told him before she passed on.

"I suppose Dad might've sold Hetty and Mike out of consideration for my mother's feelings, but Mother succumbed to her illness shortly after Mike was born. I've no memory of her at all. So Dad held on to Hetty. She was a well-trained housekeeper; it was the easiest course. I doubt he ever bedded her again."

"And the boy?"

David sighed again, seeing the unslaked curiosity on the other man's face. "Well, of course Dad kept him too. He's not the sort of man to have sold a child away from his mother. Mike and I played together when we were boys." He smiled slightly, remembering. "Once I'd started school, of course, our ways parted."

Walker frowned in thought. "Your father never gave him any schooling? Even though he was his son?"

"He couldn't have, not without sending him up North. And it was his belief that Nigras were better off not trying to shift for themselves. He was doing his best by Mike as he saw it.

"Mike managed to learn on his own though—talked other boys into teaching him his letters, then read everything he could get his hands on. Dad's retired now, but he practiced medicine most of his life. He used to have Mike help out in his office. Mike got it into his head that he could become a doctor himself if he could get his freedom. You could see Dad was secretly proud of how bright he was. But as I said, he felt the colored were better off in slavery. So he told him it was out of the question."

"So Mike ran off from your father then?"

"Not then. He was only thirteen or fourteen at the time. But he started sassing Dad more and more. Of course Dad resented his attitude. They used to have words fairly often, as I remember.

"Finally, Mike defied some order Dad gave him. I'm not sure what. I was away at university by then. But Dad felt he'd completely lost control of him and sold him to one of the slave traders in town. Luckily for Mike, he managed to escape from the trader and make his way up North."

David stopped, uncomfortably aware of the shock and outrage spreading across Walker's face. "I couldn't understand it either—how Dad could sell his own flesh and blood. It wasn't like him to do a thing like that. But he lost his temper and acted before he came to his senses.

"He regretted it afterwards. He spent years fretting over Mike. I know he missed him—even if he never said it in so many words." David stopped, feeling the onslaught of a headache. He leaned back and rubbed his forehead.

"Are you all right, Mr. Carter?" David was surprised at the concern in the other man's voice.

"I'm fine, sir. I suffered a head injury a few years ago. I've been prone to headaches since. I think the motion of the train is bringing this one on."

Walker smiled. "I feared I'd pressed you too hard with my confounded curiosity." He reached into his coat pocket for a flask. "A swallow of this may help."

"Whiskey makes it worse, I'm afraid." David smiled regretfully, watching Walker take a swig.

"I don't mean to press you, if you're not up to conversing."

David turned his head, meeting Walker's eyes. Reluctantly he smiled at the almost childlike disappointment on the bearded man's face. "I don't mind talking, Mr. Walker."

Walker beamed. "You said he was recaptured. I've covered most of the fugitive cases for the *Tribune* since the passage of the Fugitive Slave Law. I don't recall a runaway by the name of Carter."

"Mike took a new last name after he escaped: Mabaya. He claims it was the name of some African ancestor. Anyway, he was right about what he could accomplish. He found a medical school in New England willing to accept colored students. He's practicing in Boston now.

"We'd still have no idea where he was if Dad hadn't been leafing through a medical journal. He stumbled on a letter to the editor taking exception to a paper that Mike and another doctor—a Hebrew friend of his—were about to give at the medical society there. When Dad saw the name, Michael C. Mabaya, together with the information that he was a colored man, he dropped everything and went running up to Boston to see if it could possibly be Mike."

"And saw that it was, I take it." Walker beamed again. "I remember the case now. Just a few months after the passage of the Fugitive Slave Law in 1850, if memory serves. How could your father have brought himself to drag him back to slavery?"

"He didn't. Dad was delighted to see him doing so well—a lot happier than Mike was to see him. He came home intending to buy Mike back from the trading company so he could free him legally. My mother's brother—my Uncle James—dropped by that evening, and Dad told us both of his intention. He couldn't stop talking about Mike all evening, in fact."

"Well, then?"

"Well, sir, what Dad and I didn't know was that my uncle had purchased Mike as a speculation, years before—a few months after he ran off. The slave traders were willing to sell him dirt cheap, since there was no guarantee he'd be found.

"Of course, he'd long since given up hope of tracking Mike down. But when Dad told us his news, Uncle James telegraphed Boston and had him apprehended. Dad and I knew nothing about it till it was a *fait accompli*."

Walker nodded. "I see. Didn't your uncle have him jailed once he got him back to Virginia?"

"I'm afraid so. Uncle James refused to accept funds from the abolitionists to buy Mike's freedom. He wasn't interested in money; he's well off. But he had the notion that Mike's birth killed my mother—that Mother lost her will to live rather than be shamed by having her husband's nigger bastard under her roof. So he was seeking revenge on Dad as well as Mike.

"You've no idea what he put my father through. Dad walked the floor night after night, blaming himself for Mike's predicament. It was a terrible strain on his health. I've never been able to forgive my uncle for that.

"I tried reasoning with Uncle James. But he wouldn't speak to me because of a sketch I'd done at the hearing—of Mike holding his little girl after the commissioner ruled him a fugitive. She was terribly distressed. She's very attached to her father."

Walker nodded again. "I remember your drawing. A very affecting piece of work. It circulated as a broadsheet, as I recall. But I take it your uncle finally relented?"

"Yeah, finally." No need to elaborate further. "He sold Mike back to Dad, who freed him immediately."

"And your father acknowledges him as his son now?"

"Now you'd think he'd never wanted anything more than a colored family. I think he spends more time in Boston than he does at home. Well, Mike and Rachel's kids are his only grandchildren. And he always hoped to see his son follow in his footsteps," David added, after a pause.

"Your inclinations didn't lie that way, I take it?"

"I'm afraid not. Fact is, just the sight of a cut finger leaves me queasy."

Walker laughed. "If I'd followed my father's wishes, I'd have spent my days hunched in the back of a tailor's shop. I daresay you're like me in finding a correspondent's life more to your liking."

David smiled. "I'm not a newsman either. I was reporting on the trial as a favor to the *Gazette's* publisher, since I chanced to be on the scene. I'm just an artist, actually." He flushed, embarrassed to have made the claim.

"And a good one, it would seem. May I?" Walker reached for the portfolio before David could respond, nodded appreciatively as he thumbed through it. "You're fortunate if you've found work as an illustrator. There's not much demand for artists, more's the pity."

David flushed again. "I work as a freelancer. I'm hoping the editor of the *National Era* will print these."

"I know how that goes." Walker gave another laugh. "I freelanced for two years before I landed a job on the *Tribune*. Not much of a way to keep body and soul together, is it?"

"I'm afraid you're right. I've had only a handful of sketches printed, to be honest."

"How do you make your living then, if I might ask?"

"I have a small law practice. And I live simply. I'm a bachelor, so I share expenses with my father. It works out well for both of us."

"I wouldn't have taken you for a solicitor," Walker said thoughtfully.

David shifted uncomfortably, his legs cramped by the seat ahead. "I'm not much of one," he admitted. "I took up law to please my father. I'm afraid I'm ill-suited to it." He stopped, astonished to find himself blurting out still more of his private affairs to a stranger. Glancing at the other man, he noted his expression of sympathetic interest. He hesitated, then continued.

"I've always had the urge to capture what I saw on paper. When I was a boy, I dreamed of becoming an artist. Then as I grew older, I listened to reason and gave up the notion."

"And now?"

"Now, if it's not too late, I'd like to pursue it again." David searched for words. "I told you I'd been injured a few years ago. I came within a hairsbreadth of dying. It made me realize how little I had to show for my life. I don't want to live out my remaining years as nothing but a failed solicitor.

"I don't know if I've any real talent as an artist, but it's the only thing I've ever cared about." He smiled ruefully. "Determining to pursue it hasn't done me much good though. As you said, sir, there's little demand for artists."

7

"We come to a parting of the ways, Mr. Carter. I've enjoyed our conversation."

David nodded, acutely aware of how much he'd revealed to Walker over the past hours, relieved they'd be parting once the cars pulled into New York. He checked his belongings at the conductor's call, eager to catch the ferry to the Washington-bound train.

"I wish you luck in placing those. They should be seen." Walker nodded toward David's portfolio. A thought struck him. "Matter of fact, I may be able to assist you. Greeley's run an occasional woodcut if it can make a point plainer than words. If you'll entrust me with a sketch or two, it's not unlikely he'd reproduce them in the *Tribune* while the case is fresh in the public mind."

The thought of further contact filled David with renewed embarrassment. He shoved it aside. "That's very kind of you, Mr. Walker."

The newsman beamed. "Not at all. Greeley's staunchly opposed to planting slavery on free soil. If I know the man, he'll be delighted to best our competition with an eyewitness depiction of the cruelty of this damned Fugitive law."

"I'm still much obliged to you, sir," David said, leafing through the portfolio for his most telling sketches.

David set his coffee cup in its saucer with a muted porcelain click and looked up from his plate of eggs and grits. His father sat in his accustomed place across the dining room table, as they'd sat together since David's boyhood, with the exception only of the four years he'd spent attending university in Charlottesville. Displaying little weariness from his two day journey home, Dr. George Carter sat erect, with a vigor that belied his nearly seventy years, his back barely resting against his chair, his iron gray hair and firm features lit by morning sun that streamed through the archway from the parlor windows.

"I've missed your company the past few weeks," David admitted to him.

His father smiled. "It's too bad you insisted on cutting short your visit. Things settled down after you left." For an instant his face was shadowed. Burns' capture had stunned Boston Negroes. Like the rest, Mike, Rachel and their oldest youngsters, Peter and Abigail, had plunged into a frenzy of anguished protest and futile rescue attempts, that had been—David guessed—a bitter reminder to his father of how he'd inadvertently caused his own son's recapture. The instant passed, the memory was set aside. "Reverend Grimes is heading a drive to buy Burns' freedom, and he has a good part of the funds in hand already," the doctor continued.

David nodded, eager to share his own news with his father. His sketch of Burns as he was marched to the wharf under heavy guard, through streets draped in black bunting, had appeared in the *Tribune* a week earlier—in the weekly digest edition with its nation-wide circulation. *Tribune* editor Horace Greeley had run the drawing as an editorial cartoon, captioned, "Amid cries of Shame, Slavery chains the Cradle of Liberty in its Shackles."

"Their engraver didn't do much of a job of copying it," David said, frowning at the reproduction. "But at least it's in the *Tribune*." He passed his father the newspaper, its pages creased open in a permanent fold.

George Carter glanced at the illustration. "Yes, I know. I saw a copy while I was with Michael and Rachel. They were all proud of you for getting a picture published in the *Tribune*," he said, producing a smile.

"Did I mention that Grimes organized a concert at his church to raise proceeds for Burns? Abigail had a short solo. She has a lovely voice for a youngster. She's been singing with the Garrison Juvenile Choir, you know. She takes it very seriously; she's already learned to read music." He beamed across the table with a grandfather's pride.

"Dear Mr. Walker—" David paused, dipped his goose quill into the inkwell, then sighed and laid it down. Abruptly, he stood, wincing as his chair thudded into the wall of the cramped cubicle he rented for his law office. He stood a moment at the open window, hoping for a breeze, gazing desultorily down at wagons clattering along the cobblestone alley below him. The warm, humid air was as heavy as the atmosphere indoors, plastering down the locks of hair that had fallen across his forehead. Sighing again, he shoved his hair back and sat down to finish the letter.

Walker's letter had arrived with disconcerting promptness in response to his own note of thanks for the newsman's help in publishing his sketch. "I do hope to keep up our correspondence," he'd written David. "Letter writing is one of my great enthusiasms.

"Have been much occupied since our meeting with reporting the protests of right-thinking men against the extension of slavery into the Kansas-Nebraska territories by that devil, Sen. Douglas. It was a black day for our nation when his bill was passed into law by the traitors of the Senate. Greeley has hauled down the Stars and Stripes from its rooftop staff; the glory has gone out of them."

There seemed little to write in reply. Other than agreeing once again to paint the scenery for the fall production of the Alexandria Dramatic Association, there was little of interest in David's life.

He pushed the letter aside and reached into the desk drawer for the plans he'd drawn to scale of the stage area. Within moments, he was engrossed with sketching in the main elements of the scene design.

A Different Sin

The thud of footsteps on the stairs recalled him from his preoccupation. Hurriedly he began to return his sketches to the drawer before the arrival of a possible client, then relaxed as Tom Miller, the proprietor of the downstairs bakeshop, entered.

"Dotty saved you a few of the gingersnaps we baked yesterday." Tom placed a small sack of cookies on David's desk. "She remembered they're your favorites." David smiled his thanks. "She never stops trying to fatten me up."

Tom laughed. "You're in no danger of growing stout. Dotty has more luck with me; I reckon I've put on a few pounds since our wedding." He looked down at his expanse of stomach, chuckling comfortably. "You doing the scenery for the theatrical again?" he asked, waving at David's sketch.

David nodded. "I got a little ahead on my work, so I thought I'd spend a few minutes looking these over." It was a pointless pretense. He'd been acquainted with Tom since they'd been boys together. Tom knew as well as David that he'd precious little law work to keep him from the scene designs.

"I always enjoy your scenery. We'll be looking forward to the show." Tom stopped, at a loss for further conversation. "Well, Dotty'll be cross if I let my lunch grow cold." His footsteps pounded down the stairs.

David pulled the sketches toward him as Tom left, then stopped, wearying of his efforts. Putting the scene designs back in the drawer, he picked up his pen and returned to his letter to Walker.

"We share a common enthusiasm, it would seem," Walker responded. "Some of my happiest hours have been passed in the theatre. In fact, I've trod the boards myself from time to time in amateur theatricals— though I must admit, in most minor roles."

David smiled and leaned back in the wing chair. The oil lamp cast its circle of light on Walker's letter, which had been awaiting him on the hall table. The stillness in the room was broken only by the rustling of the paper. His father had retired for the night, probably hours before David had parted company from Doug and Phil, his assistants at scene painting. They'd had an extra glass of ale apiece at Gadsby's Tavern to celebrate finishing the scenery.

He returned to the letter, turning the page with fingers still showing faint streaks of paint. "Have had little time for such pleasures of late. Our struggle against the extension of slavery into the Northwest Territories continues despite the setback of this wicked law. Greeley is determined to keep up the fight for Free Soil.

"It's occurred to me that you are bound to have first-hand knowledge of the evils of slavery, situated as you are in a slave-holding state. Any illustrations you can forward to the *Tribune* will be of immense value in bringing home to our readers the cruelties of human bondage during the coming political struggle."

David set down the letter, frowning in dismay. Despite the abolitionists' trumpetings of the horrors of slavery, he'd seen little evidence of such cruelty himself. There were occasional separations of families in the slave trading establishments lining Duke Street, when circumstances made a sale of household servants unavoidable. But for the most part, his neighbors treated their Nigras with consideration.

He leaned back, suddenly tired, rubbing his forehead to forestall the beginnings of a headache. Most of the slaves he saw seemed contented enough to him. And certainly the large numbers of free colored in town bore evidence of the indulgence of their former owners.

Just look at Mike's old friend, Ned. In the hours his master had allowed him to work on his own behalf, he'd managed to buy his way out of slavery. In the years since, he'd not only succeeded in helping the rest of his family purchase their freedom, but was prospering in the carpentry shop he'd opened on South Royal Street.

David rose, extinguished the lamp, then froze as another memory surfaced. He stood a moment as remembered images filled his mind, alive before him in the darkened room, then hurried up the stairs to his bedchamber.

The blanket chest at the foot of his bed was crammed with sketches he'd saved over the years. It took several minutes to find the one he had in mind. He moved across the room, studying the drawing critically in the light of the lamp on the bureau. He'd been just seventeen when he drew it, but it was better than anything else he'd done as a boy.

He hadn't signed it when he'd done the drawing. David inscribed his name at the bottom now. He'd write Walker in the morning and enclose the sketch with his letter.

Chapter Two - 1854

THE THEATER PIT HAD BEEN CONVERTED TO A BALLROOM to celebrate the success of the fall theatrical. Jubilant actors, their faces still greasy with hastily removed makeup, accepted congratulations from the enthusiastic audience. Taffeta gowns rustled as party-goers greeted one another, admiring the production in high-pitched, honeyed tones. "The show never would've been such a success without your scenery! We've raised a record amount for the poor," Martha Ann Simpson gushed as David took her arm.

David smiled. "We'd probably never get set to put on a show at all, if you didn't manage the Dramatic Association so well."

Martha Ann beamed, her face and neck rosy with pleasure over the low neckline of her blue satin gown.

David was at a loss for further conversation, as he seemed to be whenever he found himself escorting Martha Ann. "Would you like a cup of punch?" he offered at last, making his way gratefully to the refreshment line.

Mrs. Taylor, widow of the Association's founder, presided over the punch bowl, where a colored servant was filling glasses from the commodious, cut glass bowl. "You and Martha Ann make a handsome couple, David," she said.

David glanced in bewilderment at Martha Ann as he threaded his way across a floor crowded by women's fashionably full hoop skirts. Martha Ann's soft curves swelled her lace-trimmed bodice. Her thick brown hair billowed into a loose bun caught up with flowers. Her small, shapely figure was a study in contrast to his own slender frame and height—nearly six feet when he remembered to stand up straight.

He smiled down at her as he handed her the punch, then sat listening to her earnest chatter as they drank, grateful to have little to do but nod. With a corner of his mind, he wondered why Mrs. Taylor thought they made such a well-matched pair.

"You're off to Nell's again?" Dr. Carter demanded from his wing chair.

David nodded shortly, flushing. He grasped the doorknob, shifting his weight uneasily as he awaited the rest of his father's words. Traffic clattered on the cobblestones outside; from the kitchen came the faint notes of a spiritual as their colored housekeeper did the washing up.

George Carter sighed. "David, you're not a boy. It's past time you gave up these visits to whorehouses and settled down. Have you given thought to the kind of diseases you're courting by bedding prostitutes?"

"Nell runs a clean house," David mumbled.

"That may be." His father turned to look David in the face. "But you'd be far better off to marry and settle down. You're not a boy," he repeated.

"Well, I know that," David snapped, wishing his father's scrutiny didn't leave him feeling self-conscious as a boy. He tried to smile. "I guess I'm just an old bachelor, Dad. I doubt I could find a woman who'd have me, anyway."

"You're not that old. You're still a fine looking man." George Carter looked at David fondly. "Martha Ann Simpson would marry you in a minute."

"Martha Ann?" David stared his surprise. "I scarcely know her. I never even know what to say to her."

"You've known her all your life, David." The older man's voice quickened with exasperation. "You could do a lot worse for yourself too. Martha Ann's a fine girl. It's not as if she hasn't had offers to marry, you know. She'd have been wed long ago if she hadn't felt it her duty to nurse her mother after she took to her bed."

David shifted his weight again, hoping his father would return to his reading. George Carter sat up straighter, set down his newspaper as he focused his attention on his son. David sighed. "Dad, you know I don't earn enough to keep a wife," he said finally, in a low voice.

"There's no reason why you still can't make a success of your profession if you'd just put forth a little effort, son. But in any case, Martha Ann has money of her own, now that her mother's passed on at last."

For a moment, David tried and failed to imagine a life with Martha Ann. Why was everyone so set on marrying him off? "Dad, I'm happy as I am." He shoved open the door, nearly stumbling over the sill as he made his escape.

13

A Different Sin

He frowned in dismay as he entered Nell's softly lit front parlor and saw two customers waiting their turns. "Evening there, David," tavern keeper Pete Smith boomed out in greeting. David nodded stiffly and crossed to the far side of the room.

Sinking onto the plush couch, he stared down at his hands, abashed at making such public display of his private needs. The sound of a woman's high laughter drifted down the stairs. Pete nudged his companion in the ribs; both men guffawed before returning to their talk. David glanced at the other men, wondering how they could banter with such apparent lack of embarrassment.

His own awkwardness had diminished but little since his first visit to a bawdy house, as a university freshman. He'd agreed, shyly but eagerly, to accompany John Eustis, who occupied the room next to his and was as close to a friend as he'd come to making there. He'd stood uncomfortably in the red plush parlor, admiring the ease of John's manner, the way his thick, chestnut hair brushed his neck as he tossed his head back in laughter, the proud set of his muscular shoulders...

Two of Nell's boarders sashayed into the parlor, giggling and beckoning, causing David to start from his reverie. Pete grinned as he rose, then halted halfway out of the room, addressing David over his shoulder. "Say, Nat and me are fixin' to do some business together. How's about you drawing us up an agreement Monday?"

"Be glad to, Pete." He watched in relief as the two men headed upstairs.

Nell's third boarder, Lucy, signaled him to accompany her to the familiar bedroom. He fumbled clumsily with the buttons of his pants. For an unaccountable moment his desire ebbed, the swelling of his organ that had left him flushed with embarrassment in the downstairs parlor diminished. Then his mind veered again to that first time, once again seeing John drape an arm around the giggling bawd he'd selected, the hairs glinting on the back of his hand, his stance easy with lusty masculine assurance, and his urgency returned.

Lucy spreadeagled herself on the bed, her masses of brown hair falling across her full breasts. She hid a yawn with her hand before pulling David atop her. He closed his eyes and thrust with steady, intent strokes till the dammed up tension burst from his body.

For a moment he lay limply. Lucy gave another delicate yawn beside him. David rose, shoving his legs into his trousers.

Lucy produced a smile. "Reckon I'll be seein' you in a couple of weeks, honey."

David nodded reluctantly, mumbling his farewell under his breath as he hurried from the room.

A Different Sin

Monday afternoon dragged by, the tedium of his practice more apparent after a day of leisure. David read over the agreement he'd drawn up for Pete and Nat, then slipped it into his drawer to await their signatures. He'd told Mr. McPherson he'd have the latest revision of his will ready that afternoon. Setting a clean sheet of paper alongside the old document, he dipped his quill into the inkwell, sighing unconsciously as he set to work.

Tom's footsteps sounded heavily on the stairs. David looked up to greet him, glad of a few minutes diversion, then started at the fury on Tom's face.

"What the hell do you think you're doing, David!?"

He shook his head, bewildered. Tom covered the distance to his desk in two strides, shoving David's papers to the floor as he thrust the newspaper he carried in front of him.

"Don't play dumb! That's your signature, dammit!" Slowly David nodded. "I didn't realize it had been printed. I haven't picked up my mail today."

He studied the reproduction in silence. The *Tribune* artist had done a better job of copying this drawing. The lines of the seated Negro youth were clearly etched, his shoulders bowed, head resting on one arm. His other arm lay outstretched across the table in front of him, fingers tightened into a fist. Across the tensed muscles of his bare back were the numerous slashes of barely healed whip marks.

"How Southerners Lead Slaves to Civilization: the Penalty for Reading and Writing." Tom spat out the words of the caption as if they dirtied his mouth. "What kind of lies are you trying to spread?"

David looked back at Tom. "It's no lie. That's Mike. He was caught giving lessons to Ned and Titus, and the magistrate sentenced all three of them to thirty-nine lashes. I would've thought you'd remember."

David looked at the picture again, remembering it himself as if it were just happening. The sudden growl of voices downstairs. "Gotta search all the Nigra quarters in town. Can't take any chance of another Nat Turner here!" Then the sounds of blows and curses as Mike and his friends were dragged off to jail, the geography book they'd been unable to hide in time carried along as triumphal evidence.

He didn't think about Mike much at school the next day. How much trouble could he get into just for looking at a book, even if Nigras weren't supposed to get together anymore? He had his own troubles with this new Latin master.

His mind was still on the stupidity of studying Latin as he walked home, mumbling good afternoon to old Mr. Cunningham, out for his daily walk.

"Afternoon yourself, David." The old man planted himself in David's path. "So that uppity nigger of your father's been taken down a peg or two."

David stared at him. "How do you mean, sir?"

The old man chuckled, thumping his cane. "Got what he deserved, that's how. Magistrate had him whipped good and proper. I reckon he'll know his place a little better from now on."

He rushed past Mr. Cunningham and burst through his front door. His father was home, slumped in his wing chair, his head buried in his hands. David hesitated, staring at him a second, then hurried down the hall to the kitchen. The door to Mike's lean-to of a room was shut.

"Mike?"

"Leave him be now, Mista David." Aunt Sary, their colored housekeeper, spoke in a near whisper. "He be hurt bad. Your daddy done doctored him up, but sleep be the best medicine for him now."

David nodded, staring at Aunt Sary's sorrowful face, then slowly crossed the kitchen and pushed the door open as quietly as he could.

Mike lay face down on his pallet, moaning in his sleep, his bare back covered with broad gashes that still oozed blood even through the ointment slathered on them.

"Jesus Christ!" David stood staring in disbelief, sickness rising within him. Seconds went by before he could turn and bolt from the room. He reached the backyard privy just as the sickness spewed from him, knelt and retched in horror.

David shook his head, clearing the remembered vision from his eyes, and looked back at Tom. "I thought you'd remember," he repeated.

Tom spat in disgust, missing the corner spittoon. "I remember. It happened in 1831. Nearly twenty-five years ago!

"And you know as well as I do the magistrate would've been a lot more lenient on them if it hadn't been for the whole town—the whole state, for that matter—being in an uproar over Nat Turner murdering half the whites in Southampton County. Hell, I saw Ned pull out pencil and paper just the other day, to figure the lumber he'd need for Pete's addition, without anyone raising an eyebrow."

David shrugged. "The law's still on the books, Tom."

"You don't give a damn about the law, so long as you get your precious pictures published! Now nobody objected in the least to you showing Burns being returned to his rightful owner, even if the *Tribune* did try to make their damn abolitionist hay out of it.

"But now you've dug up this ancient history and spread it all over the country. Handing out ammunition to the abolitionists, right when the South needs every man to stand by her if we're to keep our rights!

16

You don't give a damn about your own people, do you? Well, don't go expecting the people in this town to give a damn for you anymore!" Tom grabbed the newspaper and crumpled it in his fist. He tossed it in front of David again and slammed the door as he strode from the room.

David sat motionless, staring at the closed door, as the minutes ticked by. Finally he rose. He smoothed out the paper, tucked it under his arm, then walked out of his office. There'd be no clients coming by that afternoon.

His father was in his wing chair as he entered the house. He looked up at his son, a copy of the *Tribune* in his hand. "What possessed you to do this, David?"

David dropped into the chair opposite his father. "I don't know." He fell silent, pondering. "I guess I thought drawing it would help me understand, somehow, how they could do that to him. Come to terms with it, maybe. You know, that was my damn geography book. I told Mike he could borrow it."

David looked down at the picture again, at the tensed muscles and clenched fists. The memory resurfaced of how bitterly Mike had blamed his father for refusing to plead for clemency for the three boys, how unwillingly he'd submitted even to the doctor's attempts to minister to his wounds. "I'm sorry," he said at last. "I should've realized it would hurt you."

The older man gazed at him sadly. "Never mind that now, David." He dismissed his son's words with an impatient wave of his hand.

"Why did you send it to the *Tribune*, after all these years? Especially now, with the whole South alarmed that they'll be denied the right to carry their property in slaves with them if the Free Soilers win out in Kansas. I should think a lawyer would be more aware of people's attitudes. Didn't you take any thought for what it would do to you? Don't you realize how you've destroyed your position in this town?"

David rose and poured himself a glass of rum from the decanter on the table. He sat down again, cradling the glass in his hands, forgetting to drink it. "It never even occurred to me." He brooded awhile in silence. "I guess I've never had much of a position to lose," he said at last.

Chapter Three - 1855

Six months after his sketch of Michael had been published in the *Tribune*, David was still a pariah in his home town, forced to close his law office for lack of clients. Even Martha Ann sailed past him at church on Sundays without a word. He needed little persuasion to accompany his father to Boston that spring, glad enough of Mike and Rachel's welcome.

Yet, sitting in the Mabaya's front room after supper, listening to his father and Michael argue the latest developments in medicine—Michael defending Oliver Wendell Holmes' theory of a dozen years back that childbed fever was carried by midwives and doctors, Dr. Carter decrying it—David saw the heated words passing between them as evidence of their underlying bond: a connection in which he had no part.

The loss of his occupation made matters worse. Tedious as he'd found the practice of law, the dearth of clients left him high and dry: a forty-year-old man living off his father's bounty. He took refuge in his sketchpad, turning out drawing after drawing of Michael and his wife, Rachel; of his father holding four-year-old Becky on his lap with a smile of fond contentment; of Abigail, shyly earnest at eleven; of thirteen-year-old Peter who gazed at him unsmilingly, his intent young face so similar to Michael's, though with his mother's darker, mahogany coloration.

Still, it would have been laughable to proclaim himself an artist.

"Why not teach art?" Rachel proposed, one evening after Dr. Carter, as well as the children, had retired.

"I don't know anything about teaching." He fell silent, mulling over

Rachel's suggestion. But even if he had some facility at drawing, he doubted he had the ability to explain it to others. And he'd no more find art students at home than he had clients for his law practice. He'd no interest in seeking admission to the bar in some other state. He studied his hands, trying to imagine himself moving out of his familiar home, searching for students in a strange city. He couldn't.

He turned to his half brother. "How did you just leave home like that?"

"What do you mean?" Michael asked.

"How did you get the nerve to just run up North? You weren't more than a few years older than Peter is. Weren't you afraid?"

"Lord, yes, I was scared to death. The whole way to Pennsylvania I couldn't stop thinking what would happen to me if I got caught. I'd have been whipped for sure, probably sold South. I could've knelt down and kissed the ground once I'd crossed over the state line."

"I meant once you'd reached a free state though. Weren't you scared of how you'd get along, how you'd earn a living?"

"Oh." Michael gave the question a scant second's thought. "I didn't see anything to be afraid of once I was free. Of course, I didn't know if I could really become a doctor, but I knew I'd find some kind of work. What was there to be scared of?"

"I don't know." David looked down again. "I wish I knew. I just wish I knew."

The onset of summer found David no closer to starting anew. He returned home, despite Michael and Rachel's invitation to stay on with them while he tried to establish himself in Boston. "We can find room," Rachel had assured him. He'd thanked them, but declined the offer, not sure if he was simply reluctant to crowd them in their modest townhouse or afraid he'd prove himself even more of a failure in their eyes.

Still, summer brought its compensations. Free from the constraints of his law office, he wandered through the town and nearby country-side, sketching whatever took his fancy. Most often he headed for the docks to capture the muscular strength and grace of the dockworkers. His eyes would stay fixed on the rippling, powerful muscles of back and shoulders; he'd glance down at his sketch a second or two at a time, then return his admiring gaze to his subjects, his fingers moving rhythmically as he retraced lines and penciled in details.

As autumn approached though, with the prospect of being cooped up indoors with no company but that of his father, his situation weighed more heavily on him. Even Walker seemed to have lost interest in pursuing their correspondence. He'd received just one letter from the newsman since spring—a hastily scrawled missive preoccupied with the efforts of the *Tribune* to aid Free Soil settlers in Kansas in their struggle against "border ruffians," who'd thronged across the state line from Missouri to cast fraudulent votes for a pro-slavery legislature. Doubtless Walker was too caught up in the conflict to write—though, as far as David could see, it seemed likely to produce nothing but turmoil and bloodshed.

Perhaps, David told himself as he headed for home one fall afternoon, the newsman simply had no further use for him since he'd forwarded no additional sketches illustrating the horrors of slavery.

His father called to him from the parlor as David entered the house, beaming as he handed David a letter from Michael. David skimmed it. The opening of school had gone well, Michael wrote. The Massachusetts legislature that spring had passed a law prohibiting school boards from restricting colored children to separate schools. The new legislation ended a boycott of the public schools by Negro parents in Boston; Michael and Rachel's youngsters were now enrolled in public school, rather than alternative schools set up by colored parents.

"Peter's entered the Boston Latin School," Dr. Carter reported proudly, before David could finish reading.

David nodded, handed the letter back to him.

"Oh," George Carter added, as David turned to head upstairs. "You've got another letter from that friend of yours in New York."

He ripped open Walker's letter.

"Please accept my apologies for not having written sooner. Have been much pressed for time of late.

"I have news which may prove of interest to you. A new weekly, modeled after the *Illustrated London News*, is to be launched this fall. The publisher, Frank Leslie, is a man with much experience in illustration and engraving, and the sound judgment to make a success of the undertaking. Expect he will be hiring staff artists shortly. Advise me without delay if you are interested, and I will arrange for you to meet at the earliest opportunity."

An inkstand and pen stood on the writing table in the parlor. David sat at the table and dipped the quill into the inkwell, calculating the length of time it would take for his answer to reach the newsman.

He set the pen down. By the time additional letters traveled to and from New York, Leslie might well have engaged all the illustrators he needed. If he caught the morning train, he could reach New York City tomorrow evening.

He took the stairs two at a time. Packing a few extra clothes wouldn't take long, but he wanted to take his time selecting sketches for his portfolio.

Chapter Four - 1855-56

Alexandria was a mere hamlet compared with the tumultuous, traffic-filled streets of New York City. David looked across Printing House Square to the five-story building that was the home of the *Tribune*, briefly wishing he'd heeded his father's advice to have the sense to reply in writing rather than take the first train north. He waited for a break in the speeding stream of coaches, then crossed the square, skirting steaming piles of horse dung.

The news offices were on the third floor. Walker was sitting with his back to the door, jacket slung carelessly over his chair, his shoulders rounded as his pen moved swiftly across his paper. David crossed the newsroom to his desk.

"Mr. Carter!" Walker's look of surprise gave way to a beam. "I'd expected to hear from you by post, but I see you've come in person instead."

David smiled, embarrassed. "I guess I thought I'd lose my courage if I waited."

Walker laughed. "Have a seat. I'll be finished up here in a minute." He rained a fine spray of ink drops over his manuscript as he waved his quill at an adjacent chair.

David perched on the edge of the seat. Some half dozen newsmen at nearby desks glanced at him with curiosity, then dismissed him from their thoughts as they returned to their copy. He began to relax, watching Walker frown in concentration as he scribbled.

"Well, there's an end to that!" Walker stood and stretched, tossing his pages into the basket for outgoing copy. "Here, follow me and I'll introduce you to Greeley." He strode off, still dressed in his shirtsleeves.

A Different Sin

Horace Greeley's office was a cubicle at one end of the newsroom. A tacked-up sign read, "Editorial Rooms: Ring the Bell." Walker pushed open the door, ignoring it.

David followed him, looking around in wonder. The famed editor sat hunched over a desk by the window. Dangling from the ceiling over the desk was a large pair of shears—apparently to prevent their loss in the sloping mound of clippings, pamphlets and correspondence in which the desktop was buried. Newspapers and books overflowed the bookcase, covering a sofa and several rickety chairs.

Greeley continued writing as Walker spoke. David wondered uneasily if he'd heard them come in at all.

Suddenly Greeley turned and extended his hand, his high voice a contrast to his bewhiskered countenance. "I'm glad to meet you, Mr. Carter. I was darn pleased with that last drawing you sent. It's the kind of evidence we need to give slaveholders the lie. Wish I could use you myself as a sketch artist for the *Tribune*."

David murmured his thanks. Walker turned to him when they'd left the editor's office. "Let's go somewhere we can get a drop of refreshment while we talk. There's a beer cellar favored by *Tribune* men, if you don't mind a bit of a walk. None of us care to imbibe under Greeley's nose. Though walking suits me in any case, as my name might suggest."

David smiled, falling into step with Walker's brisk stride. Pfaff's beer cellar, a flight below the lamplit bustle of Broadway, was a cavernous vault, ripe with the mingled odors of lager beer, tobacco smoke and spicy German sausage. Walker led the way to a vacant table, greeting cronies as he went, then ordered tankards of beer and plates of steaming sauerkraut and frankfurters. David dug into the unfamiliar supper with relish; he'd been too nervous to eat more than a few crackers and an apple during the hours on the train.

Walker lifted his tankard, took a long draught. "Ah, that's better. I see eye to eye with Greeley on most things, but not his zeal for outlawing Demon Rum."

David laughed. "I think he'd have a harder time of it than if he tried doing away with Southern slavery."

"You're probably right." Walker sobered. "Well, now you're here, the first order of business is to arrange a meeting with Frank Leslie. Once that's done, you'll have a little time to get situated in New York before work starts on the first issue." He sliced a frankfurter in two, his round face cheerful once again.

"I hope you're right," David said. "About the certainty of my gaining employment, that is. I'm afraid I burned my bridges behind me. My neighbors haven't forgiven me for aiding the abolitionist cause with the sketch I sent you last winter."

Walker's face fell. "I didn't intend causing you harm. Leslie's in the market for talented illustrators though. I'm sure he'll take you on. Your misfortune may well prove a springboard to work more to your liking," he added, brightening.

The newsman's optimism was contagious. David set down his tankard and smiled at him. "Well, I'm grateful to you for informing me of the chance in any case, Mr. Walker."

Walker beamed. "If we're to be colleagues in the news business, it's high time we dropped this formality. I'm Zachary. Though my friends mostly call me Zach."

"And mine, David."

David prayed his trepidation was not in evidence, as Frank Leslie thumbed through his portfolio. The black-bearded editor set the drawings on his desk and leaned back in his chair, eyeing David thoughtfully.

"I'm of two minds, Mr. Carter," he said, intertwining stubby fingers. "On the one hand, your work's competent enough. You render your subjects accurately, an important consideration, especially now that the public's grown accustomed to the verisimilitude of the camera."

"Thank you, sir," David murmured, waiting anxiously for the rest of Leslie's words.

"On the other hand, this is a fledgling operation. By and large, the artists I'm considering are just starting out in life, whereas you, sir, are a man of mature years. Might I venture to guess thirty-five?"

"I'm just past forty," David said, disconcerted.

Leslie nodded. "You look younger than your years. But my point is borne out all the more. To put it plainly, the amount of recompense I'm able to afford is unlikely to be attractive to a man who's already established himself in a profession."

David swallowed, understanding Leslie's intent. "I've grown weary of the practice of law, sir," he said, praying his voice didn't reveal his desperation. "What sort of recompense did you have in mind?"

"I'm afraid the most I can manage is six dollars per week." Leslie looked at David blandly.

No more than a common laborer. David recollected what Zachary had told him about prices in New York and sighed under his breath, watching Leslie's shrewdly composed face. Clearly, the editor realized he wouldn't turn down any offer.

"I assume once your publication has turned a profit, salaries will be raised accordingly," David said at last.

Leslie smiled broadly. "By all means, Mr. Carter. Well, if you're agreed then, I'm happy to welcome you aboard."

A Different Sin

Leslie's assessment of the youth of his fellow illustrators had been correct. Of the dozen or so artists contributing sketches to the new weekly, not one was over thirty. Elliot Gareau, one of the few other full-time artists, was a worldly twenty-five. Several contributors were less than half David's age, such as Arthur Lumley, a student at the National Academy of Design, and Thomas Nast, a brash fifteen-year-old.

More disquieting was the realization that, like young Lumley, the others had all been trained in the arts, either through private instruction or academy study. David was the only one with no formal training whatsoever; his father had refused to pay even the small fee demanded by the drawing master at the academy he'd attended in boyhood.

The worry nagged him even as the staff of *Frank Leslie's Illustrated* newspaper gathered to celebrate the weekly's first issue. With Christmas ten days off, the atmosphere was doubly festive. Leslie had brought in several bottles of good whiskey, and artists, reporters, engravers and compositors drank to the success of the new venture.

David set down his glass to look over his copy of the paper. He gazed with satisfaction at his sketch of a crowded street scene, holiday shoppers swaddled in scarfs and muffs, juggling armloads of parcels as they dodged through horse-drawn traffic. Slowly he studied the other artists' illustrations: courtroom spectators at a heralded murder trial; Dr. Kane's expedition of Arctic exploration; a scene from the play *Little Treasure*, enjoying an extended run at Wallack's Theatre; and a depiction of defiant free-staters—rifles at the ready—meeting in convention in Topeka, Kansas, drawn from a telegraphed account.

His work was a match for the others, even a trifle livelier than some. Little by little, like a cake of soap left accidentally in the wash basin, David's anxiety melted away. He folded the newspaper and joined the others in a toast.

The craze for ice skating had swept New York by winter of 1856, as it had Boston and a dozen other eastern cities. Zachary Walker—who'd become a fast friend—persuaded David to join him one Sunday afternoon for a skating party arranged by a senior *Tribune* reporter, at his rural home near the village of Harlem.

David sat alongside Zachary on a log at the edge of the pond, fastening his skates to his shoes with trepidation. "I'm afraid I don't know how to skate. I've never been, to tell the truth."

"It's not hard. I'll show you." Zach beamed with anticipation, his frozen breath puffing out of his round, bewhiskered face.

David smiled nervously. Accepting Zach's helping hand, he edged onto the ice, already filled with circling skaters from mere tots to gray-bearded grandfathers.

"Don't lift your feet as if you were walking. You want to glide from one foot to another." Zach let go of David's arm, moved smoothly across the pond, circled back in a neat figure eight. David watched the burly newsman skim over the ice with admiration. "It must've taken you years to learn to skate like that," he said, as Zachary glided to a stop.

Zach laughed. "I'm Dutch on my mother's side. She had us kids skating soon as we could walk." He grasped David's arm lightly above the elbow, repeating his instructions as they slowly circled the pond.

"You've got it now. Try it on your own."

David struggled to keep his balance and move as Zach had shown him. Glide with the right foot, glide with the left. He began to enjoy himself. The cold air felt clean and crisp on his face.

"Betcha can't catch me!" A towheaded boy cut in front of him, chased by a second youngster. David swerved. His feet tangled together and he fell, thrusting his hands out in panic. His palms stung as they slid along the ice.

Shaken, David sat back, one hand automatically probing his head. Zachary appeared at his side. "You all right?"

David nodded, pulling himself up with Zach's help. Carefully he edged off the ice. A few feet from shore a bonfire had been started, where several women tended a kettle of hot cocoa. He made his way clumsily toward the fire and settled himself on a log.

Zach followed. "Ready to try again?" he asked, as they drained their cups.

"You go ahead. I think I'll just watch."

"You weren't doing badly. Everyone falls when they're first learning. It's no reason to give up."

David smiled apologetically. "I'm a little afraid of hurting my head again. I suppose I'm overly cautious."

"Your head?" Zach stared quizzically, abruptly nodded. "I remember. You mentioned it on the train when we first met. You didn't say how you'd been injured."

"It's a long story." No reason not to tell it, David supposed, seeing his friend's face brighten with interest.

"I was trying to help Mike escape from the Alexandria jail. You remember—my half brother who ran off and became a doctor. My uncle had him jailed after he recaptured him."

David continued, not waiting for Zachary's startled nod. "I told you Uncle relented and sold Mike back to my father. Actually, he intended to ship Mike down to Georgia and sell him there. When word got out, a colored man, Ned—a boyhood friend of Mike's—found a pretext to visit and show him an escape route."

A Different Sin

"Ned's a carpenter. He helped build the jail and knew the ceiling of Mike's cell was really nothing but plaster. So Mike could break into the attic and climb out a window there. It took courage on Ned's part to help him that way."

"But what *happened*? How did you—?"

"I was to meet Mike with a buggy once he let himself out the window. We planned to smuggle him onto a British ship, get him out of the country."

"That must have taken courage on *your* part."

David shook his head. "I've never been known for courage, I'm afraid. I didn't have any choice. Dad was distraught worrying over Mike as it was. If Uncle had sold him South, he might never have recovered.

"Our plan misfired though. Tell the truth, I don't remember what happened, just what I've been told. The last thing I remember is waiting down the street from the jail till the night watchman had gone by.

"I'd driven the buggy up to the jail where Mike was to let himself down to the street with a rope he'd made of his bedding. I'd climbed out of the buggy to watch him, was standing alongside it. God knows why.

"Anyway, we were surprised by the watchman. He fired a warning shot and spooked the horse. It bolted. I was hit by the buggy and thrown backwards, striking my head on the cobblestones."

David held his hands out to the fire to warm them. "You know my father's a doctor. The jailer sent for him. Dad told me afterward the shattered bits of skull bone were pressing on my brain so the only way to save my life was to cut out the fractured section. He didn't dare do it himself. Instead he persuaded the jailer to move Mike from his cell so he could operate."

Zach whistled. "Right there in the jail?"

David nodded. "Dad had brought his medical kit, so Mike had the instruments he needed."

"Still." Zach shook his head wonderingly. "He must be a good doctor."

"He is."

Zach waited a moment. "You were still unconscious?"

"Thank God! My uncle arrived next morning before I'd come to. Mike had sutured my scalp back in place, but apparently there was still a lot of blood." David shuddered involuntarily. "Uncle took one look and leaped to the conclusion Mike had killed me."

Zach stared at him, spellbound.

26

"When I came to my senses, he was holding his revolver to Mike's head, threatening to shoot him in retaliation."

"Good Lord!"

"Of course I was pretty groggy, but I remember Dad and the jailer trying to reason with him. Dad was pleading that Mike was his son too, which just infuriated Uncle more.

"Thank God I was able to attract his attention before he could carry out his threat. When he saw I was alive, he came to his senses and agreed to sell Mike back to Dad."

"Well," Zach said after a pause, "at least it ended well."

David nodded. "Mike and Dad were reconciled, after all those years. Dad and I've been closer too, matter of fact."

At least he's doing his best not to let me know I'm a disappointment. He dismissed the thought, gazed at the pond.

"It's pretty cold just sitting here, Zach." David pulled his cap securely down on his head and stood, balancing gingerly on the skates. "Suppose you show me how to stop with these things on."

After a few shaky months, the trickle of subscribers to *Leslie's Illustrated* grew. By spring it seemed the brainchild of the swarthy, energetic publisher might yet prove a success.

By spring, too, Leslie's pages were filled with reports of violence over the issue of slavery. On May 19th, after a fiery anti-slavery speech, Massachusetts Senator Charles Sumner was attacked in the Senate chamber by South Carolina Representative, Preston Brooks, and beaten senseless with a cane.

In Kansas, where free state and pro-slavery legislatures contested for recognition, seven hundred pro-slavery men mounted a raid on Lawrence, killing one resident and burning stores, hotels and newspaper offices. Armed marauders led by fiery abolitionist John Brown, seized five pro-slavery settlers in retaliation, splitting their skulls with broadswords.

Newsboys cried out the latest bloodshed as David and fellow artist Elliot Gareau turned off Nassau Street's "newspaper row" in the direction of Pfaff's to meet Zachary and two companions from the *Tribune*—both bachelors as were Zach and Elliot. They hurried downstairs to the beer hall, pausing an instant for their eyes to adjust to the dim, smoky room.

"The free staters in Kansas say Brown's a hero," Dick Potter, a fervent abolitionist, was saying as David and Elliot joined them. "It's true. He has the Lord's strength in his sword." David sighed, wishing they could talk of something else for once. Dick turned on him. "You disagree?"

"I just don't see how bloodshed is going to change anyone's mind about slavery," David said mildly.

"He's not talking about changing minds, David," Zach put in. "It's a little late for Garrison's way of leading slaveholders down the path of sweet reason. Dick's right. It'll take willingness to fight before Kansas can win admission as a free state. Anyhow, the violence was started by the slaveholders themselves."

"An eye for an eye, the Bible says," Dick intoned.

Elliot snorted, fine droplets of ale flying from the ends of his ginger mustache. "You'll make the whole Northwest territory into an asylum for the blind, at that rate. Who gives a damn whether they come in slave or free or not at all? It's their worry."

"We know you don't give a damn about anything, Elliot," blond, chubby Stephen Van Dyjk said with unaccustomed vehemence. "But bloodshed's not the only way. I see a good deal of promise in this new Republican party."

"Their platform proposals are half measures, Steve," Dick argued. "It's not enough to keep slavery from spreading. We've got to wipe it out, no matter where it exists." A teetotaler, Dick washed down his sausage with a swallow of cider.

"I'm afraid you'd have a harder time than you realize," David said. He picked up his tankard, wishing he'd kept quiet as Dick launched another offensive.

"I keep forgetting you're a Virginian, David. I suppose you're going to defend the South's peculiar institution now."

"I wasn't defending it. Matter of fact, I agree with you it's an evil. But it's existed for hundreds of years. You can't end it overnight."

"So you'd reward evildoers for their past sins by giving them your blessing to continue?!"

David flushed as heads at nearby tables turned toward them, took refuge in a shrug.

"You've no business hounding him, Dick." Zach's voice boomed out warmly. "Anyway, I'll warrant David's the only one of us sitting here who's endangered his own hide helping a man escape from slavery."

David flushed again, not at all happy at having the family history he'd shared with Zachary repeated to the whole table. It was too late to protest though. Zach was already launched on the story.

Elliot spoke up as Zach concluded. "Well, David, sounds to me as if you're the only practicing abolitionist among us." His long fingers hid a sardonic smile as he smoothed the ends of his mustache.

David shrugged, smiling with embarrassment. He looked down, recalling Mike's recapture five years earlier, reliving his father's distress and Mike's unhappy pacing, penned up in the tiny cell with only his fears for company.

Of course he'd wanted to help his own flesh and blood. What did that have to do with his political views?

He shrugged again, not bothering to argue the point. Let them think what they pleased.

The violence continued into summer. James Redpath, the *Tribune* correspondent in the Northwest Territory, sent daily dispatches on "bleeding Kansas." Southern newspaper editors hailed Sumner's assailant as a hero.

The continuing bloodshed sent newspaper circulation soaring. By June of 1856, Leslie announced that "an American illustrated newspaper of a high order is no longer an experiment, but a necessity to the reading public."

True to his word, with the success of the fledgling newspaper assured, Leslie raised wages. At last David could move from the shabby boardinghouse that had been the best he could afford. He made up his mind to ask Zach to recommend a decent roominghouse, when his friend returned from covering the Republican convention.

"Six dollars a week," Mrs. Chapman said firmly. "And worth every penny." David looked slowly around the room, as Zach and Elliot waited.

There chanced to be two vacant rooms in the very boardinghouse where he lodged, Zach had said, beaming. The smaller of the two was on the second floor, at the front of the house, and almost directly across the hall from Zachary's room. Elliot, who was on the lookout for better quarters himself, had already agreed to take it. David stood indecisively in the second vacant room, at the opposite end of the narrow hallway. Like Zach's room, it occupied a choice corner spot, though at the front of the house rather than the quieter rear.

"Hell of a lot better than that hole you're living in," Elliot murmured, too low for the landlady to overhear. David nodded, looking appreciatively at the clean counterpane and Franklin stove. There was no comparison to the unsavory waterfront boardinghouse that sheltered seamen on leave and newly arrived immigrants. And the location of Mrs. Chapman's, on Broad Street near the corner of Wall, was just a fifteen minute walk to Leslie's.

Still, six dollars was a lot, over half his weekly wages. Zach caught his eye. David smiled at him, unaccountably pleased at the thought of moving into lodgings with this friend.

"I'll take it, ma'am," he told Mrs. Chapman.

Chapter Five - 1856-57

A̲T LEAST HE'D MOVED TO A DECENT BOARDINGHOUSE before his father's visit. David sat stiffly on the horsehair sofa in the boardinghouse parlor, searching for a topic of mutual interest. George Carter gazed around the parlor, which they had to themselves on this warm Sunday afternoon, equally at a loss for conversation.

In the two days since his father's arrival, David had shown him through Leslie's, explaining the publisher's innovation in dividing the wood blocks into sections of ten, twenty or more parts, tightly joined with screws on the back. "Then after the drawing's completed, the block is taken apart for the engravers, so each section can be engraved by a separate man. It's how we publish illustrations in the paper so soon after events happen. Otherwise it would take days to finish one picture. The engravers have to cut away the entire surface of the wood, except for the lines of the drawing. It's an incredibly painstaking process." George Carter had nodded dutifully at David's words. He'd looked with polite interest at the steam engine that powered the printing press and the overlay forms that produced the effects of tone and shading in the printed illustrations.

That morning, they'd attended services at Trinity Church, returned to Mrs. Chapman's for Sunday dinner. Now George Carter pulled out his watch. There were several hours yet till the scant supper Mrs. Chapman served on Sundays. He cleared his throat. "Your landlady sets a good table, though a bit heavy for this warm a day."

David nodded. "How was your visit to Boston?" he inquired, certain he'd asked the question at least once.

"Very pleasant." The older man brightened. "I accompanied Michael to a lecture by Dr. Bowditch on thoracentesis. It's a procedure developed a few years ago to remove fluid accumulations in the chest. It's quite simple really. A long needle is inserted into the chest, and then—"

"Good Lord!"

"Well, I suppose it wouldn't interest you that much." His father smiled ruefully.

"I'm afraid not."

There was another silence. "We went to the Common for the July Fourth celebration," George Carter said finally. "It was quite spectacular. The highlight was a balloon ascension."

David smiled. "I know. Elliot—he's the younger man I introduced you to—made a copy of the balloon on the wood block, from a sketch done at the site. The children must've found it terribly exciting."

"Yes, Becky especially. She talked about it for days." His father shook his head, smiling. "She's growing up so fast. She'll be starting school this fall, you know."

"It hardly seems possible. It seems just yesterday she was a baby."

"That reminds me. Have I told you Rachel and Michael are expecting another child? A little after Christmas, they think." He sat back, beaming.

"No, you hadn't. Well, they must be pleased."

"Very much so." George Carter fell silent a moment. "I'm hoping, if it's a boy, they'll consider naming him after me," he added, his voice suddenly shy.

"He'd still have a different last name though." David wished he could call back his words, as his father's face fell.

"Even so, it would be something. Though you're right. I'd always hoped to have my son carry on my name." The older man's voice trailed off wistfully. He straightened his shoulders and looked at David. "Haven't you ever felt that desire yourself?"

"I've never given it much thought." David fell silent, plunged into introspection by his father's question.

"I'm afraid I can't picture myself the head of a household," he said finally. "What I really hope for, to tell the truth, is to be remembered as an artist. That is, if I ever grow good enough," he added, embarrassed.

His father nodded slowly. "I see. Well, you may yet change your mind about wanting a family."

There was no sense upsetting him further. "Well, perhaps so, Dad," David answered, sighing under his breath.

A Different Sin

The supper dishes had already been cleared from the boardinghouse table Monday evening, by the time David returned from New Jersey, where he'd seen his father onto the overnight train to Washington.

"I knew you'd be late," Zachary told him, "so I thought I'd wait and join you at Pfaff's. I'll be glad of a change from boardinghouse food."

David smiled, glad of Zach's company.

"Your father didn't visit very long," Zach said, once they'd settled themselves at a table and given the waiter their order.

"No, he's eager to get home. He's been away over a month."

"He's been up in Boston all that time?"

David nodded. "He likes to spend as much time as he can with his grandchildren. And Mike and Rachel too, of course." He fell silent, reaching into the bread basket for a roll.

Zach reached into the basket without taking his eyes from David, his thick brows rising in silent inquiry.

"To tell the truth, I'm afraid Dad and I don't have much in common." David tore the roll in two. He stared down at the two halves. "I've always been a disappointment to him. He wanted a son like Mike," he said, unable to stop himself.

Zachary stared in astonishment. "I don't see how you can say that. You've told me he could never even bring himself to acknowledge him."

"Well, of course, he was ashamed to admit he'd fathered a colored son. That's not what I meant." David hesitated, his fingers shredding the roll into crumbs.

"I think Mike spent more time with Dad than I did," he said finally. "Dad always had him doing some job around his office. And he was always pleased with Mike. Well, not when he'd grown old enough to defy Dad, though I'm sure he cared for him, even then. But when he was a child, nine or ten, maybe...."

His words trailed off as his mind shifted back in time to another hot August evening. He sat in his room, staring idly out the open window, watching the shadow of the shed slowly creep across the yard. He could see his father's stocky figure pass the entrance to the alley, Mike trotting alongside him, lugging the heavy medical kit proudly. He could hear them talking, though their words were too faint to make out.

David crossed the hall to his father's room, looking out the window as his father and Mike came around the corner and passed beneath him. He could hear Mike's words clearly now.

"Yassuh, but how you knows when his leg be healed enough so he don't need the splint no more?"

David watched another moment as his father turned his head

toward Mike, his expression softening into a smile as he started to answer. He didn't feel like hearing any more. He walked back to his room and sank down on his bed.

He heard the door open. His father's footsteps sounded on the stairs as he headed to his room to wash up for dinner. He looked in on David. "Good evening, son." He paused. "What are you doing?"

David shrugged. "Nothing much, sir."

His father sighed. "Surely you could find something worthwhile to fill your time. If nothing else, you could review your school lessons from last term. I'm expecting you to bring home better school reports than last year."

"Yes, sir," David mumbled.

He forced his thoughts back to the present, surprised to discover that his dinner had been set in front of him. Zach was still staring at him in surprise.

"He was always so damn eager to learn. Mike, I mean." David smiled ruefully. "He was just the way Dad wanted me to be, to tell the truth."

"The father...manly, mean, anger'd, unjust. The blow, the quick loud word."

David blinked. "What's that?"

"A poem, or part of one anyway. By a man named Whitman. He's had a number of poems published in the *Tribune* the past few years. I'd like you to meet him one day. I warrant you he'll be known as one of the great American poets, one of these days."

"Oh. It didn't sound much like poetry. Dad wasn't like that though. I mean, he wasn't harsh. He didn't beat me. He never raised his voice much, for that matter. It's just that he always let me know he was disappointed in me."

Zach's wide mouth curved upward in a smile, goodhumored lines forming above his silvery wreath of whiskers. "I didn't mean Whitman's words as a literal description of your father, David. They just came to mind." He took a bite of his food, chewing with relish, then set down his fork.

"That's not quite true, either. I guess you could say that quoting him was my roundabout way of saying it's the nature of fathers and sons to disappoint each other."

"Oh. Dad's not disappointed in Mike though," David blurted. "I mean, they're always arguing about something, but you can see they like each other. And Dad's forgotten he was ever ashamed of fathering Mike, he's so proud to have a son who followed in his footsteps."

"Not every son turns out the way his father hoped."

"I suppose not." David picked up his fork and pushed his food around his plate.

A Different Sin

Zachary watched him a moment. "Perhaps it's none of my business, but I am your friend. Why worry what your father thinks now? You're not a boy, after all."

David flushed. "That's just what Dad's always saying."

"Well, he's right. About that." Zach smiled. "But far as I can see, you've turned out fine. You needn't doubt yourself."

David smiled back, warmed by his friend's regard. "I try not to. Anyway, thanks for saying so." He looked down at his plate again, in mingled pleasure and embarrassment.

By the time a year had passed, David was surprised how much at home he felt in the chaotic, noisy metropolis. Lodging with friends helped, and agreeable evenings drinking with Elliot and Zach. He spent more hours with Zach alone, attending theater or wandering through one of the many art galleries that lined lower Broadway.

An exhibit at the National Academy of Design, early in 1857, attracted all three men. As usual they ended up at Pfaff's. The smoke-filled cellar was crowded with hard-drinking, argumentative newsmen, tired doctors from New York Hospital, the clique of Bohemian artists and writers that out-of-towners flocked to see.

"I thoroughly enjoyed the exhibit," Zach said, hoisting his tankard, "especially the Hudson River landscapes. They put me in mind of the country upstate, when I was a boy."

David voiced his admiration of William Mount's rural Long Island scenes. Then, his tongue loosened by the beer and companionship, he blurted, "When I was a boy I used to dream of seeing my drawings hanging in a gallery."

Elliot snorted. "We're a damn sight better off with steady jobs. For every artist whose work's in the Academy, there's twenty sleeping in their studios because they can't afford a boardinghouse."

"Still, it would be good to have our drawings last longer than yesterday's newspaper."

Zach touched his arm. "More people read the daily papers than ever set foot in an art gallery, David."

"I suppose."

"And our work has an influence on the public. Yours more so than mine: one picture's worth a thousand words. Take your drawing of those new immigrants just landed at Castle Garden."

David nodded, pleased that Zach remembered his sketch of the sweating, stoic immigrant women, nursing their infants under the furtive privacy of a woolen shawl, keeping anxious watch over frightened, eager children while their menfolk went in search of ticket agents and information bureau.

34

"Even the Know-Nothings among Leslie's subscribers were bound to see they're just families no different than their own. And at least a few will see immigrants as being a little more their fellow men as a result. Just as Greeley's efforts at hammering away at the institution of slavery will change our readers' sensibilities on that score."

"Huh!" Elliot scoffed. "Nine out of ten of those immigrants are ignorant, Pope-ridden scum! Is there anything that isn't a mission with you, Zach? You don't even have the excuse of being a churchgoer like Dick."

"You don't have to sit in church to feel the sufferings of your fellow men! I learned my zeal at my mother's knee. More than one occasion, she fed some poor runaway at our table, and rested uneasy till she knew him safe."

Elliot snorted again. "Anyhow, drawing's just a trade like any other. And a damn sight easier way to make a living than most. There's no need to make more of it."

"I doubt you'd find many at Leslie's agreeing with you," David said. "Most of them would give notice in a minute if they could live off the sale of their paintings."

He fell to thinking of Zach's words. He'd rarely made a conscious effort to influence others with his sketches; in fact, his own feelings toward a subject were often unclear till he'd captured it on paper. "I'm afraid I never gave thought to changing the Know-Nothings' views," he confessed, hoping he hadn't lowered his friend's opinion of him.

Zach smiled. "I daresay you give yourself too little credit," he said, laying his hand warmly on David's a moment.

The night air struck their faces in chill contrast to the crowded tavern as they climbed back to the street. Zach shoved his hands in his pockets. "We're in for another cold snap. A fire in our stoves will feel good tonight."

Elliot laughed. "I intend warming myself at a better fire than that. I won't bother asking you to join me, Zach. David?"

David hesitated, feeling urgency stir within him. But he'd accompanied Elliot to one house or another some half dozen times, joining in hurried, joyless union with women whose faces and bodies he barely remembered by the morning after. Each time, the warnings voiced by his father sounded louder in his mind. This wasn't some small town. Who knew who had lain with these women or what diseases they carried? He'd thought of asking Zach to recommend a clean place, but it didn't seem a thing he could ask this friend.

He shook his head. The chance of infection wasn't worth the brief respite from lust lying with whores afforded.

Elliot turned away with a nonchalant wave of his hand. David turned his collar up against the wind and fell into step with Zach as they headed back to Mrs. Chapman's.

Sleep eluded him that night. He tossed restlessly, his efforts to summon drowsiness driving it further from him. He turned onto his back, trying to ignore the urgent throbbing in his member, regretful now that he hadn't accompanied Elliot to the brothel despite his fears.

Yet he'd never found more than brief, unsatisfactory respite lying with women. He thought suddenly of that first time he'd gone to a bawdy house, in company with his college friend, John Eustis. He'd been far too embarrassed to admit his disappointment to John afterwards. He'd walked alongside him in silence as they returned to the dormitory, trying to emulate John's cocky, carefree grin.

He'd never approached—then or afterwards—the ecstatic heights that John had boasted of as they ambled back together, John smelling pungently of rich, masculine sweat, his broad shoulders straining his carelessly fastened shirt, his arm circling David's shoulders in brief, warm comradeship.

David's hand crept down of its own accord. Moaning in reluctance, he gave in to his pulsating need, surrendering himself to the relief of the familiar, lonely massage.

"The Glory of Young Men is their Strength." Elliot's voice wavered midway between scorn and envy as he read the caption printed under David's sketch of a massively bulging bicep. "I suppose it's all right for those with nothing better to do than stand around posing like Greek statues."

David laughed. "That is a statue, so to speak. I drew it from a plaster cast Ottignon keeps in the lobby of his gymnasium to demonstrate his results. But the exhibition *was* impressive. I've never seen feats like some of his athletes performed."

Zachary turned over his copy of Leslie's, studying David's half-page sketch of the gymnasium, the spectators in the flag-bedecked hall gazing open-mouthed at the gymnast soaring effortlessly on the flying rings—the highlight of the establishment's semi-annual public exhibition. "I've let a few years go by since I last set foot in a gymnasium. I wouldn't mind using some of Ottignon's apparatus myself," he mused.

Elliot guffawed, causing several heads to turn toward him with disapproval in the crowded boardinghouse parlor. "I'd like to see that, Zach, at your age."

"You needn't be so quick to sneer. I wasn't referring to the rings.

But I daresay this muscle building apparatus could benefit any of us. You'll note," Zach added, his finger lighting triumphantly halfway down the accompanying text, "that the list of members includes many persons of mature and even advanced ages.'"

David smiled. "Ottignon invited me to come back and try out his facilities with no charge."

"By all means, let's take him up on his invitation."

Zach folded his newspaper, beaming.

Without the hoopla of flags and orchestra, the gymnasium presented a different spectacle. A lone gymnast hoisted his body slowly above the level of the flying rings, toes pointed as he raised his legs to the horizontal, his biceps quivering as he held the position, then lowered himself into a straight-armed back somersault. The young men using the various pieces of apparatus paid him no more attention than they did the oversized mottoes on the walls. Their grunts and explosions of breath came at regular intervals in their rhythmic, self-absorbed repetitions. David stood a moment, eyes glued to their powerfully developed bodies.

Ottignon welcomed them effusively. The muscular proprietor led Zach and David through his establishment, pointing with pride to climbing ropes, vaulting horse, horizontal bars, pulley weights, dumb-bells and curved boards for the development of abdominal muscles. David breathed deeply, savoring the pungent aroma of liniment mixed with sweat pouring from the bare chests of the straining athletes.

Zach cast his eye along the rack of graduated weights as Ottignon left them with an invitation to try their strength. "I lifted bar bells in my younger days," he said, as he laid aside his jacket and shirt. "Though I suppose I'll not be able to match the strength I had back then." He hefted a set of weights, then reluctantly exchanged them for a lighter pair and fit them onto the bar.

David paused in the midst of unbuttoning his own shirt to watch him. Zach's muscles tensed as he lifted the bar bell to chest height, then slowly raised it above his head. His bare chest was solid and firmly muscled beneath its crop of curling gray hair.

He's not stout at all, David thought, realizing he'd expected him to be from his bulk and round face. In fact, unclothed, he looks nearly as well muscled as any of the men here. He stood motionless, unable to take his eyes from Zach as he started on another repetition of the exercise.

Zach lowered the bar, then caught David's eye, smiling as if he'd guessed his thoughts. David flushed as he smiled back, embarrassed to be caught staring. Hurriedly he undid the rest of his buttons, and turned toward the rack of weights.

He should've paid more attention to Ottignon's caution not to overdo exercising the first time, David told himself ruefully that night. He could already feel the soreness in his shoulders as he pulled on his nightshirt. Doubtless he'd be stiff by morning.

A firm knock sounded on his door. Zach smiled ruefully as he stepped into the room. "I'm not in as good shape as I like to pretend. You're a bit sore yourself, I'll warrant."

"I'm afraid so," David admitted.

"It's fortunate I have this, then." Zach held out a jar of liniment. "It's good stuff. Here, take off your nightshirt and I'll rub it in for you."

The liniment was good. He could feel its heat entering his muscles as Zach's strong hands kneaded his shoulders, his thumbs pressing firmly between the blades. He closed his eyes, savoring the warm, pleasurable sensation.

Zach stripped off his shirt and settled himself in turn on the room's one chair. David's palms and fingertips tingled as he rubbed the liniment slowly into Zach's firm shoulders and upper arms, feeling the warmth of his body under his hands.

Zach rose. He smiled as he shrugged his arms into his sleeves. David smiled back, realizing he'd forgotten to pull on his nightshirt again.

"David—"

Zach paused. He looked at David, his expression oddly wistful, then slowly shook his head. "I've forgotten what I meant to say." His eyes dropped to his shirt buttons as he rapidly did them up. "Well, it's late. We'd both do well to get a good night's sleep."

"I intend to," David assured him.

He wasn't sleepy though. He sank onto the chair, reaching for a novel he'd started a few days ago, decided after a few pages he wasn't in the mood for reading either.

His sketchbook lay on top of the bureau. He hadn't drawn much for his own pleasure since taking the job with Leslie's. He reached for it, then closed his eyes to summon an image from memory. His fingers darted across the paper, recreating Zach's solid figure as he prepared to heft the bar bell that afternoon.

David studied the drawing, remembering the warmth of Zach's flesh under his hands, suddenly wondering how it would feel to run his hands down Zach's muscled, hairy chest, then slide his palms downward till—

The sketchbook trembled in his hands. What in God's name was he thinking of? He ripped the sketch from the book and shoved it into his bottom bureau drawer.

He was scheduled to cover the first graduation ceremonies of the new school for the blind in the morning. Quickly he turned down the counterpane and climbed into bed, fixing his mind firmly on the upcoming assignment.

Chapter Six - 1857

"Drop what you're working on for now and get these copied onto the blocks," Frank Leslie directed his artists. He handed a photograph apiece to David, Elliot and William Waud, a young Englishman Leslie had recently taken on. "Our correspondent in St. Louis persuaded Dred Scott and his family to sit for daguerreotypes. We're featuring them in the next issue. Give me quarter-page copies of Scott and his wife, and an eighth of a page on the daughters. Stick with it as long as it takes; you'll be compensated for overtime."

"Damnation!" Waud muttered after Leslie strode off again. "I had plans for this evening. The Supreme Court handed down its ruling on the poor blighter three months ago. Back in March. What's he in such a bloody hurry for?"

Elliot grinned sardonically. "Leslie's had a bee in his bonnet ever since Harper started his illustrated. Scared they'll steal his thunder. Though you'd think people would be sick and tired of the nigger question by now."

"I'm afraid we haven't heard the last of it," David said. "Take Greeley. Since the Court ruled that living in a free state didn't free Scott legally, hardly a day goes by without Greeley running some story on the horrors of slavery. The decision's turned a lot of moderates like him into abolitionists. It seems to be dividing the country even more."

David turned back to his drawing table, propping the daguerreotype of Dred Scott up on the slanted board. The face of the black man in the portrait gave no hint of the fire that had caused him to sue his master for freedom after being returned to the slave state of Missouri. At least, there was nothing apparent to David in the man's expression but a mixture of the dignity and weary resignation he'd often noted in the faces of elderly slaves back home.

You'd think he'd have had the good sense to stay up North when he had the chance, if he was so eager for freedom, David thought, instead of causing himself and everyone else so much trouble.

David had to agree with Elliot. You'd think Greeley and his staff would be sick of the slavery issue by now, but day after day, week after week, the *Tribune* badgered its readers with horror stories collected from abolitionist travelers and culled from Southern newspapers. As the off-year, state election neared, Greeley's campaign intensified. You could scarcely leaf through the paper without seeing a copy of an advertisement for some hapless whip-scarred runaway, or a lurid account of an innocent mulatto maiden, delivered into a den of iniquity to satisfy the debts of her impecunious half-brother.

It was a relief to sit down in Pfaff's with his friends and hear talk on another topic, as Stephen Van Dyjk's round face, alight with quiet joy, told Elliot, Zach, Dick Potter and David of his forthcoming marriage to the young woman he'd been courting for the past year.

"She'll be sending out formal invitations," Stephen said. "But I wanted you to know when it'll be. We've planned the service for the Saturday after Thanksgiving. We're hoping you'll all be able to attend."

"We'll be delighted to," Zach said heartily. He sat back, lifting his tankard, looking nearly as pleased as the prospective bridegroom.

David smiled regretfully. "I'm afraid I won't be able to make it. I already promised Mike and Rachel I'd come up for Thanksgiving."

"Well, we'll miss you, but of course family comes first."

Dick leaned forward, suddenly intent. "That's the *Negro* branch of your family, am I correct? Isn't Mike the fugitive Zach told us about, whom you helped escape from slavery? You're going to his house for Thanksgiving dinner?"

"Well, I think Mike wrote we'd be eating at his sister-in-law's. They have more room for company. It's the same size house, actually, but Mike uses what was meant to be the dining room to see patients, so that leaves the kitchen the only place to eat, and that's not really big enough for a crowd." David stopped, feeling foolish. Dick wouldn't be interested in Mike's room arrangements.

But Dick was staring at him intently. "I find it hard to believe you're intending to sit down at table with a tribe of Africans."

"Mike's not African. He was born in Virginia, same as I was. I don't see why I shouldn't eat with him. We grew up in the same house. He used to sleep on the floor of my bedroom when we were boys." David flushed, thinking how that must sound to them.

He looked back at Dick, his perplexity changing to annoyance. "I don't see why you should object, Dick. I thought you were such a strong abolitionist."

"An abolitionist, yes. I do my utmost to obey the will of the Lord in all things, including his words in Deuteronomy that 'Thou shalt not deliver unto his master the servant which is escaped from his master unto thee.' But that doesn't mean we need to live cheek by jowl with heathen savages. The Lord intended Africa as the home of the Negro people. Blacks liberated from bondage should be colonized there as soon as practicable."

"I can't imagine Mike and Rachel wanting to go live in some jungle." David glanced at the others, wondering if they all felt the same as Dick. Stephen seemed barely aware of the conversation, his mind still on his upcoming wedding. Elliot was turning from David to Dick like a spectator at a tennis match, an expression of obvious amusement on his face.

Zach cleared his throat, turning toward Dick. "I know you think I'm little better than a heathen myself, Dick, but it may surprise you to learn that my upbringing included a thorough grounding in the scriptures. I believe the rest of that passage you just quoted goes, `He shall dwell with thee, even among you, in that place which he shall choose in one of thy gates, where it liketh him best'."

Elliot laughed.

David smiled at Dick's look of dismay, then nodded his thanks to Zach for his support. Zach smiled back warmly. He continued looking at David a moment, then pulled an envelope from his breast pocket, scribbling on it with the stub of a pencil.

He looked across the table at David again. "Just you, your father and Mike lived in your house together?" he asked.

David nodded, startled. "And Hetty, of course, till she died. Mike's mother. He must've been about twelve then. Let me see. Yes, she died right after the big fire in twenty-seven, when I was thirteen. We were all out the entire night passing buckets up from the river. She took a chill, passed on just a week or two later."

"Do you know how long your father owned Hetty when Mike was born?"

"No, I have no idea."

"Well, it's not that important." Zach looked at his scribbles again, frowning in concentration.

"What did you want to know for?" David asked.

"Just an idea I had. You told me your father was always fond of Mike, that he had him run his errands, do odd jobs in his office. I suppose he realized, even then, that Mike was his son?"

"Well, of course he did. He always knew that." David stared at his friend. "I've already told you all about Dad and Mike."

Zach smiled. "I know. I just wanted to check my facts before I started writing. Yet your father sold him to a slave trader. He wasn't much more than a boy then, either. Didn't you tell me seventeen or eighteen?"

"About that." David was filled with sudden unease. "Before you start writing what?"

"Well, I need to check with Greeley first, but a man selling his own son— You can see what kind of an impact that would have on our readers."

"On your readers! Forget it, Zach! I don't want you writing a story about Dad and Mike!"

Zach leaned toward David. "I don't think you realize how much a piece like this can turn public opinion against slavery. I should think you'd appreciate that more than most, David."

"I don't give a damn about slavery! You're not spreading scandals about my family all over your paper," David said, angrily aware of the others turned toward them, listening. "And I'm sick of hearing you all talk about them like they were an exhibit from Barnum's!" He rose, shoving his way through the tables, still furious as he slammed the front door of the boardinghouse.

Mrs. Chapman stuck her head out of her room, glaring at him in annoyance. David sighed. "I'm sorry, ma'am." He closed the door to his room quietly, trying to calm down. At least he'd nipped Zach's notion in the bud.

David overslept the next morning, missing breakfast, just as glad not to see Zach and Elliot. He bought a sweet roll, eating it on the ferry on the way to his assignment in Brooklyn.

He was still put out at suppertime. He nodded shortly to Elliot and Zach, then dug into his food, making desultory conversation with Mr. Wilson, the elderly bank clerk who had the room next to his.

"David." Zach caught up to him as he left the dining room. "Don't just rush off without a word."

David turned, reluctantly smiling at Zach.

"I need to talk to you about the piece on your family."

David's smile faded. "There's nothing to talk about. Just forget it, will you! I've had a long day. If you'll excuse me, I'm turning in." He took the stairs two at a time, his mood sharp with annoyance again.

"Care to join me for a beer, David, or are you still in a huff?"

David looked up as Elliot leaned against the edge of his drawing table early the next evening.

"A beer sounds good. I've been copying these onto the blocks since morning." David smiled apologetically. "I'm afraid I got a little peeved the other night over Zach's notion to do a story on my father."

"So I saw." Elliot smiled. "Fact is, I was kind of surprised to learn you changed your mind."

"What do you mean?"

"Well, since he's gone ahead with it, I just assumed you had."

"Gone ahead with it!? You're sure?"

Elliot nodded. "I ran into Dick a couple of hours ago, and he said Greeley was enthusiastic about the idea, told Zach to finish it up this morning so he could make the weekly edition." He smoothed his mustache and smiled crookedly. "I gather it wasn't with your okay. Well, Zach can be pretty pigheaded when he gets on his high horse about slavery."

The pencil fell from David's fingers. He rushed into the street, dodging heedlessly through the traffic in front of the *Tribune* building.

Zach looked at him in surprise.

"Elliot told me you went ahead with your story on my father."

Zach nodded. "I tried to talk to you about it, but—"

"Goddamn it, Zach!" David took a breath, trying to calm down. "I want you to kill it."

"It's too late." Zach spread his hands. "It's already gone down to the compositors. David, listen to me—"

"Shut up! Just shut up!" Tremors of rage shook David uncontrollably. His hands tightened into fists. He took two steps around Zachary's desk and swung. The shock traveled up his arm as his fist thudded into Zach's cheekbone.

Zach rocked back, grabbing at his desk to save himself from falling over. His chair crashed to the floor. He scrambled to his feet, a look of astonishment on his face.

David stared at him, finally thinking to draw back his hand for another blow.

Zach reached him before it could land, grabbed David's arms just above his elbows and pinned them to his sides. "Keep your shirt on, David. Just listen to me—"

"Get your hands off me!" David struggled to free himself from Zach's grip, humiliation warring with fury. He gave a last, desperate heave and wrenched loose, rushing from the news office past the staring faces of the *Tribune* reporters.

He reached the Murray Hill Reservoir, three miles uptown, before exhaustion forced a halt to his flight.

From the broad walls of the reservoir, it was possible to see both the East and Hudson Rivers, plus the village of Harlem in the distance. David didn't glance at the view.

The weekly digest edition of the *Tribune* circulated nation-wide. There was virtually no chance his father wouldn't see the story. David stared down into the dark waters of the reservoir, visualizing his father's shock and humiliation as he read it.

How the hell was he going to face him?

And why had he fled here like a fool, instead of marching into Greeley's office and demanding he kill the story?

He pulled his watch from his pocket. The editor would be gone by now. He resumed his fruitless pacing along the promenade though it had long since grown too dark to see even the waters below.

Only two or three fellow lodgers still occupied their favorite seats in the parlor when he entered Mrs. Chapman's. David ignored their greetings, heading straight for his room. He couldn't settle down. He paced restlessly from the door to the window and back again, hearing the remaining tenants climb the stairs for the night.

There was no point even trying to sleep. David pulled out a sheet of writing paper. If he could somehow explain to his father—

It was no use. He threw the crumpled paper into the stove, pulled out a fresh sheet, then tossed it away too, resumed his unavailing pacing.

There was a rap on his door. David yanked it open. Zachary stood in the doorway. His broad shoulders were slumped with weariness, his normally ruddy complexion pallid with fatigue. The purple bruise on his cheek stood out in sharp contrast.

"What the hell do you want?"

"To give you this." Zach thrust several sheets of closely scrawled manuscript into David's hand. "I was going to burn it, but I saw your lamp through the window and thought you'd prefer to see it done yourself."

David stared at him blankly.

"You rushed off before I could tell you that I'd see Greeley about pulling it."

"It's not in the paper?" David looked down at the manuscript, weak with relief. He sank onto the edge of his bed.

"No it's not in the paper. I thought Greeley was going to have a fit of apoplexy, but he finally agreed to break up the forms. I suppose I'd let him think you were agreeable to running the piece in the first place.

"I would've let you know sooner, but I had to crank out a story to fill the hole, and then I stayed on to help with the typesetting." Zach rubbed his eyes. "Mind if I come in a minute?" He slumped onto David's chair without waiting for an answer.

David looked at him. "Do you ever wait for permission before you go ahead and do what you damn well please?"

Zach smiled ruefully. "I suppose that's one of my failings. I was sure you'd see it my way once you thought things over. I didn't understand how distressed you were till you burst in and punched me this afternoon."

"I don't recall ever hitting anyone before," David said slowly.

"I didn't think you had." Zach gave another rueful smile and felt the bruise gingerly with his fingertips. "It was an honest mistake on my part though. I assumed you'd drop your objections once you understood how such a story could aid the anti-slavery cause. Especially after what you've told me of the suffering that slavery caused your brother.

"And it isn't as if you kept your connection a secret. Your father even showed us a daguerreotype of his grandchildren when he was here."

"That doesn't mean you need to brand him an adulterer in front of the whole country!"

"I didn't look at it that way. I daresay I completely misapprehended how you felt."

"How the hell would you feel if it was your father?"

"I don't know. I don't think about my father very often." Zach lapsed into silence, staring down at the backs of his hands. "He threw me out of the house when I was fifteen," he said finally.

"Threw you out! How could he? What for? Because you wouldn't follow the occupation he wanted?"

"What? No, it was nothing like that. He— he caught me doing something he didn't approve of."

"You never said—"

"It's not a subject I'm fond of talking about."

David stared at Zach, trying to imagine a circumstance that would have made his own father evict him from his home when he was still a half-grown boy. "But what did you do? I mean at fifteen—"

Zach gave a thin smile. "Oh, I didn't have to fend for myself. I had an aunt in the next village, who was charitable enough to take me in. I found work in the local printing shop so I could at least repay her for my keep. And my mother stood by me. She slipped over to see me once or twice a month, till she took ill with pneumonia a year later. I attended her funeral service, of course." He paused. "My father wouldn't speak a single word to me, even then. The day after we laid Mother to rest, I packed up what possessions I had and struck out on my own. Worked here and there, at printing and reporting, till I ended up in New York City. I haven't seen my father since that day. I don't even know if he's alive or dead." Zach's voice trembled slightly. He attempted a shrug.

David studied him, taking in the rigid set of Zach's shoulders, the way his fingernails dug into the palms of his hands. He walked over to him and laid a hand on his shoulder.

"Well, so far as I can see, it's his loss, not yours, Zach," he said at last.

Chapter Seven - 1859

Dᴀᴠɪᴅ ʀᴇᴀᴄʜᴇᴅ ɪɴᴛᴏ ʜɪꜱ ʙᴜʀᴇᴀᴜ ᴅʀᴀᴡᴇʀ for his woolen underwear, stowing it in his carpet bag with his extra shirts and collars. Charles Town, Virginia would likely get cold nights, though it was still early autumn.

Nor was there any telling what sort of accommodations they'd find, with the town already jammed with spectators come to see John Brown and his followers brought to justice. Excitement over the slavery issue had died down somewhat in the two-and-a half years since the Supreme Court ruling on Dred Scott, but now flared to new intensity with Brown's raid on the arsenal at Harper's Ferry. He opened the door to Zachary's knock. "You still packing, David?"

"I'm nearly done. We've got over two hours though."

"I know." Zach smiled. "Actually, I'd appreciate the use of your shaving things before you pack them up. I've had these whiskers so long, I'll be damned if I know what I did with my own razor."

"You're going to shave them off?" David watched in surprise as Zach filled his wash basin with water, then began lathering up the soap. "How come? I'm not sure I'd even know you without them."

Zach continued working the soap into a lather, then unfolded David's razor, testing its edge gingerly against his thumb. "That's my hope. Though it's not *my* notion to shave, I'll tell you that. Greeley insisted on it. He's had one reporter run out of Charles Town already. The *Tribune's* not exactly welcome south of the Mason-Dixon line."

David laughed. "I'm not surprised."

"I have to admit, my face is well known among my fellow newsmen. Fact is, Greeley was still reluctant to send me, despite my promise to shave." Zach hacked at his growth of beard with a scissors, then began brushing the lather onto his cheeks. The shaving soap foamed over the top of the jaggedly trimmed beard. Thin rivulets of soapy water trickled back into the wash basin.

"You look like a mad dog, Zach." David grinned. He shoved the last of his clothes into his bag and sat on the edge of his bed to watch. Zach drew the razor down his cheek, squinted into the mirror and repeated the operation, wincing as the blade bit into freshly denuded skin. His soapy chin whiskers slithered into the basin.

"And now?"

David studied him. Zach looked younger, his face vulnerable without its heavy wreath of hair. "Like a man who's just shaved off his beard. Your skin's lighter where it was growing, not as weathered." He stood, stretching out his hand involuntarily. Zach's newly shaven skin felt soft to his touch. David dropped his hand, flushing in momentary embarrassment. "Well, I doubt anyone will examine you that closely."

Charles Town's unpaved streets were coated with dust kicked up in thick clouds by the shuffling feet of volunteer militiamen. Members of the parading companies dangled their muskets with casual threat as they spat out challenges to newly arriving visitors.

The few rooms at the town inns had long since been taken.

"Landlord here says there's a chance a Mrs. Jackson, a little ways out of town, might be able to put us up," David reported to Zach, as he exited from the third one they'd tried. "'Go about a mile,' he said, 'then look for a white house on the left.' Better let me do the talking, Zach," he added, as they turned down the short lane leading to the sagging, white house.

David smiled disarmingly at the plump, suspicious farmwife. "Afternoon, ma'am. I'm David Carter, with *Leslie's Illustrated*, and this is Mr. Walker. We were told in town you might have rooms to let."

"That depends." Mrs. Jackson pushed a strand of gray hair back into her bun and placed her hands on her hips. "Mr. Jackson and myself don't hold with having no abolitionists under our roof. Where y'all say you're from?"

"From New York now, ma'am, but my people come from down near Fredericksburg. I was raised in Alexandria."

"Fred'ricksburg?" She nodded, pleased. "I thought you sounded like a home boy. What you doin' up in New York with all those Yankees?"

David shrugged. "It's the only place I could find work as an artist, ma'am."

"Well." She paused. "I knew a Silas Carter came from down round Fred'ricksburg, let me see, 'bout 'thirty-six or thirty-seven. Married up with Sue Jenkins. Had themselves six, seven young'uns. He any kin to you?"

"Well, not any close kin that I know of, ma'am, though I think my granddaddy might've had a cousin named Silas. His name was Enoch Carter. He farmed most of his life, raised tobacco mostly."

Mrs. Jackson smiled. "Well, we ain't got but the one room, but I reckon you're welcome to that."

"We can share it," Zach put in quickly.

"You'll have to share a bed, too, mister. Ain't got but the one. Follow after me, and I'll show you."

Zach sank onto the sagging mattress after Mrs. Jackson left them, stretching himself out comfortably, head pillowed on his hands. "It's fortunate for Leslie he had you to dispatch down here, even though he's bent over backwards not to offend the slave-holders. It's not so easy being a *Tribune* correspondent, I'll tell you that. I'm forced to disguise myself like a play actor and send my copy in secret through Greeley's man in Maryland."

David grinned at him. "And you're enjoying every minute of it. Come on, let's get back to town and find out what's going on."

The town square was teeming with the tramping militia, correspondents from papers up and down the East Coast, giggling girls in twos and threes talking excitedly and casting sideways glances at the militiamen, rifle-toting farmers on horseback down from farms in the surrounding hills, small boys scrambling up trees for a better look at the doings and busy housewives who had found an errand in town a sudden necessity.

The jail stood catty-cornered from the stately, columned courthouse where the Jefferson County grand jury had already indicted Brown for murder and treason to the Commonwealth, a week after his capture. David drew a rough sketch of the jail and its heavy guard of militiamen in full dress uniforms.

Zach tapped him on the shoulder. "I've been talking to some of these fellows while you were drawing. They say the jailer isn't averse to admitting newsmen in to see Old Brown. I suppose you'd better do the talking again."

David nodded eagerly. They edged their way through the guards, up the half dozen steps of the narrow porch fronting the jailhouse. The guard at the door moved back a reluctant half step as David identified himself.

"Wait a minute, David!" Zach grabbed David's arm, pulling him back the way they'd come. "Don't look now, but that son-of-a-bitch from the *Herald* was coming right toward us. Blasted pro-slavery rag. He'd like nothing better than to expose me."

David glanced over his shoulder. The *Herald* correspondent had climbed onto the porch from an opposing set of stairs, and was turning into the doorway of the jail.

"Yeah, I see him. And we were practically inside too. It's a good thing Leslie doesn't know we're traveling together. He'd blow his stack if he knew I missed a chance like that." He shook his head, smiling ruefully at Zach. "Well, I guess we can try again tomorrow. We might as well get some supper."

"Lumpy as this mattress is, I daresay we'll sleep well anyhow." Zach hung his shirt on a wooden peg on the wall. "I'm getting past the age where I relish such a long journey."

David glanced at him. Zach had stepped out of his trousers and stood momentarily nude as he reached for his nightshirt. His bare thighs boasted the same firm musculature as his chest, his stocky body still showing only the hint of a paunch. David forced his eyes away. "You've a long way to go till old age, Zach."

"Well, our sessions at Ottignon's may have done me a bit of good." Zach chuckled. "But I daresay I'll sleep well, in any event." He stretched luxuriously, then arranged himself comfortably under the counterpane.

David shifted uneasily on the sagging mattress alongside him, feeling the closeness of Zach's comfortably sprawled body. He couldn't remember ever sharing a bed before.

Well, it didn't matter. He relaxed, letting himself be lulled by Zach's rhythmic snores.

Despite his closed eyes, David could still see Zachary standing across the small room, just a few feet from him. He watched, helpless to turn away, as Zach stepped lazily out of his clothes, stretching his bare, muscular body. Zach met his eyes then, smiling at David's fascination.

He moved toward Zach, unable to stop himself, reaching out to touch him. The smooth skin of his side was warm under his fingertips, soft and unprotected like his newly shaven face. David caressed him. His hand moved down of its own accord, stroking Zach's firm, hairy thigh.

His fingers were inches from Zach's member. He trembled.

David woke. He lay pressed tightly against Zach in the sagging bed, his nightshirt up in a tangle around his waist. His own member had grown hard and throbbing as his nude flesh rubbed Zach's flank. My God! David held his breath, terrified to move. Dear God, don't let him waken!

A Different Sin

Zach stirred, turning toward David, his arm outstretched. David flung himself convulsively back to his side of the bed.

He lay still, barely breathing till he heard Zach's snores start up once more. Thank God he hadn't been discovered!

How could he dare even close his eyes again? David turned onto his stomach, sliding to the edge of the bed. He hooked his right arm and leg over the side, then lay rigidly, waiting for morning.

"Better get up, David, if we're to get breakfast before the trial. We'll have to be at the courthouse when the doors open just to get inside, with this mob in town."

David opened his eyes to daylight. Zach stood in his shirtsleeves, lathering up David's shaving soap. He'd gone back to sleep after all then. Christ, how could he have had such a dream?

He glanced at Zachary. Zach gave the soap a last stir with the brush, then picked up the razor. He grimaced as he drew it down his cheek. "It's getting late, David," he repeated.

"I'm up." There was nothing on Zach's mind beyond his impatience to get to the courthouse. David was sure of it. Zach couldn't know about the bizarre dream he'd had. David thought of how he'd awakened lying practically atop Zach. He must have dreamt that too. He put it out of his mind as he pulled on his clothes.

The courthouse was as crowded as Zach had predicted. John Brown, weakened by the wounds he'd received at his capture, lay on a cot before the bench. David edged through the crowd till he had a clear view of the bearded fanatic lying placidly under a counterpane.

Brown's court-appointed lawyer, Lawson Botts, moved to the bench, entering into evidence a letter from the defendant's former Ohio hometown avowing that madness was a family curse. The prisoner should be declared innocent by reason of insanity, Botts argued.

A stir went through the courtroom as Brown drew himself painfully to his feet, glaring at his lawyer. "I look upon it as a miserable artifice and trick. I am perfectly unconscious of insanity, and I reject, so far as I am capable, any attempts to interfere in my behalf on that score."

The crowded courtroom was silent as he lay back. David looked around, startled at the expressions of reluctant respect on the faces of onlookers, then returned to his sketch.

The inn that evening was as crowded as the courtroom. Nearly an hour went by before a table was freed up. It looked to be an equally long wait to get any dinner. David pulled out his sketches. The one of Brown standing before the court could use more work, he thought critically.

"I see you haven't made him out to be quite as dastardly a brigand as your counterpart from *Harper's*," Zach said, leaning across the table for a closer look. "Well, what do you think?"

David looked up. "I was just hoping that Leslie gives these to Bill Waud to copy and not to Elliot. Elliot's too satisfied with a halfway job. He has the talent to be a really fine artist but he doesn't give a damn about doing anything with it."

Zach chuckled. "I meant what do you think of Brown?"

"Oh." David put his sketches away. "He's more impressive than I expected. But he's crazy, no matter what he says. How else could he have believed that twenty-two men could do away with slavery? And kill half a dozen innocent people in the attempt?"

"He's guilty of misjudgment, I'll grant you that. But I warrant you he'll be remembered as a martyr to the cause of freedom."

David looked around uneasily. "Come on, Zach. If anyone's martyred it's the people he murdered. And the first one a black for God's sake."

"That was a regrettable accident. And he'll doubtless hang for his pains. But his cause was righteous."

"Not his deeds though. The court has no choice but to hang him if it's to do justice."

"Not a year ago, David, Charles Lamar smuggled three hundred Africans into Georgia on his accursed sloop. Three hundred human souls! And for every African he succeeded in landing alive, another died from his sufferings en route. Murdered as surely as if they'd been shot in cold blood!"

"Zach—"

"I covered Lamar's trial for Greeley." Zach raised his voice a notch higher, ignoring David's interruption. "The evidence was conclusive that he operated the Wanderer as a slaver in clear violation of Federal law. Yet not only was he acquitted, but allowed to buy back his ship at auction after it was seized. Now tell me the slaveholders care for justice!"

"Zach, shut up!"

"You disagree? You think Brown deserves a noose for his efforts while Lamar is toasted throughout the South for kidnap and murder?"

David leaned across the table, speaking as quietly as he could."I think you're probably right about Lamar. But this isn't the place to bring it up, for God's sake."

"Good Lord!" Zach looked cautiously around, then turned to David, abashed. "I forgot myself."

"That's evident. Let's hope no one overheard you." David sighed, then smiled ruefully at Zach, unable to stay annoyed at him. "Well, noisy as this place is, there's probably no harm done."

After the tumult of the inn, the quiet of the country road leading back to the Jacksons' was welcome. David strode alongside Zach, letting his mind wander.

The hoofbeats of galloping horses suddenly shattered the evening's silence. David edged closer to the side of the road as half a dozen mounted men rode into view.

The riders pulled up rein, forming a semicircle around the two men. David swallowed nervously. He glanced at Zach, then back at the riders. At least three or four of them wore the uniforms of local militia.

The lead rider, a heavily bearded man of middle years, gazed from one to the other in angry scrutiny, then turned to Zach. "Mister, we don't want no *Tribune* reporters in this town.

"We're givin' y'all notice that the citizens of Charles Town ain't puttin' up with no nigger lovin' flapjaws incitin' our slaves. There's a train leaving out of here in an hour, and we aim to see you're on it."

Zach spread his hands disarmingly. "Sir, I give you my word I have no purpose in Charles Town other than to report on the trial."

The militiaman spat. "Your word don't count for nothin' round here, mister. Now you can either get on that train peaceable or ride out on a rail. And that goes for your friend here, too."

David winced. Zach smiled ruefully. "You leave me little choice, sir. But Mr. Carter here has nothing to do with the *Tribune*. We fell into each other's company by chance on the train to Charles Town. He's a Southerner himself, hardly an abolitionist."

"That so, mister?" The bearded man gave David a suspicious stare.

He nodded slowly. There was no point in them both getting thrown out of town. "I've been drawing for *Leslie's* a few years, but I was raised in Alexandria. My people are still there."

The man turned away to talk in whispers with the other mounted men. David strained unsuccessfully to make out their words.

"You swear you ain't no abolitionist?" David nodded. "My father owned slaves, sir."

"Well, reckon as how you can stay then," the man said, his voice still reluctant. "But better watch who you 'sociate with from now on."

"I intend to, sir."

The man nodded briefly. He spat once more, in the direction of Zach's feet. "We'll be keeping a lookout to see you get on that train, mister."

"You needn't have walked all the way back to the station with me."

David smiled. "I want to make sure you're safely on the train myself."

"I'm probably safer from our friends there than from Greeley, when he learns how I muffed this assignment." Zach smiled wearily. "Well, at least I can stop scraping the skin off my face every morning."

Zach picked up his bag as the chugging of the train grew louder. "You'd best stay out of sight. I'll— I'll miss your company, David." He walked quickly across the platform. The walk back seemed longer than he'd remembered, without Zach's company. David fell onto the sagging bed, exhausted.

At least, with Zach gone, he needn't fear any more disturbing dreams, he thought, before sleep overtook him.

John Brown's conviction was a foregone conclusion. The fiery raider was sentenced to be hanged on the third of December, a month hence; the trials of the four followers captured with him remained on the docket. It had been four years since David had been home. He dispatched his sketches to Leslie's and caught the train to Alexandria for the weekend recess. The town seemed smaller than he'd remembered, the cobblestone streets less trafficked, as he hurried from the station.

He found his father at home, sitting in the front room with his Uncle James. "Dad." David embraced him, nodded coldly to his uncle.

George Carter held onto his son a moment, looking at him fondly. "It's good to have you here. I was hoping, when you wrote you were going to Charles Town, that you'd be able to manage a visit."

"I wasn't sure if I could. But they're trying each of Brown's men separately, so I was able to get away during the recess."

His uncle looked at David with a smile. "I take it you still enjoy illustrating court cases more than arguing them."

David nodded shortly. "Yes, sir."

"You know, I haven't heard from you in all the time you've been up North, excepting through your father."

"I haven't had anything to say to you, Uncle James." James Harrison's face tightened. He rose. "I'll leave y'all to get some visiting done, George." David sat in the chair his uncle had vacated. "Why do you go on seeing him after what he did to you?"

"He's a lonely old man, same as myself. Why spend what few years are left us feuding? I don't have many friends in this town, you know." There was a moment's silence. "I miss your company, son."

"Well." David looked at his father awkwardly. "You'll be going up to Boston for Christmas?"

"Yes, I'm looking forward to it." He paused. "I've given some thought to moving there altogether."

A Different Sin

"To Boston? You're going to move up there?"

"Well, probably not. I don't want to wear out my welcome. And it would be hard to uproot myself, at my age. Still, it would be good to see the children more often. They grow up so quickly. You know, Peter's graduating from Boston Latin this year. He's going on to college. Oberlin, I think. He's made up his mind to become a lawyer." His face lit up with fond pride.

"Oh. I imagine he'd make a good one."

"Very good, I should think. He's a bright boy, same as his father."

"Still, it won't be easy for him."

"No, it won't. He's very determined, though." David smiled. "He takes after Mike in that too." His father sobered. "If only I hadn't been so shortsighted. I could've freed him, sent him to school."

"I used to wonder why you didn't, when I was a boy." David looked at his father's face and stopped himself. "Mike did all right though."

"All those years, when I didn't even know if he was still alive."

"No use crying over spilled milk, Dad."

"You're right." George Carter sat up straighter. "I want you to stop harping on the past, too."

"What do you mean?"

"I'm talking about your attitude to James." He paused. "He felt he had a legitimate grievance against me. Maybe—maybe with some justification."

"He had no justification."

The older man waved his words aside. "But in any event, you know how much he's always cared for you. And he's alone now. You can at least call on him while you're here."

David sighed. "Yes, sir."

"So you've decided to come pay your respects after all. I suppose I have your father to thank." His uncle gave David a slight smile.

David flushed. "I take it you see as much of Dad as ever."

"When he's at home and not on one of his infernal trips to Boston."

"He told me he's thinking of moving up there," David blurted. He studied his uncle. James Harrison's blue eyes were sharp as ever, but new lines had etched themselves into his face since he'd seen him last. He picked up his drink from the table between them and gave David another ironic smile.

"I wouldn't be surprised. Wouldn't be at all surprised. I don't mean to criticize your father to your face, but George is making a laughing-stock of himself running back and forth to see those nigra brats. And the way he was so godawful pleased they gave the last one Carter for his middle name. Joshua Carter Mabaya! My God!"

David shrugged. "He wanted his name carried on."

"Now that's what you should've done for him. If you'd given him grandchildren, he'd never have bothered with those halfbreed brats."

He might be right, David thought. He envisioned his father looking forward to visiting him with the same eagerness and pride he lavished now on Michael's household, dandling his children with the same affection—

Hell, what he was dreaming of? He'd never had any inclination toward marriage. Just this afternoon he'd run into Martha Ann Simpson, married over three years now, with two infants and another on the way. He'd been hard pressed to fill five minutes with small talk.

"He has grandchildren, Uncle James. Mike and Rachel's children are his flesh and blood, you know that perfectly well. And they're a nice bunch of kids, too."

"You're as big a fool as he is, David, though it's right generous of you to take up for them." His uncle smiled. "Let's talk of something else. I don't mean to put you in an awkward position when you've come round to see me at last. How about telling me a little more of what you've been doing the last few years?"

David took a swallow of bourbon and looked at his uncle. He'd always favored him in looks, and doubtless his own hair would fade to just such a silver in time. Would he inherit James' lonely old age as well? he wondered a moment.

He set down the glass. "What would you like to hear about?"

Chapter Eight - 1859-60

D<small>AVID STOWED THE LAST OF HIS CLOTHES IN HIS BUREAU DRAWER,</small> relishing the comfort of his familiar room after a month spent covering the trial and execution of Brown and his followers. A quick knock sounded on his door. "Come in." Elliot entered as David spoke.

"Good to have you back, David. Say, you have a pair of cuffs I could borrow? I'm on my way to see a lady friend and I just realized mine are all in the wash."

Elliot was nearly always fresh out of something. "In the top drawer," David told him.

"Thanks." Elliot slouched against the bureau while he wriggled his cuff holders into place.

"It's good to be back. I hope I never have to witness another hanging." David sat on the edge of his bed. "But I have a hunch Zach's right: Brown'll be remembered by history. He must've been kicking himself for getting thrown out of Charles Town like that."

Elliot laughed. "He was. He's been stewing about it for weeks." He slipped his jacket on and headed for the door. Halfway there he turned back to David. "Maybe it's just as well for you, though. I've heard some funny stories about Zach. It might be for the best that you didn't have to bunk with him all month."

"What are you talking about?"

"I don't mean to blab, but just between you, me and the bedpost, I've heard that Zach's given to unnatural acts."

"Unnatural— I'm not even sure what you mean, but I thought Zach was a friend of yours! What the hell are you spreading rumors about him for?"

"Keep your shirt on, David. I like the guy. It's just that since he's such a good friend of *yours*, I thought I oughta warn you to watch your step with him. Forewarned is forearmed, they say." Elliot shrugged. "Well, I've probably shot my mouth off too much already. I'd best get going."

David stared after him, shaken, his mind going back to the night he'd spent with Zach in Charles Town. There'd been nothing unnatural in Zach's behavior then.

The only thing odd about that night had been that dream he'd had.

Thank God Zach hadn't wakened! He'd have had good reason to accuse David of unnatural lusts rather than the other way around.

David shook his head, willing away the memory. It was past time to forget the dream. Dreams didn't mean a damn thing anyway.

Zach wasn't alone in his prediction of John Brown's place in history. Ralph Waldo Emerson prophesied Brown's death would "make the gallows as glorious as the cross." Southern hostility toward the North swelled as prayer meetings passed resolutions memorializing Brown and church bells tolled in solemn commemoration of his execution.

By April of 1860, when the Democratic party convention assembled in Charleston, South Carolina, calls for secession mounted. Southern delegates demanded the inclusion of a slave code plank in the platform, affirming the rights of slaveholders to take their human property into the territories. Northerners voted them down. The 1856 plank calling for popular sovereignty in the territories was reaffirmed, 165 to 138.

Southerners marched out in a bloc. With insufficient delegates remaining to nominate a presidential candidate, the Democrats adjourned, postponing their convention six weeks.

"I daresay Leslie's relieved he decided to rely on sketches from correspondents, rather than send you to Charleston," Zach said, as they left the dining table for the boardinghouse parlor that evening.

David nodded. "Though we wouldn't have been traveling together, in any event." He stopped short. Why in the world had he said that?

On his other side, he caught a glimpse of Elliot's quickly hidden smirk.

David flushed. Despite himself, he'd kept dwelling on Elliot's warning. He glanced at Zach, meeting his quizzical gaze, turned quickly away. "I'm feeling a little unwell," he muttered. "I think I'll turn in early. Nothing serious," he added, as Zach's face took on a look of concern. "Probably something I ate hasn't set quite right."

He made his way to his room. Elliot's hints and his own disturbing memories refused to vanish. A second disquieting memory surfaced. David crossed to the bureau, pulling out his sketch of Zach—stripped to the waist at Ottignon's gymnasium—which he'd shoved into his bottom drawer and never brought himself to discard.

He stared at the drawing a long time, unwillingly recalling the stirrings he'd had as he gazed at Zach. For a moment, he allowed himself to relive that night in Charles Town.

Suppose, just suppose, Zach had awakened, had turned to him—

David sat trembling, his imagination faltering. Finally he pulled himself from his unwanted reverie. He thrust the sketch back into the drawer, crumpling it in his haste.

Southern outcries continued as the Republicans passed over radical party leaders Chase and Seward to nominate the moderate Illinois favorite son, Abraham Lincoln.

Democratic regulars balked at admitting Southern bolters to the new convention that convened June 18th. The party split in two. Northern loyalists nominated Stephen A. Douglas, while a Southern rights convention named John Breckinridge of Kentucky. The remnants of the Whig and American parties formed the Constitutional Union party, nominating John Bell of Tennessee.

The slavery controversy that was the focus of the presidential campaign overshadowed other news, even the tumultuous reception of the first envoy from the mysterious Japanese islands. Summer evenings in Pfaff's resounded with arguments between pro-slavery sympathizers, Garrisonian disunionists and the holders of a dozen other shades of political opinion.

David listened with unwonted concentration. If he could just keep his mind on the election, and off the disturbing thoughts that still plagued him.... It seemed impossible that Zach hadn't sensed his shameful, furtive notions, despite the efforts he'd made to drive them from his mind over the past few months, the care he'd taken to look anywhere but Zach's body on their visits to Ottignon's.

If only Elliot hadn't spoken as he had! David glanced at the younger man, sitting happily oblivious to the turmoil he'd caused him, his arm around the bare shoulder of a heavily rouged young actress. David rubbed his forehead, feeling the throbbing onset of a headache.

Zach paused in the midst of a spirited defense of the Republican presidential candidate. "You're feeling unwell? It's no wonder, in this damnable heat and noise. Let's call it a night. I daresay you'll feel better when we've gotten out in the fresh air."

David followed him upstairs, nearly running into a florid, bewhiskered man in workman's clothing, a red undershirt showing at his open collar. Zach greeted him, beaming.

"You recognized Walt Whitman?" he asked, as they walked down the street. "I would've stopped for a few minute's conversation with him, if you'd been feeling better."

David nodded, glad of the distraction. "I've seen him at Pfaff's before. He doesn't look much like a poet though."

"Yet I warrant you, he'll be remembered as one of the finest poets of our day, no matter how he dresses. In fact, he's just had a new edition of *Leaves of Grass* published by Thayer and Eldridge of Boston. I've treated myself to a copy, matter of fact."

"But I thought you already owned a copy."

Zach chuckled. "I do. But Whitman is forever expanding his magnum opus. This new edition has a number of poems he's completed in the past year or so. If you're feeling a little less under the weather, why not stop by a few minutes and I'll show you it," he added, as they entered the boardinghouse.

David sat on the edge of Zach's bed as Zach thumbed through the book. "Here, this whole section—Calamus is new in this volume." Zach settled himself next to David, reciting aloud as he held the opened book between them. "...the soul of the man I speak for rejoices in comrades... Resolv'd to sing no songs to-day but those of manly attachment... Bequeathing hence types of athletic love..."

David swallowed. "I'm not sure I follow his meaning."

"He's not always an easy man to understand. But I greatly admire his sentiments of friendship." Zach turned a few pages, murmuring lines aloud from time to time. "Publish my name...as that of the tenderest lover...whose happiest days were far away through fields, in woods, on hills, he and another wandering hand in hand, they twain apart from other men..."

He paused, settling himself more comfortably. David felt the pressure of his thigh, warm against his own. The pages rustled as Zach turned to a new poem.

"...when I thought how my dear friend my lover was
on his way coming, O then I was happy...
For the one I love most lay sleeping by me under the same
cover in the cool night,
In the stillness in the autumn moonbeams his face was
inclined toward me,
And his arm lay lightly around my breast-and that night
I was happy."

Zach's voice trailed off, the last words nearly a whisper.

David turned toward him questioningly, just as Zach turned on his own account to David. Their lips brushed lightly, momentarily, accidentally. David drew in his breath, willing himself to draw back. He couldn't. He sat motionless, feeling Zach's breath warm against his face.

"David?" Zach's voice was still a whisper. He took David's face gently between his hands. His kiss was soft but deliberate.

David closed his eyes, feeling the warm pressure of Zach's lips on his. He sat helpless a long moment, then his lips parted, and he caught Zachary in his arms, pulling him closer.

Zach's fingertips brushed his face lightly as they finally drew apart. "I've wanted to do that for so long," Zach murmured. "You're trembling," he added softly. "We needn't do anything further."

"I—" David's words caught in his throat. "I want to," he whispered finally. He reached out for Zach and pulled him down on the bed beside him, trembling still as they undressed.

He lay in Zach's arms then, his friend's strong, male body hard against his own. Slowly he let his hands roam over Zach's naked skin, his tentative touch quickening with the incredible pleasure of caressing him freely at last.

He'd hadn't dared even imagine the tingling excitement of Zach's caresses on his own body. Zach's beard brushed David's face as he kissed him again. His hands moved down David's back, firmly cupped his buttocks, stroked his member with tantalizing gentleness.

David gasped. Waves of pleasure swelled within him, rising higher and higher like an incoming tide. Zach drew David closer as he moved against him in accelerating, urgent rhythm. His exploding release subsided into smaller ripples. He gave a shuddering sigh and lay back in Zachary's arms, his body fitting itself to Zach's as if they'd lain together always.

Chapter Nine - 1860

FOR A MOMENT, AS HE CAME SLOWLY TO CONSCIOUSNESS, David thought he'd dreamed again. He woke fully then. Morning sunlight illuminated Zach's room, the rumpled bedclothes, his shirt and trousers tossed on the floor alongside the volume of poetry. David turned stiffly, feeling Zach's warm bulk next to him. He took a deep breath, wincing at the odors of their mingled sweat and semen.

Zach stirred. He threw his arm lightly across David's chest and gave a long, contented sigh. He lay quietly another moment, then kissed David on the forehead and sat up, stretching. "We'd best get up. We'll want to have time for a good wash before breakfast is ready."

David watched him numbly. It seemed impossible that Zach could be going cheerfully about his morning routine, pouring water into his washbasin as if nothing had occurred between them. He lowered his feet slowly to the floor, unable to move further. "My God, Zach, what have we done?" he said at last.

"Nothing to regret." Zach crossed the room and laid his hand on David's shoulder. "We'd best get dressed now. There'll be time to talk later." David managed to nod. It was Sunday; at least he didn't have to show himself at *Leslie's*. He'd had thoughts of attending services at Trinity this morning, but that seemed equally impossible now.

He pulled on his discarded clothing, opened the door a crack and peered out. He'd been in and out of Zach's room dozens of times in the years he'd boarded at Mrs. Chapman's, but now he made certain the hallway was empty before scurrying down it like a sneak thief.

They walked without speaking till they reached the Murray Hill Reservoir.

"I never intended to cause you distress," Zach said at last, as they paced around the broad esplanade, out of earshot of other strollers.

"You're not to blame. I wanted it as much as you. You make me feel like—like a woman is supposed to," David admitted, his voice barely audible.

"I feel the same way about you." Zach laid a hand lightly on David's shoulder.

"Zach, for God's sake, people will see us!" David jerked away before Zach could drop his hand. He stared down at the water. "It's a sin," he said, not looking up.

"Perhaps. But I daresay there are worse sins than loving."

David glanced at Zach. "I've been lusting after you for months," he muttered.

"It's more than lust, David, on my part at any rate, I promise you that."

"Zach, for God's sake, we can't let it happen again!"

Zach sobered. He moved toward David, stopped a few, careful feet away. "It made me very happy to be close to you last night. But it'll not do anything to change our friendship."

"We'd best get back." David strode off, barely waiting for Zach. How the hell could they go on with their friendship as if nothing had happened? He ought to move out of Mrs. Chapman's, stay away from Pfaff's—

"David!" Zach's strong arms yanked him from the path of a hurtling coach. The driver's flung curses rang in his ears.

"You all right, David?"

"Yeah, fine. God, I didn't even see it!" David leaned back against Zach, starting to shake at the near miss. Zach tightened his grip on David reassuringly.

David took a deep breath. He straightened and turned to Zach, taking in his anxious expression. He managed a smile. "I'm fine, Zach. Thanks!"

How could he give up Zach's friendship? He'd just have to make sure his unnatural lust for him didn't lead to a repeat of the shameful episode of the night before.

His first thought had been right, David told himself more than once as summer mellowed into fall. He should've left Mrs. Chapman's. It would've been easier than seeing Zach daily, making casual conversation with him, all the while trying to forget the feel of Zach's naked body next to his.

True to his word, Zach didn't press him to repeat their sin. Still, David didn't dare be alone with him. When he wasn't on assignment for Leslie's at one of the numerous election rallies, he spent his evenings in the stuffy boardinghouse parlor or nursing an ale at Pfaff's.

Despite his efforts to put his lust out of his mind, he was reminded of it everywhere. The sight of Whitman, sitting in silent magnetism at a corner table of the beer cellar, induced a rush of remembered passion.

Retreating to the privacy of his room was no help. More than once he found himself staring at the sketch of Zach he'd done so long ago, crumpling it to toss into the stove, then pulling his hand back at the last moment and returning it to its hiding place. It was better to spend his time with others, sick as he was of the parlor under Mrs. Chapman's gaze, trying to read or pass the time with small talk against the steady background of rustling newspapers and clearing throats.

At least in his hours at work he could lose himself in concentration. With just over a month to go till the November election, campaigning intensified. David's pencil skimmed over his sketchpad as he watched the torchlight parade of Wide-Awakes, uniformed squadrons of youthful Republican supporters, as they poured down Broadway. From his vantage point at the front of the cluster of reporters, David could clearly see the napless caps that gave the young men their nickname, the shiny material of their capes, their flaming torches, mounted atop the rails that had become Lincoln's symbol, swaying in unison as they marched. As he gazed further down the street, the raised torches seemed to blend into a stream of flames.

Zachary tapped his shoulder, speaking into his ear to be heard above the cheers and singing of the marchers. "An impressive showing for the Railsplitter."

"It makes me wish I had brush and paint instead of my pencil, to capture that torchlight." David stepped a foot or so away from Zach. He squinted at his sketch a moment, lifted his eyes back to the parade.

"I was thinking more of the numbers of Honest Abe's supporters." Zach raised his voice. "This country'll be in a bad way if the Republicans fail to carry the election."

The final marchers were in sight. The assembled reporters scribbled the last of their notes and shoved their pads into coat pockets. David continued to squint at his sketch, reworking the lines of the massed flames as the torchbearers passed from view. Finally he tucked the sketchbook under his arm. The street had become virtually deserted. Zach stood waiting.

David fell into step beside him. Their footsteps crunched on the cobblestones as they walked. "I'm afraid we'll be in a bad way if Lincoln does win," he said finally. "At least if the fire-eaters are sincere in their threats to secede."

A Different Sin

"Better disunion than carry slavery a foot further into free territory! But I wouldn't worry, David. The Southerners'll back down from their threats when the election's over, I'll warrant you that."

"I hope you're right." David fell silent, swinging his free arm as he walked. The back of his hand brushed Zach's. David jumped, pulling his hand away. He brought his mind back to the threat of disunion. "Dad writes that more and more people at home are calling for separation."

He fell silent again, thinking of the Southern fire-eaters' threats to wage war rather than remain in the Union if Lincoln was inaugurated. A shiver of unease ran through him.

Zach guessed his thoughts. "The slaveholders' talk of making war is sheer bluff. Outside of their slaves, what resources have they? No industry to speak of, precious few rail lines. Their real aim's to bully the Northern voter into voting against Lincoln." He talked on in lowered tones as they entered the darkened boardinghouse. David listened, for once preoccupied by their conversation, automatically walking alongside Zach as he turned down the hall to his room.

"There's no need to be concerned," Zach said again. "Well, I daresay we'd best say goodnight." He grasped his doorknob, hesitated a second, then slowly turned the knob.

David's preoccupation ended. He was suddenly intensely aware of Zach's body, mere inches from his in the dim hall. He sensed Zach's unspoken longing echoing his own. His own lonely bed waited down the hall.

He stood motionless, trying to force himself to turn away. He trembled, then slowly covered Zach's hand with his. The door pushed silently open under their hands.

David bowed his head as Michael asked grace, glad to avert his eyes from his father's gaze. He was being foolish, he told himself. His father couldn't know about the act he'd repeated with Zach almost nightly in the weeks since the torchlight parade. He'd fled to Boston for Christmas, relieved at removing himself at least temporarily from the occasion of sin, but the knowledge of his deed traveled with him. It seemed impossible that his act was not writ as large to the world as the letter A worn by the adulteress in Hawthorne's novel.

Michael ended the grace to a chorus of soft amens. His father turned to David. "I'm glad you were able to get time off work for a visit. The way things stand, there's no saying when we'll be able to be together like this again."

David managed a smile. His father's last utterance registered belatedly. In his preoccupation with his private torment, he'd paid scant attention to the still seething controversy that had culminated in South Carolina's proclamation of secession four days ago.

"You think it'll come to war, Dad?" he asked. George Carter turned up his palms in a helpless shrug. "I pray not, though if Lincoln tries to hold the secessionists by force...."

The rest of the family gazed at him solemnly. Only little Joshua, just a week short of his fourth birthday, plunged his spoon happily into the oyster stew Rachel had prepared for Christmas Eve dinner.

"It won't come to war, Grandpa Carter," Peter—Mike and Rachel's oldest—said bitterly. "The North finds trade with the South too profitable to fight a war over slavery. More likely they'll grant the slaveholders every concession they can to keep them in the Union. There's already been three states repealed their personal liberty laws."

David looked at Peter in astonishment. "You can't mean you'd welcome a war!"

"If it would free my people, I would!"

"David, you're a newsman," Rachel put in. "You must have more knowledge than we do of what's likely to happen."

"I'm afraid not. I don't do much reporting, except for a few scribbles to explain my sketches. And I've never paid much attention to politics."

"We'd be better off with disunion," Peter said. "At least there'd be no more fugitives returned to slavery like my father was! And the government wouldn't be bound to protect slavery anymore, so revolts would have a better chance. John Brown might've succeeded if not for the power of the army."

"He might have," David said slowly. "But I can't agree with shedding blood over slavery. I mean, I can understand how you feel about it—"

"Not really," Michael stated.

"What?"

"You can't understand how we feel, just seeing it from the outside, even coming up as close to it as you did. You've no idea what it's like to be another man's property. You've never been whipped or sold or—" Michael broke off. His face seemed graven in stone. He looked across the table, meeting his father's eyes.

Then he's never really forgiven Dad after all, David thought. He stared in fascination at his father and half-brother. A moment went by. Michael's expression softened. A look of affection slowly grew between the two men as they continued to gaze at one another.

David looked down at his plate, abashed at his sudden dismay.

"I missed you," Zach told him. He propped himself up on one elbow and smiled at David, running his fingers gently down David's jawline.

"I—" Hell, he'd missed him too. His visit to Boston hadn't changed a thing. "I was just gone a week. For God's sake, let's get our clothes on."

He shoved his shirttails into his trousers. "I thought about you a lot," he said finally. "But it was good to see my family while we still have a chance to get together."

David managed a smile. "Mike and Rachel gave Joshua a pair of skates. We took him over to the Frog Pond the day after Christmas. You'd have enjoyed seeing it."

He'd stood there as the three older children took turns guiding Joshua in circles around the crowded pond, barely seeing the scene before him, thinking of Zach's love for skating, thinking of Zach's unnatural love for him—

"You all right, David?" He started at his half-brother's question. "Yeah, fine."

"You seem troubled. You still worrying about war?" David managed a smile. "No, I think Peter's probably right about that. I was just thinking how peaceful the Common looks under the snow, and what a contrast it is to the pond. I doubt you could squeeze in another child. I thought I might do a sketch of it." He opened his sketchbook, glad he'd brought it along to give credence to his lie.

He brought himself back to the present. Zachary was smiling at him wistfully. "I envy you your family," Zach said.

"It's good to have them." David studied Zach a minute. "What you told me about your father— This is why he threw you out, isn't it?" His hand made a semicircle, encompassing their hastily clad garments, the rumpled sheets.

Zach slowly nodded. "Yes, it's why. I had a friend, a year older than myself. Ephraim. We were very— very drawn to one another. He looked a little like you must've done as a boy, tall and thin, with yellow hair forever falling in his eyes." Zach smiled painfully. He reached out and pushed a few strands of hair off David's forehead.

"Pa caught us fondling one another," he said after a long pause. "We'd gone into the woods behind our homes after firewood—we often helped one another with our chores. There was a hollow half filled with fallen leaves we'd lie in. Pa came out to see what had kept me at so simple a task. We were too taken up with one another to hear his footsteps.

"Pa used to lean on a hickory staff when he walked, on account of his rheumatism. When he took in what we were doing, he raised it over his head as if he would smite us. Then he looked at Eph and said,

'You're not my son, Ephraim. Your own father must do with you as he sees fit.' He stood there with the stick in his hand all the while Eph was taking to his heels, and I shrank back, waiting for it to fall. Then he lowered it, and looked at me—the way you might look at a rat you'd just killed in your pantry. 'Neither are you, Zachary. You're no more son of mine.' I'd have rather he'd beaten me, I'll tell you that. Even if he'd struck me dead."

"Oh God, Zach." David laid his hand on Zach's, pulled it back. He sat looking at him numbly. "How can you be so easy about us now?" he whispered finally.

"I wasn't easy about it then, I'll grant you. I was certain my father's God would consign me to eternal hellfire, though Mother promised me the Lord hated the sin, not the sinner. But I couldn't repent of it. I spent hours on my knees trying to pray for forgiveness, but whenever I closed my eyes I'd see Eph lying there with the leaves in his hair and that crooked smile he had, and I couldn't be sorry for what we'd done."

"I don't see how you bore it."

"It came to me after a while that I was as the Lord made me." Zach shrugged mightily, as if he were shaking off the memory as a dog shakes off water. "I didn't ask to be fashioned this way—to love men instead of women."

"I've been with women!"

"I didn't say you hadn't. But not half so eagerly, I daresay."

David flushed, not answering.

"At any rate, I've come since to a different view of sin."

"Christ, Zach, what other view can you come to!"

Chapter 10 - 1861

Davɪᴅ sᴇᴛ Bɪʟʟ Wᴀᴜᴅ's sᴋᴇᴛᴄʜ ᴏғ ᴀ Soᴜᴛʜ Cᴀʀᴏʟɪɴɪᴀɴ ʀᴇɢɪᴍᴇɴᴛᴀʟ review in the top rack of his drawing table, ready for copying. He picked up his pencil resignedly, thinking a moment of the argument he'd had with Leslie when the editor had announced his decision to assign a staff artist to Charleston, two days after Lincoln's election. "Why are you picking Bill to send? I'm a Virginian, after all," he'd pointed out. "I'm at home in the South."

"And equally at home, I'm given to understand, in the company of Greeley's correspondents."

David flushed. Surely Leslie knew nothing of what had occurred all fall between Zach and himself! The editor couldn't have guessed that his eagerness for the assignment stemmed as much from his desire to get away from temptation as from interest in the convention called by South Carolina to vote the state out of the Union.

Leslie looked at him shrewdly. "It hasn't escaped my notice that you came within a hairsbreadth of being expelled from Charles Town during John Brown's trial, along with Greeley's man."

"Oh."

"At any rate, young Waud's English and the Southerners want to court allies abroad. And reporting on the new Southern government will take a good deal of moving about in society. To be frank, your own strength lies solely in your facility as an artist." David nodded in resignation. He didn't have half Bill's social graces, he knew.

He turned his attention back to Bill's drawing now, automatically reversing it left to right as he copied. Earlier in March Leslie had published Bill's portrayal of Jefferson Davis' inauguration as Confederate president, in the same issue with illustrations of the inauguration of Abraham Lincoln. Outside of that, during the four months he'd been in South Carolina Bill had sent little besides portraits of secessionist leaders, sketches of rallies, parties and gallantly posing soldiers, and chatty notes describing the fervor of the South Carolinians for their new nation.

Despite the South's revolutionary fervor, conservative Northerners still cherished hopes of mollifying the Southerners sufficiently to restore the Union. Abolitionist meetings were set upon by mobs led by lawyers and clerks as well as lower class ruffians. In the abolitionist stronghold of Boston, anti-slavery meetings were broken up with the unofficial blessing of the police. In January and February, Zach—dispatched to upstate New York for the *Tribune*—had wired reports of attacks on abolitionist gatherings in Buffalo, Rochester, Rome and Auburn. Only in Albany did an anti-slavery meeting proceed uninterrupted, protected by the police and the presence of the city's mayor, seated on the platform with a revolver in plain view on his lap. David had read the account with a shiver of fear for Zach's safety.

He'd missed Zach, he admitted to himself, however much he told himself a period of separation would cool their ardor. He sighed, redirected his attention to the drawing of the strutting Southern regiment.

With the approach of April, Bill Waud's dispatches from Charleston took on a grimmer tone. South Carolina pressed her claim to the Federal fort, Sumter, on an island commanding the entrance to Charleston harbor. Bill forwarded sketches of entrenched guns on Morris Island, the Charleston armory and the batteries ringing the Charleston harbor.

April sixth, a month after his inauguration, Lincoln informed the governor of South Carolina that he intended reprovisioning Fort Sumter, nearly out of supplies since an attack by South Carolina shore batteries had repulsed a Northern relief ship.

The new Confederate cabinet replied with a demand for the fort's surrender. On April 12th the Confederates opened fire on the unyielding fort. Two days later, Sumter's commander formally surrendered Fort Sumter to the superior Confederate forces. On Monday, April 15th, Lincoln proclaimed the South to be in a state of insurrection, and issued a call for 75,000 state militia.

The attack on Sumter wrought a "wonderful transformation," Leslie's reported. War fever took over the North; the Stars and Stripes waved from every building. David filled his sketchpad with scenes of mass rallies in Union Square, the fervent faces of cheering men and women mirroring those of the Confederate celebrants in Bill's dispatches from South Carolina.

Northerners of every persuasion rallied behind the President. The prominent abolitionist Wendell Phillips abandoned twenty years of calls for disunion to welcome a war which, he now felt, would bring freedom in its wake.

Dick Potter, in accord with his abolitionist views, gave notice to the *Tribune* and enlisted in the newly mobilizing militia. David felt alone in viewing the conflict with misgivings. He sat silently at Dick's farewell party in Pfaff's, listening to other young reporters boast of their plans to join up. At least he was past the age where anyone would expect him to volunteer for military duty, not that he could imagine taking up arms against his home state, any more than he could see himself fighting in defense of slavery.

On April 17, a Virginia State Convention adopted an ordinance of secession, voting 88 to 55 to submit the question to popular referendum in May. The western counties, at least, seemed reluctant to leave the Union. It was possible the populace would override the action of the convention.

It was a slim hope at best.

"If I were a few years younger, I warrant you I'd be in uniform myself," Zach said in David's ear as they watched the first squadrons of Colonel Ellsworth's New York Fire Zouaves march smartly down Broadway. The onlookers were crushed so tightly together that David felt Zach's beard rubbing his face, yet he had to strain to make out his words over the noise of the crowd.

"They're damned impressive," he answered, his eyes fixed on the flamboyant Zouaves—the 11th New York Infantry—in their colorful red and blue uniforms. At their head, drawing excited yells of admiration, stepped young Colonel Ellsworth, more dashing than any of his men.

"It's amazing how he's formed such a splendidly turned out regiment in so short a time," David added. He'd sketched the Fire Zouaves as they drilled the day before, admiring the precision of their acrobatic maneuvers in the exotic, Arabic-inspired uniforms Ellsworth had adapted for them. Only twenty-four years old, Elmer Ellsworth— a one-time student in Lincoln's law office—had outfitted and trained his men at his own expense. In just a few weeks, he'd turned the volunteers he'd recruited from New York City firemen into a military unit of dashing verve and precision.

David turned his attention back to the parade. The Fire Zouaves marched by in colorful unison, the rhythms of their regimental band nearly drowned out by the shouts of the watching throng. David's enthusiasm swelled with that of the crowd, his reservations about the war momentarily set aside as the Zouaves trooped by in glorious pageantry.

The lead steamer moved silently across the Potomac under a moonlit sky, trailed closely by two sister ships bearing the men of the llth New York. Ellsworth surveyed his troops with satisfaction, then turned to the accompanying newsmen. "The lst Michigan will cross into Alexandria over the Long Bridge while we take the Secesh by surprise, landing at the foot of the town. We're not expecting much resistance."

David let himself be reassured by Ellsworth's prediction that there'd be no bloodshed such as had greeted Federal troops passing through Baltimore five weeks before. In the days that had passed since Leslie assigned him to accompany the Fire Zouaves to Washington City, David had come to respect the quick thinking and daring of the handsome young officer.

His opinion was shared by the inhabitants of the Federal city. The Fire Zouaves became local heroes as the former firefighters swarmed up a human chain to douse flames threatening Willard's Hotel.

David jotted a few notes now, to one side of the new sketchpad Leslie had supplied him, with the publisher's copyright in the bottom left corner. A half-finished sketch of Ellsworth occupied the rest of the page. David returned to it as the young officer busied himself with preparations for landing, penciling in Ellsworth's mobile, sensitive face in its frame of wavy brunette locks, his contemplative expression as he gazed across the water to Alexandria, one hand resting lightly on his sword.

David followed his gaze, suddenly touched with a sense of unreality. He'd hoped to squeeze in a visit home during the course of this assignment. Instead, he found himself aboard a troop ship, accompanying an invading army to his home town.

Less than twenty-four hours before, on May 23rd, Virginia voters had approved the ordinance of secession drafted by the state convention in April. Much as he wished Lincoln would let the Southern states go in peace, conflict seemed inevitable. It would be folly for Federal forces to ignore the presence of what was now enemy territory, so close to the capital city.

The steamer docked with a slight thud. The Fire Zouaves scrambled off the steamships as the sun rose, greeted by the news that Confederate soldiers had already begun a retreat from the city. David breathed a sigh of relief.

Ellsworth ordered his men to fall into companies, seemingly

disappointed at the lack of a fight to test their mettle. The young officer drew himself up decisively. "There's the railroad station and telegraph office to secure still." He detailed the main body of his men to reinforce Michigan troops at the Orange and Alexandria depot, while he headed for the telegraph office with a smaller detachment. David fell into step with Ellsworth's file.

They marched double-time up King Street toward the telegraph office, met by stares of sullen curiosity from onlookers in doorways and windows. David wondered a moment how many of his old friends and neighbors were accounting him a traitor as they watched him walk up King Street in company with the occupying soldiers. He forced the question from his mind. If the choice had to be made, the Union was still his country.

Many shops and houses were deserted, abandoned by townsfolk fleeing South in anticipation of a Federal attack. "We'll be marching through Richmond by fall," Ellsworth predicted, as he studied the scene. He stepped jauntily, his bearing commanding despite his short stature.

David's spirits rose at the thought that the rebellion would surely be of short duration. He strode along a few feet behind Ellsworth, exchanging comments with Bobby Maguire, a redheaded Fire Zouave from Brooklyn, and Edward House, a *Tribune* correspondent with whom he had a nodding acquaintance.

The detachment reached the corner of King and Pitt streets. Ellsworth halted. "What's that rag doing up there?" David followed his gaze to the Confederate flag flying from the roof of the shabby Marshall House hotel.

Ellsworth grinned. "I'll soon have it down." He bounded into the tavern, followed by a half dozen of his men.

David entered the dim lobby after him. Ellsworth's footsteps were already pounding up the stairs to the roof. David waited a moment till his eyes adjusted to the dimness, then headed upstairs.

The trapdoor to the roof thudded shut above him as David neared the second landing. Ellsworth appeared again, his grin curving up into his mustache, the Confederate banner clutched triumphantly in his hands.

A man suddenly stepped from a doorway on the landing, leveling a double-barreled shotgun. David gasped. He opened his mouth to yell a warning, simultaneously with the shotgun's blast.

There was a short, anguished cry as Ellsworth fell. A second burst of gunfire sounded and his attacker fell to the floor beside him.

David's feet continued the climb to the landing without his volition. A shocked hush had fallen over the huddled soldiers, broken only by the sobbing of Ellsworth's lieutenant as he cradled the youthful officer's body in his arms. A young private, rifle shaking in his hand, stood over the body of the second dead man: Jim Jackson, the tavern's proprietor, David saw numbly.

He looked back at Ellsworth. The dead man's mouth gaped open, his sightless eyes stared upwards, blood spurted from the cavity in his chest, drenching his brass-buttoned uniform and the Confederate trophy still dangling from his fingers. The stench of loosened bowels hung over the stairwell.

David was overcome by nausea. He grabbed for the bannister behind him, clutching the hard wood railing as he retched. Long minutes went by. Finally he straightened up shakily and rubbed his mouth with his handkerchief. He stood trembling another moment, then slowly opened his sketchpad and set to work.

Chapter 11 - 1862

THE HORROR AND DISBELIEF THAT SHOOK THE NORTH at Ellsworth's death had given way to grim expectation of mounting casualties. The abandonment of hope for a quick victory after Bull Run was followed by the bloodbath at Shiloh and mounting losses in the Virginia peninsula as the war entered a second summer.

David set his pencil down on his drawing table and rubbed his aching fingers, studying his copy of Henri Lovie's sketch of a skirmish on the Western front. Shock and anguish mingled on the faces of soldiers drawn as they fell, mortally wounded.

"Hey, David, you'll be all night getting those on the blocks if you just sit and stare at them."

David started at Elliot's voice. "I was thinking how much bloodshed there's been. It's hard to picture so many men dying in just a year."

"Be glad you're here copying those and not with the army getting shot at."

David picked up his pencil again, glancing at Lovie's scribbled instructions before adding a line of trees to the top of the drawing. "To tell the truth, I find it pretty tiresome. As many new artists as *Leslie's* hired to cover the fighting, there's precious little chance for us to do much else besides copying."

"I thought Leslie offered you the chance to stay with the troops before he sent Art Lumley down."

"He did." David smiled ruefully. "After Ellsworth, I couldn't face up to seeing anyone else get shot."

Elliot snorted. "Or getting yourself shot either. Not that I blame you. It's all the same to me what I draw, so long as my hide stays in one piece. You got much more to do on those? I'm tired of that damn boardinghouse food. Join me for beer and sausage at Pfaff's after we knock off?"

"I've already told Zach I'd meet him there, to tell the truth."

"So? I'll join you, then. You two courting or something that you can't stand a little company?"

David winced, then prayed Elliot hadn't spotted his twinge of fear. Elliot was given to shooting his mouth off, he told himself. His remark meant nothing.

He managed a weak laugh. "Listening to Zach rehash McClellan's mistakes for the hundredth time, more likely. I'll be glad to have you turn the talk to cheerier subjects."

The din of Pfaff's bar and dining room assaulted David as he entered. He stopped at the foot of the stairs and peered through the haze of tobacco smoke. Zach was already seated, at a table close to the far wall. He waved at David and Elliot as they threaded their way through the crowded room, then turned back to talking with two of the *Tribune's* writing editors.

Pfaff's never changed, David thought, as he squeezed into a seat across from Zach. Most of the young reporters who'd been their regular drinking companions had scattered—a few enlisted like Dick, others as correspondents with the Army of the Potomac or on the western front. Elliot, lounging comfortably alongside him, was one of the few familiar faces. Yet the packed tables and echoing arguments were no different than the first day he'd walked in here.

True to David's prediction, Zach was engrossed in discussion of McClellan's generalship. "If the man had attacked instead of falling back after Malvern Hill, I daresay we'd be reporting now on the fall of Richmond!"

Elliot nudged David in the ribs. "If it's cheerier conversation you want, you won't find it in our present company." He glanced toward the stairs. "Bessie told me she might be bringing someone for you to meet. Yeah, here they come now. Take a look over there."

David looked across the room where the latest of Elliot's lady friends was settling herself at a table, smoothing her skirts as she chatted animatedly with a second heavily-rouged young woman.

"That's the sort of company you need to cheer you up. Take a look at those tits, will you!"

The young woman's breasts bulged roundly above the tight bodice of her gown. As David watched, she produced a handkerchief and daintily patted her cheeks and forehead, then languorously passed the cloth over her expanse of bosom. Elliot's lady friend leaned over and whispered in her ear. Both young women turned to smile in their direction, then leaned together again, bursting into subdued giggles. David flushed, lowering his eyes. He felt Elliot nudge him again. "Bessie's cousin. Whaddya think?"

"She's very— very good looking."

"A beaut. And Bessie says she's hoping to be shown a good time while she's in New York. If you get my meaning."

David smiled faintly.

"C'mon then. I'll introduce you."

"I— I don't think so."

"Hey, you don't need to worry about disease with her. She's not a hooker, she's just looking for a little fun."

"Maybe some other time, Elliot."

"Suit yourself." Elliot smoothed the ends of his mustache and pushed back his chair. "But for chrissake, David, you oughta get yourself a woman before people get to thinking you're as big a nancy as your friend Zach."

David froze, unable to move as he watched Elliot saunter across the restaurant. Why the hell couldn't he have brought himself to take Elliot up on his invitation?

He managed a glance at Zach, hoping he hadn't heard.

Zach nodded goodnight to the two editors and turned to David. "I didn't mean to leave you sitting alone." He paused. "You all right, David? You look troubled. I keep forgetting the fighting's been largely in your home state."

He couldn't have heard Elliot, David told himself. "I'm fine. I wouldn't mind getting my thoughts off the war, though."

Zach smiled and gestured toward the table behind them, adjacent to the one Pfaff saved for his fashionable crowd of literary Bohemians. The men at this table were young, dressed in the rough clothing of stage drivers and ferryboatmen. At one end sat Walt Whitman, garbed in sturdy blue flannel, his eyes riveted on a swarthy, muscular young man in workman's coveralls.

"There's an empty seat or two there," Zach said, "and I daresay the talk will be livelier." David sighed under his breath as he picked up his tankard and followed Zach.

Whitman greeted them with a nod, then turned his attention back to the young man, prompting his words with a question now and then, in a voice as unexpectedly soft as a caress.

You'd never take him for a poet, David mused, uncertain he'd ever understand the fascination Whitman held for his friend. Zach sat in unwonted silence, happily spearing sausages with his fork. He resembles him a bit, David thought, that mane of a beard and gray head of hair, and their size. If Zach were to dress as unconventionally as Whitman—

"Zachary! What a pleasure to see you!"

David looked up from his reverie at a smiling, well-tailored man in his mid-fifties, silk cravat elegantly knotted about his neck. Zach was pumping his hand heartily, beaming in turn.

"This is my good friend, David Carter, one of Frank Leslie's prize sketch artists. Byron Roosa, David. We labored on the *Tribune* together before he left to pursue the higher callings of essayist and novelist."

Roosa took David's hand between both of his own, bowing slightly as he spoke. "A most valuable apprenticeship, and one I've often recalled with pleasure. I'm delighted to make your acquaintance, Mr. Carter, and to renew Zachary's. I've been traveling about the Continent so long, I fear my old friendships are in sad disrepair."

David smiled, watching Zach and Roosa launch on a spirited reminiscence, the two men a study in contrast. Zach beamed happily, sitting comfortably at ease in his rumpled coat. Roosa sat straightbacked, his long fingers balancing his tankard as delicately as he might a crystal wine goblet. He pulled a gold watch from his pocket, then gestured gracefully. "My affairs call. Another day, I hope." He turned to David, pressing his hand once more.

"Perhaps we'll meet again," he murmured. "Do you ever take occasion to visit any of the public baths?"

David started, taken aback at such a personal question from a stranger. "Once in a while, but I generally content myself with my washbasin," he stammered finally.

Roosa chuckled softly, his voice even softer. "Ah yes, cleanliness is next to Godliness, I daresay, but I had other enjoyments in mind." His hand lingered on David's. "It would be my pleasure to show you, sir."

David stared at Roosa in slow, unwilling comprehension, his flush of embarrassment mingling with the heat of rising anger. He jerked back his hand. "You can go straight to hell!" He glanced momentarily at the consternation on Zach's face. "I'll settle my bill with you later, Zach. I'm getting out of here."

He'd reached the front door of the boardinghouse when he heard Zach's footsteps behind him.

"You might've refused him a little less rudely!"

"Rudely! Do you know what he wanted!"

Zach gave a slight, breathless chuckle. "I can imagine. But I fail to see why you were so offended by it."

"You don't see— For God's sake, Zach!" The silence following his words stretched between them.

"He picked me out as a— a sodomite."

Zach sighed deeply. "David, if you want to talk, we can do better than Mrs. Chapman's front stoop."

"I don't want to lie with you, Zach."

"I daresay we can be in a room together without that."

"C'mon to my room then."

David crossed to the mirror above his bureau and looked into it a long moment, irritably watching Zach shuck his coat and toss it onto the chair. His own face stared back at him: clean shaven, angular featured, blond hair falling lankily on his forehead. He shoved it back.

"I doubt he accosts every man he meets. What in hell was it he saw about me?"

"Likely nothing but the fact that you're a friend of mine. We knew each other fairly well at one time." Zach sat on the edge of David's bed and slipped off his shoes. "Ah, that's better.

"We're not the only men in the world to prefer the affection of other men, David. I daresay Byron misspoke himself, but I fail to see what harm's been done you by it."

"Dammit Zach, just because we— because we've— I'm not some damn nancy like Elliot calls you!" He drew in his breath. "Christ! I didn't mean to repeat that."

"Perhaps not. Though you wasted no time in doing so. Why in damnation do you think us any worse than Elliot, with his parade of fancy ladies?"

"At least it's not unnatural. He's not some kind of— of pervert."

"In that case, I fail to see why you didn't join him!"

"I should've! At least it would keep him from shooting off his mouth about me too." David looked at Zach's unwontedly rigid posture, his hands clenched on his knees. "Hell, I'm sorry, Zach. I never think of you as—"

"David, we are as we are."

"I'm not— I've never— I never had a real friend before we met. I guess I felt such affection for you it spilled out of its proper boundaries."

Zach relaxed back into his customary easy posture. "You know how dear your friendship is to me, as well. I cared for you for years before I dared express my feelings to you." Zach smiled gently. "But we do seek after a different sort of love than other men."

"Zach, for God's sake, do you think I would do what we've done with any other man— with that, that friend of yours, say?"

"He was heartily embarrassed by his misjudgment, as a matter of fact. Byron's a bit full of himself, but he's not a bad sort. I've known him a long time."

"I don't want to know how well you knew him!"

Zach chuckled softly. "It was a long time ago, David. I have no desire now for anyone but you. And I'm delighted that my feelings are reciprocated." He hoisted his feet onto the bed, propped the pillow against the headboard for a backrest and stretched out his legs. "There's room for both of us to sit here in comfort. It's wearying me just watching you pace."

David smiled painfully. "Every time I sit on a bed with you, we end up sinning again."

"There's no sin in enjoying the love of another man if you broaden your sights beyond a narrow-minded view of Scripture. The Greeks believed it the highest form of love. Plato speaks of it, if I'm not mistaken."

David lowered himself slowly onto the bed alongside Zach. "You probably know more of Plato than I do. I'm afraid a college education was wasted on me. But, hell, Zach, the Greeks weren't even Christians."

Zach chuckled, and draped his arm lightly around David's shoulder. "I doubt that Christians are in sole possession of the truth."

"Perhaps not." David sighed. "I wish I had your ease about it." He sighed again and moved closer to Zach, letting himself rest comfortably against his warm bulk. His friend's arm tightened around his shoulders.

David closed his eyes, savoring their silent closeness. He could feel Zach breathing with him in companionable, rhythmic unison. He turned his head, smiling at the familiar tickle of Zach's beard.

Zach's arm crept further around him. Slowly he undid the top buttons of David's shirt. His fingers made gentle semi-circles around David's nipples. David gave an involuntary shiver of delight, feeling the first stirring in his penis. Zach's strokes quickened, passing in electric tingles over the sensitive tips of his nipples. David abandoned any remnants of reluctance, surrendering himself to his enjoyment of the sensation.

Zach brushed David's eyelids and temple lightly with his lips. "Still regretting you didn't take Elliot up on his invitation?"

David opened his eyes. He turned toward Zach and traced Zach's smile with his finger. "You know damn well I'm not." He let his fingers trail through the lushness of Zach's beard, then slipped his hand behind Zach's head and kissed him hungrily. Their lips met with near-bruising intensity. David pulled Zach closer still, his tongue darting caresses as Zach's lips parted in eagerness.

He drew back for breath, still holding Zach to him. "You know damn well there's no one in the world I want to lie with but you." He closed the distance between them and covered Zach's lips with his once again.

A Different Sin

The unaccustomed hum of Zach's snoring awakened him. David rolled over and fit his body closer to Zach's, his arm thrown loosely across Zach's chest. He gave a contented sigh and began to drift back to sleep, lulled by his friend's warm, comforting presence, his chest rising and falling under his arm.

It would be damn good to lie like this till morning, David thought sleepily. My God! Morning.

He jerked awake and shook Zach. "Zach, c'mon, wake up. You've got to get out of here!" Zach's rhythmic snores broke off. He gave a protesting moan. "It's nighttime yet."

"Thank God I wakened before morning! You've got to get out of here before anyone sees you!"

"Mmmn. It's so good just to lie next to you like this."

"Hell, I know it, Zach." David ran his hand lightly over Zach's chest, smiling at the furry feel of his hair. He reached down and gently patted Zach's private parts. His fingers closed lightly around Zach's balls, cupping them tenderly.

A long, peaceful moment passed. David forced himself to renewed alertness. "If we fall asleep again, half the boardinghouse will be watching you troop out of my room tomorrow morning!" He gave Zach a last, affectionate pat. "Now go on and get out of here before I grow horny again."

Zach stretched sleepily and began to fumble around for his clothes. David held his door open a crack as he listened to Zach shuffle barefoot down the hall, holding his breath till he heard the quiet click of Zach's door. He lay back on his empty bed with a sigh of relief.

Without Zach's presence the bed felt clammy, the sheets unpleasantly sticky with semen. David was unable to return to sleep. He rose to use the chamber pot, then stretched out uncomfortably.

He thought a moment of his disgust at Byron Roosa's proposition the evening before. Did the affection he and Zach felt for one another make their lust any less a sin?

He'd meant to avoid the sin of sodomy for once. He should've known better. Hell, he was as eager for it as Zach, maybe more so, to be honest with himself.

How the hell could he want it so much and regret it so sharply? He lay awake, wrestling with the dilemma as the night wore on.

"Where you been, David? Leslie's been looking for you for an hour," Elliot greeted him as he hurried into work the next morning.

David winced. "Overslept, I'm afraid."

Elliot laughed. "It should've been me who overslept, left with both young ladies to entertain."

Christ, David thought. Did he bed the two of·them? He stared at

Elliot. The ginger-haired artist smoothed the ends of his mustache, his drawing pencil dangling carelessly from his fingers. He gave David a wink.

David managed a weak laugh in return. Doubtless Elliot had never suffered a moment from the sorts of compunctions that had kept him awake till nearly dawn. He sighed under his breath and hurried on to Leslie's office.

"I overslept, I'm afraid," he apologized.

"Sit down, sit down. I wasn't seeking you to complain about your hours." Leslie waved toward a vacant chair and proffered a box of cigars. "Ah, yes, I'd forgotten you don't indulge. Too bad. They're good Havanas." He selected one and busied himself lighting it.

"I've had word from Art Lumley that he's leaving my employ for *Leggett's Illustrated*. I needn't tell you, that leaves me in a pinch. I must have an artist I can depend on stationed with McClellan.

"I'll be hiring on as soon as I can, but I'd rather have a new employee under my direct supervision." Leslie paused and puffed hugely on the cigar. "It hasn't escaped my notice that you've been a bit restive with the amount of copying that's been your lot of late."

David nodded, his surprise turning to thoughtfulness. Perhaps he ought to take the chance to get away from New York. If he'd stayed with the army last year, he might've broken himself of the habit of sin he'd fallen into with Zach. For a second the memory of Ellsworth's death surfaced vividly in his mind. Still—

"I don't know what to say," he said finally. "I'm past the age of most of the field artists."

"I did give your age a bit of thought. But to all appearances, you're in as good condition as many a younger man."

David smiled. "I try to maintain my health. I exercise at Ottignon's gymnasium once or twice a week, if I've time."

"A practice most of us would do well to emulate. May I assume you're agreeable then?"

"I— I'm not sure. I'd like to give it some thought." Damn. Why the hell couldn't he just agree to go?

Leslie smoothed out a grimace of annoyance. "Think it over a day or so, by all means. In the meantime, I want you to stop by the New York Hospital tomorrow, do a few sketches of the wounded from the second Bull Run engagement."

David nodded, wondering again why he hadn't just agreed to take the assignment and be done with it.

"I'm damned if I know why I put him off," he told Zach that evening. "I should've just told him I'd go instead of hemming and hawing."

David glanced out Zach's window, then continued pacing restlessly around the small room.

"Well, I'm damned glad you didn't, I'll tell you that. Especially without even talking it over first." Zach set the book he'd been reading next to him on the bed and swung his feet to the floor. "Will you stop walking in circles and sit down."

David lowered himself onto Zach's chair.

"You turned down Leslie's request to stay at the front last year, and very sensibly so. Why the sudden urge to see bloodshed?"

"It's not so sudden. I've hardly done a damn bit of work outside of copying since then. I've gotten sick of sitting at my drawing table day after day. For that matter, I'm sick of sitting in that damned tavern every night listening to you all second guess McClellan's strategy. And of seeing that damn poet you're so fond of, who can't even write two lines that rhyme, and watching you all fawn over that damn bunch of Bohemians who think because they're authors they can look down on everyone else!" David stopped short, surprised at his own vehemence.

"Sick of our friendship?"

"Of— No, not of our friendship. Never of that." Zach's breath escaped in a sudden rush.

David stared at his hands, absently picking at the calloused pencil bump on his third finger. "We should leave it at friendship. We never should've carried it further."

"That's a far cry from your words last night."

"Christ, I know that. When we're together, it just feels so natural and good, I forget everything except how much I want you." David stared down in silence. "It's afterwards...." he said, finally.

"I know how you feel. I don't much relish creeping down the hall, shoes in hand, myself. In fact, I've been thinking of late. If we were to pool our resources, I daresay we might afford to take lodgings together."

David drew in his breath, imagining lying nightly by Zach, waking up next to him, talking to him freely without the listening ears of a dozen fellow lodgers. He fought down a surge of longing. "For God's sake, Zach, have you gone crazy? Isn't there talk enough already to suit you?"

"There's nothing to cause talk if two bachelor gentlemen pool their funds to secure better lodgings. As you said, sometimes I get confounded sick at the thought of spending the rest of my days in a boardinghouse. I'd dearly love some little place that would be more of a home."

"No! Damn it, Zach, no!"

"Calm yourself, David." Zach stood and walked behind the chair.

He placed his hands on David's shoulders, kneading the tense muscles of his back and neck. "You've let Byron distress you unduly."

"He has nothing to do with it! Oh hell, I guess you're right. I think he's made me see us a little more clearly."

"Us?"

"We're as perverted as he is. It's good Leslie wants me at the front. We need to get away from each other a while to break ourselves of it."

"I've no desire to break myself of you!"

"You think I want to do without your company?" David reached up to touch Zach's hand. Zach's fingers entwined with his. David fought back another wave of longing. He jerked free and rose. "We can't keep on like this."

"David, listen to me—"

"I've made up my mind." David yanked open the door and fled down the hall.

The clatter of silverware on breakfast dishes mingled with the clearing of throats and mumbled "good mornings" as David took his place at the table. He muttered a greeting to old Mr. Wilson on his left. Zach sank into his accustomed chair at David's right. "You're heading in to tell Leslie you'll take the assignment?" he greeted David.

"As soon as I've done the sketches at the hospital."

"I hoped once you slept on it, you'd change your mind." David busied himself with his eggs, washing them down with hasty swallows of coffee. "I told you, I've decided." His chair clattered against the wall as he shoved it back, bringing a frown from Mrs. Chapman. He muttered a quick apology as he fled.

Zach followed him into the hallway. "Listen to me a minute—"

"Zach, I'm in a hurry."

"I daresay you can spare me five minutes." Zach laid a hand on David's shoulder. "You've not thought this through—"

David jerked away. "Dammit, Zach, do we have to make a spectacle of ourselves in front of the whole boardinghouse?" He looked at Zach's face and sighed. "All right, walk with me to the hospital then."

They strode two blocks in silence. Zach cleared his throat. "There's more to take into account than just your feelings about our friendship. In fact, I'm damned if I can understand your eagerness for the front, considering how little stomach you have for bloodshed."

"I suppose I can accustom myself to the sight of bloodshed."

"It's more than the sight, David."

"I don't understand what you're talking about."

"I'm talking about the risk to your own life!"

A Different Sin

"I'm going as an artist, not a soldier." Zach halted. He caught David's arm and pulled him around to face him. "David, to sketch scenes of the fighting like those Lumley's been sending, you'd have to expose yourself to fire as much as if you were a soldier!"

"I don't think—"

"Give it some thought, will you!"

"I'm not intending to endanger myself. I've got to get going now." David forced himself to put Zach's words from his mind. He hurried down Broadway, not slowing till he reached Pearl Street and the New York Hospital.

One wing of the hospital had been turned over to the military. The cots of injured soldiers filled the wards in closely packed rows, a neatly printed name card set in the rack nailed to the foot of each bed. A stream of visitors—nurses, doctors, anxious parents, sweethearts, curious onlookers and straightbacked society matrons bearing the charitable gifts of the Sanitary Commission—bustled up and down the aisles. David stood to one side and studied the ward. A few aisles over, a bearded veteran shuffled a deck of cards, dealing them onto a thin board propped between the edge of his cot and that of his neighbor. A third player sat at the foot of one of the cots, a pair of crutches tossed to the floor.

The man's right foot was missing. David made his way toward the players. He took his eyes from the pants leg, pinned neatly below the knee, and joined the small group of recuperating patients who'd gathered to watch the game. The group shifted their attention to the scene forming on David's sketchpad. "Hey, he can draw, Jake! Sure caught that shnoz of yours! You gonna make us out heroes in the ill-us-trated, mister?" David smiled shyly, noting down the soldiers' names and regiments.

Other aisles held soldiers suffering more deadly wounds. David walked through them quickly, uneasily trying not to disturb the wounded men, though the ward was filled with the constant undercurrent of groans and calls.

"Mister, hey mister!"

David turned. A freckled boy of seventeen or eighteen lay propped up on a pillow, bedcovers neatly drawn to his chin. He grinned weakly at David. "Can you help me to a drink, mister? Nurse left a jug of water, but I ain't got any way to get to it."

"Yeah, sure." David spotted the water pitcher on the floor by the edge of the cot, and filled the cup lying alongside. He held it out to the boy.

"You gotta hold it to my mouth, mister. One of them shells took both my arms clean off. Damned if I wasn't clear back of the lines, too, helpin' carry my buddy to the surgeon's tent. Reckon I was lucky the doc was near to hand when it happened." The boy attempted another grin. He grunted as he tried to heave his body into a sitting position. The sheet slid down, revealing bandaged stumps ending inches below his shoulders.

David froze in shock. He struggled not to stare at the boy with the expression of horror he knew must be on his face. The water shook in the cup.

He felt the cup eased from his fingers, heard a man's soft, steady voice. "Here, give me that. I'll take over here. You've other work to do." He fled halfway across the ward before he turned to look back. The poet, Whitman, sat on the edge of the cot, cradling the boy's tousled curls against his chest, holding the cup to his lips as tenderly as a mother nursing her babe.

Slowly David raised his pencil to his pad. He tightened his grip on the pencil till his hand stopped shaking. The gray haired poet was easing the boy back onto his pillow, kissing the freckled young face as he arranged the covers. David glanced down at his pad, surprised to see the scene taking form without his conscious volition.

He stood, breathing deeply till he felt in control of himself again. His fingers held the pencil lightly now, guiding it over the paper in swift, automatic response to his mind's commands, nerves and muscles working in sure, accustomed harmony.

Other soldiers called out, "Hey, how's about drawing my picture, mister?" David did quick sketches of as many as he could. From time to time he glanced down at his hand, imagining it being ripped from his body in a swift, bloody explosion.

He'd finished far more sketches than Leslie had requested. Doubtless the editor would be impatient to see them. David lingered in the ward, nevertheless, presenting small sketches to several of his more eager models. He was in no hurry to face Leslie with the news that he wouldn't be going to the front after all.

Chapter 12 - 1862-63

THE LINE OF PEOPLE WAITING TO ENTER MATTHEW BRADY'S GALLERY turned the corner of Broadway and stretched down Tenth Street. After a long summer of Union defeats, McClellan had whipped Lee in the battle of Antietam.

Brady's photographs of the battle—the first photographs of the war to be publicly exhibited—were attracting jubilant throngs.

David inched after Zach as the queue advanced a few shuffling steps; the hoop skirt of the woman behind him grazed his ankle as the line jerked to a halt again. He gave a sigh of resignation and tapped Zach on the shoulder. "I got a letter from Mike today, did I tell you? Though he didn't write much, except how pleased the colored are over Lincoln's proclamation—that the slaves in the Secesh states'll be free after New Year's."

"And about time! Though it doesn't go nearly far enough, I'll tell you that!"

"Well, I don't see how he expects to enforce it where he's no power, in any case."

"The power will come, I'll warrant you! Now that Lincoln's taken the first step to abolishing slavery, the Union's bound to show new resolve."

"I suppose. Though the Copperheads are strong enough here in New York. Anyhow, Mike writes that Peter's more unhappy than ever that Lincoln won't allow colored to enlist. He's been champing at the bit to join up."

David shuffled forward a few steps as the line moved up. "Mike and Rachel feel the same. They've been petitioning Massachusetts to let colored into the state militia. I can't really understand their thinking, to tell the truth. You'd think they'd be pleased to have Peter out of the fighting."

Zach turned and looked at him. "It's how I feel, at any rate," he said quietly. "Damned pleased to have someone I care for out of harm's way." David flushed and looked down.

Zach smiled. "Though there's much to be said for allowing the blacks to fight for their own freedom. Especially—" He broke off as the line surged forward.

The door to Brady's gallery opened and a stream of visitors emerged. In contrast to the talkative, waiting crowd, the men and women leaving the exhibit were silent, their faces blank with shock. The line moved again. David entered the gallery and followed Zach upstairs.

Brady's long reception room was filled with viewers clustered around each of the photographs. The gallery was unnaturally quiet, sounds more muffled than could be accounted for by the thick carpeting alone. David could hear the hiss of gas in the chandeliers as he and Zach moved down the line of photographs.

The camera had recorded the battle with a grim realism no artist's pen could match. A line of Confederate soldiers lay in the country lane where they'd fallen, their bodies heaped on one another like bloody flour sacks tossed in a wagon. Other Confederates sprawled along a cornfield fence they'd died defending, rifles dropped from out-stretched, stiffening arms. David tried not to wonder which old friends and acquaintances might lie among them.

A Union burial detail labored to dig a mass grave for a row of Federal dead. A half-dozen Southern artillerymen stared lifelessly toward heaven, a few hundred yards from a shell-pocked country church. A dark-haired boy lay crumpled on the ground, eyes open in blank, arrested shock, one of the 26,000 casualties in a single day of battle at Antietam.

A young, fashionably attired woman swooned, saved from falling only by the press of the crowd. The onlookers parted as her escort assisted her to a couch.

"They should have better sense than to admit the ladies to a sight like this," a balding man standing behind David muttered. David nodded. He felt a bit queasy himself as he gazed at the dead boy. Zach pressed his hand a second, his motion hidden by the crush of the throng.

The gallery visitors filed out to Broadway in nearly complete silence. "It's a damned disgrace!" the bald man suddenly cried out. "White men dying like flies to free a bunch of nigger savages!"

Zach spun around to confront him. "I warrant you, sir, the niggers would fight for their own freedom if they were but given leave."

"Freedom!" The man spat a mouthful of tobacco juice in the direction of the gutter. "To overrun the North! Mark my words, letting the niggers loose'll prove our undoing. Damned abolitionists dragged us into war against the Southerners and now that ape in the White House means to steal the Sechesh's rightful property! It's the destruction of the Union he's brought on us!" Most of the dispersing crowd had stopped to listen; half a dozen loudly seconded him.

"I daresay, sir, it's Southern sympathizers like yourself who'll destroy the Union quicker than any proclamation of emancipation!"

A heavyset man nodded emphatically at Zach's response. "I've two boys fighting for the Union and no use for Copperhead traitors!" Others rallied to his side. David eyed the angry crowd uneasily, trying in vain to signal Zach to move on.

The bald man raised his voice to carry over the shouted epithets opposing factions had begun to fling at one another. "At least the Southerners know how to keep their niggers in check! Mark my words, niggers by the thousands'll be roaming our streets, living off our bounty, attacking our women! Hordes of savages—"

Zach's voice boomed out again. "Given half a chance the colored can act as civilized as whites." He caught David by the arm. "You can testify to that better than I can."

David winced and pulled back. "For God's sake, Zach! Let him talk. It's not worth starting a fight over."

"Not worth—" Zach dropped David's arm, turned back to the bald man. A hack approached, wheels clattering noisily on the cobblestones. The wrinkled Negro driver reined his horse as he searched the crowd for fares. The man spat again. "Goddamn niggers stealing a livelihood from white men!" The black driver hesitated an instant, then whipped the horse down the street.

"Now listen here!" Zach thundered. "You've no right—"

"I've a right to live in a white man's country, by God, without nigger lovers like you forcing your amalgamation on me!"

The gallery door opened and another group emerged. A slender, elegantly dressed man stopped at the edge of the crowd. His well-modulated voice cut through their yells. "Gentlemen, may I remind you we're in the presence of the gentler sex." The bald man looked abashed, hurried off with a muttered apology.

The man who'd chided him moved closer as the crowd drifted away: Zach's friend, Byron Roosa. Zach greeted Roosa with surprised pleasure. David nodded curtly, then spun on his heel and strode up the street. Zach caught up to him, puffing angrily.

"You could've at least spoken to Byron. It wouldn't hurt you to be civil."

"I have nothing to say to him."

"Listen to me, David, he's offered you his apology—"

"I don't want to argue about it, Zach."

"David—"

"I told you, it's not worth arguing about."

"Not worth— What in damnation do you find worth arguing about? Your own brother's colored, yet you wouldn't say one word in their defense to that Copperhead bigot."

David winced. "It was a waste of breath. You weren't about to change his mind."

"At least I was standing up for my beliefs!"

"And nearly got yourself in a brawl over them! What the hell good would that've done? Even that perverted friend of yours had the sense to see that. Oh, hell, I'm sorry, Zach."

The curses of a coachman cut off by traffic drowned out whatever reply Zach might've made. David glanced at him.

Zach stalked on in tight-lipped, fist-clenched silence.

David matched his stride in accompanying silence till they were forced to wait for traffic at the cross street. "I'm sorry," he said again. "I didn't mean— I guess I let Brady's photographs upset me."

After a moment, Zach shrugged. "Perhaps so." David shoved his hands into his pockets and retreated into his thoughts. "How could it be worth it?" he muttered, as they reached the boardinghouse steps.

"What in tarnation are you mumbling about?" Zach asked, his voice still gruff with anger. "What's not worth it? Arguing for what's right?"

"All those men killed. Half of them no more than kids. How the hell could anything be worth it?"

The victory at Antietam seemed destined to be the last for Union troops. On November seventh, Lincoln removed McClellan from command of the Army of the Potomac, replacing him with Ambrose Burnside. Two weeks later, Lee and Jackson repulsed Burnside's troops, suffering 5,000 casualties to the Union's 12,000. General Grant was stalemated in the West in his drive to take Vicksburg. With the coming of spring, the Confederates outmaneuvered Northern troops at Chancellorsville, driving them back across the Rappahannock River.

A discouraged Union electorate gave Democrats a gain of 32 House seats. Democratic denunciations of Lincoln's Emancipation Proclamation grew, New York's governor, Horatio Seymour, terming it "bloody, barbarous, revolutionary."

A Different Sin

On May 1, 1863, Clement L. Vallandigham, campaigning for the Democratic gubernatorial nomination in Ohio, exhorted a Copperhead constituency to depose "King Lincoln" as the first step to a negotiated peace. Four days later Vallandigham was arrested and imprisoned by a military commission for his words.

"And no more than he deserves," Zach told David, waving the latest issue of the *Tribune* triumphantly.

David shrugged. Much as he hoped the Democrats' calls for a negotiated peace would bear fruit, there was no point arguing the matter with Zach. Since their quarrel over Roosa at Brady's gallery, their differences of opinion had all too frequently ended in angry exchanges. Over the past winter it seemed to David their easy friendship had changed into an uneasy truce interrupted by suddenly flaring combat—and by bouts of eager, explosive lovemaking.

Boston Common was packed with an expectant crowd come to see the Fifty-Fourth Massachusetts: the regiment of colored volunteers raised by Massachusetts Governor Andrew in the months since Lincoln had authorized the enlistment of Negro soldiers. David stood at the edge of the area roped off for newsmen, Mike and his family just outside the reserved area. They'd left home early that morning to get the spot; the sun was nearly directly overhead now. David gave a worried glance at his father, wishing he hadn't insisted—at his age—on seeing his grandson march with his regiment to Battery Wharf and the troop ship South. The elderly doctor stood patiently, his head bent to catch the words of his youngest grandchild, but his facial muscles looked slack with fatigue. David's eyes met Mike's, seeing his concern echoed in his half-brother's face. Strains of band music sounded from the direction of the Charles Street gate. Mike swiveled, straining for a first glimpse of the regiment.

The music of "John Brown's Body" grew louder. The first ranks marched into view, led by their young white colonel, Robert Gould Shaw, sitting his horse lightly with upraised sword. Cheering broke out, swelling as the white commissioned officers were followed by the six hundred colored troops, crisp in their dress uniforms and waving aloft the flags of country, state and regiment. There seemed no trace in Boston today of the opposition to the war that had grown in New York in the three months since the enactment of conscription in March.

David felt a tug on his arm. "Can you see Peter, Uncle David?" Joshua was standing on tiptoes, his dark eyes shining against the lighter brown of his skin. David smiled down at his nephew, hoisted the youngster to his shoulders a moment. "I see him! I see him!" Josh cried.

Peter turned to grin at his family a split second, then marched on in unison with his regiment, his face proud and solemn, his grip firm on his Enfield rifle.

Rachel reached for Michael's hand. A twinge of fear moved across her face; David thought he saw a corresponding emotion shadow Mike's expression. He turned his attention back to the regiment, which was lining up in military formation at the foot of the reviewing stand. His fingers flew over his pad, sketching the straight-backed troops and their aristocratic young colonel, the dignitaries on the platform, the leonine mane of the Negro orator, Frederick Douglass, surrounding a face fierce with pride as he looked at his own sons in their Union blue.

He glanced back at Mike and Rachel. Their eyes were fixed on the colored volunteers as the regiment marched across the Common toward the wharf, their fingers still entwined, their faces showing nothing now but hard won pride and determination.

David closed his eyes, trying to clear his mind of images from the long tiring day and get some sleep. Despite the open window, Peter and Josh's attic room was stuffy, adding to the discomfort of the unfamiliar bed. Still, you'd think he could sleep, tired as he'd gotten traipsing from one end of the city to the other to bid Peter goodby at the wharf. They'd all been tired from the excitement of the day. Little Josh had nearly fallen asleep at dinner.

Dad looked exhausted too, despite napping the rest of the afternoon. After all, he's up in his seventies. But when did he get so damned frail? Of course it's been upsetting for him seeing Peter go off like that. Though Dad's never been as close to Peter as he is to Abigail and the younger kids. But then on top of that—

David's thoughts returned to the evening meal. Tired as he was, Dad kept smiling so at Josh's chatter. And the way Becky never misses a chance to reprimand him. I suppose just to show how grown up she is: nearly through grammar school already. Seems just yesterday Abigail was that age. And to think she's actually graduating from normal school. Dad's so proud of her. Well, he should be. She must've worked damned hard. It couldn't have been easy for her, probably the only colored student in the whole school. Not that she'd ever complain. Damn sweet kid. I don't suppose you'd call her pretty, even if you were colored yourself, but as nice a girl as you could find.

It's too bad she had to pick this evening to tell Dad she's going down to the Sea Islands to help teach the contrabands there. Or maybe she's mentioned it to him before. You could see he was trying to take it in stride. And she ought to be safe, there's enough Union troops occupying those islands. But then Mike had to announce that he's made up his mind to enlist as an army surgeon.

Through his closed eyes David could see his father's face lose its color, his hands shaking on the tablecloth. Hell, he wasn't as upset at Peter's going off to fight, and it's not like a doctor's going to the front lines. Though I suppose there's always the danger of a stray shell. And of course, Mike's his son.

David turned restlessly. You'd think Rachel would be upset, but she didn't seem distressed. Not that she'd be likely to let on in any case. Look how the two of them held up this afternoon. They must be scared to death for Peter, but they're not about to show it. The image formed once more of Mike and Rachel's proud faces, their hidden fear betrayed only by the grip of hand on hand.

At least they have each other to turn to. They needn't be ashamed of their affections.

The image of Mike and Rachel faded, replaced by the memory of Zach's angry face the week before. They'd had another of their quarrels. Over that damn pervert, Roosa. "I'm damned if I know what you're afraid of," Zach had said. "I told you, Byron's just asked a few friends in for the evening to celebrate moving into new lodgings."

"And I told you I'm not going."

"Well I'll be damned if I can understand why not. It's just for an evening of talk, for Lord's sake. And if I know Byron, there'll be a sight better food and drink than any we'd see here or at Pfaff's either. The Fifth Avenue Hotel's supposed to have the best kitchen in New York. You've complained enough about how sick you are of sitting in Pfaff's night after night. I don't see what you're so afraid of."

"I'm not afraid dammit! I'm just not interested in spending an evening talking to a bunch of perverts like—"

"Like me!?"

David winced as Zach stormed toward him, bracing himself for a blow. Zach grabbed his arm and swung him to face the mirror. "I see two perverts here if that's what you choose to call us!"

"I didn't call you— I— I've told you before, I'm not— It's only our friendship that's made me—"

Zach sighed gustily and dropped his arm. "Whatever you call me, David, I'm at least honest with myself. Which is more than you can say. And I'm not ashamed of wanting to spend an evening in the company of people who accept me for what I am." The door clicked shut on his rigid back.

David turned again, trying to rid himself of the memory. It had been three days till they'd made up the quarrel. Though they'd forgiven each other readily enough then.

A breeze came through the window, touching his face lightly, recalling Zach's first tentative caresses when they'd finally mumbled their apologies. They'd grown in intensity as they buried their differences in urgent, heated lovemaking, Zach's hands pulling him closer, fondling him hungrily, Zach's mouth moving down his body, engulfing his member with hot, rhythmic strokes till he'd had to stifle his sudden outcries of pleasure.

David moaned. God, how he'd like to reach out and touch him right now, let his own mouth move on Zach's body, feel his throbbing, joyous release. He tossed restlessly in the narrow bed. His hand crept down and closed on his erect penis.

Christ! Not here! Not in Mike's house, for God's sake. With Josh asleep on the trundle bed just a few feet away. If he couldn't sleep, he'd get up, get a glass of water, maybe read awhile.

David padded downstairs to the kitchen and worked the pump handle in the sink. He set down the glass, thirst quenched, but sleep no closer. He'd find something to read then. He'd left the novel he'd been reading in his room at Mrs. Chapman's, but there'd surely be something in Mike's bookcase.

He felt for matches in the dark, then lit the lamp in the front room. The books seemed to have been set haphazardly in their case, the family Bible sharing a shelf with the children's schoolbooks and Mike's old medical texts. David looked through them, shoving aside *The Narrative of Frederick Douglass, The Condition and Elevation of the Colored People, Colored Patriots of the American Revolution*, a book of verse by John Greenleaf Whittier. He saw only two novels: *Uncle Tom's Cabin* and *A Tale of Two Cities*. He had no desire to reread either.

He pulled a book at random from the top shelf. Darwin's notions on the origin of species. David thumbed through the pages. God. How could Mike read this? He set it back on the shelf and sank into a chair. The table alongside it was cluttered with magazines and newspapers. Well, it might be interesting to take a look at the Boston papers.

David reached for a newspaper from the pile, managing instead to knock one of the magazines from the table. The Boston Medical and Surgical Journal. He flipped through it idly. It was even duller than Darwin's book. He gave a final glance at the advertisements filling the back pages.

"IMPORTANT ANNOUNCEMENT: New improved douche chair prevents wasting of vital fluids from the vice of self-abuse. More effective than genital cage in cooling impulses of unnatural venery."

David stared at the illustration, unable to take his eyes from the description of the chair, its seat open like that of a privy, the zinc pan underneath to be filled with ice water or medicated refrigerant fluid that would be pumped onto the genitals at the first stirring of sexual excitement.

The journal slipped to the floor. David lowered his head into his hands, uncertain whether to laugh or cry. What in hell would the inventor of this damned chair prescribe for the type of unnatural venery that existed between Zach and himself?

Was it possible a doctor could actually cure those desires? Mike was a doctor. For a moment David imagined himself coming to Mike with such a shameful complaint. How the hell could he ever face him again after such a confession?

He couldn't. If he were ever to break himself of his sin he'd damn well have to come up with the strength to do it on his own.

Chapter 13 - 1863

I<small>F HE COULD JUST GET Z</small>ACH<small> TO SEE THINGS HIS WAY FOR ONCE.</small> David knotted his cravat by feel, without bothering to look in the mirror. Hell, he had to struggle against the temptations of the flesh as much as Zach. Zach knew that.

Not that he gave a damn for David's struggles though. He must've told Zach a dozen times in the six weeks since his visit to Boston that he meant to break himself of sinning once and for all. And Zach had dragged out his volume of Plato to argue it was no sin, or those lousy poems by Whitman celebrating the love of comrades.

"Comrades, sure. You know damn well how I treasure our friendship," David had told him last night. "But we've gone way beyond simple friendship."

"I daresay Whitman had more than simple friendship in mind when he composed these."

"I don't give a goddamn what he had in mind!"

"Nor, I daresay, for my feelings for you. I'm not able to turn my affections off so easily as you."

David sighed. How the hell could Zach accuse him of lacking affection for him? He knew damn well— A rap on the door broke into his thoughts. "Yeah, come in," David called. The door opened simultaneously with his words. Elliot breezed into the room.

"Hey David, you have a spare collar I can use?" David fished in his bureau. "Don't you ever buy anything of your own?"

Elliot laughed. "I've gotta save up three hundred bucks in case my name comes up in the draft. I don't want to be caught short if I need to buy an exemption. You're lucky you've no need to worry about it. Well, I've gotta get going. Thanks for the loan of the collar."

A Different Sin

He'd best get going too, David told himself. No use stewing over last night. Let Zach think his affections had cooled. It might make it that much easier to keep them in check.

Sweat trickled down David's neck as he threaded his way up Sixth Avenue two hours later. He yanked at his cravat, loosening it along with his collar. The steamy heat was worsened by the closely packed bodies of the crowd. Sixth Avenue overflowed with angry men and women carrying placards demanding an end to conscription, shoving their way toward a platform at the edge of Central Park where speakers shouted protests against the opening of the draft lottery in New York City two days earlier.

The air was heavy with the mingled odors of sweat and exhaled whiskey. Streams of tobacco juice splashed trousers and shoes. Laborers and longshoremen, who'd walked off their jobs to show their hatred of the draft, wet hoarse throats with whiskey bottles passed hand to hand and roared their applause for the speakers in tones of mounting fury.

David winced as a gob of tobacco spittle hit his ankle. He shifted his position fruitlessly, too hemmed in by the mob to move, and flipped his pad to a new page. At least he'd gotten a few hour's respite from his drawing table to cover this unexpected rally.

It was far more hours than he'd anticipated before he managed to make his way past blockaded and destroyed street car tracks back to *Leslie's*. Outrage against the draft had exploded into violence across the city. News and rumors flew: An angry mob had burned the Provost Marshal's office at Third Avenue and 46th Street to force an end to the draft selection. Police Superintendent John Kennedy had been beaten. Union veterans in the Invalid Corps had been shot down as they tried to restore order.

David had watched an angry mob set fire to the Colored Orphan Asylum on Fifth Avenue. The mob had allowed mere minutes for orphanage staff to evacuate the children before looting and burning the building. Even after the youngsters were lined up outside, holding hands in wide-eyed fright, women and men glowered and threatened them, stopped from actual attack only by the arrival of a company of firemen, who stood guard with axes and hook poles. David sketched automatically, staring in disbelief at women, faces contorted with hate, screaming, "Kill the damn little niggers!"

He repeated his horror to Elliot as they stumbled exhaustedly from *Leslie's* late in the night.

"Hell, David, you know the Celts have it in for the niggers, afraid they'll steal their lousy jobs from them."

"But these were kids for God's sake! If you'd seen the way they looked at them— How the hell can they? Don't they have kids of their own?"

Elliot shrugged. "They're a bunch of animals, lousy Irish scum, that's how." He laughed shortly. "It's not just the niggers they have it in for. They've threatened to hang Greeley for his support of the draft. A bunch of drunken scum tried to burn down the *Tribune* building earlier this evening."

David stopped dead on the sidewalk. "My God! What happened? Is— Are—" He tried to keep his voice casual. "Have you seen Zach?"

"Nope. I've been stuck at my drawing board since I got back, same as you. But I heard Greeley hightailed it out the back way, hid himself under a table at Windust's restaurant." Elliot snorted. "I'd like to have seen that-New York's mightiest editor huddled under a tablecloth."

"But his staff—"

"They were right on his heels, every last man of them." Elliot laughed again. "And didn't set foot back in the building till the police drove off the mob for them. I hear they've got a regular arsenal in there now though. They're not about to be made laughingstocks a second time."

"My God!" David turned and stared in the direction of the *Tribune*. At this hour the street appeared quiet, a few stolid policemen walking their beat. "Are they still inside? Have they gotten the final edition out yet?" He took a few tentative steps toward the newspaper building.

"By this hour they better have, or they might as well call it tomorrow's. C'mon, will you." Elliot glanced at David with sudden curiosity. "You worried about Zach, for pity's sake? He'll be fine. He's probably having a grand time playing soldier."

It was hard to believe only two days had passed since the riots had flared up on Monday. David slogged along uneasily at the rear of a crowd of some fifty hard-drinking, yelling men and women. Thank God Zach was safe! Despite Elliot's reassurances, he'd been tense with fear till he'd seen him with his own eyes. But Zach had been fine— fatigued, but oddly exhilarated as he told David how he'd spent the night on sentry duty at an upstairs window, helping stand guard for the compositors, once his own copy was in.

Rioting mobs still howled for vengeance on Greeley and his newspaper though; Zach could yet be in peril. There was no telling— David stumbled on a loose pavingstone, nearly falling against a burly, unshaven man alongside him. "Watch where ya goin', goddam ya," the man growled.

A Different Sin

David winced, muttering an apology as he drew back. He'd best pay attention to his own peril now. Though he'd followed Leslie's caution to his artists to dress in shabby, workmen's clothing before mingling with the rioters, it would still be all too easy to give himself away. He shoved his hands into his pockets, feeling the folded pages he'd torn from his sketchpad, and concentrated on memorizing the scenes he'd commit to paper afterwards.

They'd reached Twenty-seventh Street, a neighborhood of poor Negro shanties. The mob's shouts took on new viciousness. David shuddered. In the past two days he'd seen some half dozen bodies of Negroes dangling slackly from lamp posts. He'd no desire to witness a hanging with his own eyes.

The street was deserted, its colored occupants fled or in hiding. The rioters milled about aimlessly. There was a sudden shout of triumph as a woman pointed to the end shack of a tumbledown row, where a darting movement had been spotted behind a window. Empty bottles and pavingstones were hurled through the window, their crashes nearly lost in the screams of the mob. David shuddered again and edged his way out of the crowd.

A narrow alley ran behind the row of shacks. David circled the rear of the mob in the direction of the alley, peering over the rioters' heads for a view of the ringleaders. A sudden movement in the alley caught his eye. The back door to the house opened a crack and a Negro girl of eleven or twelve slipped through. She darted a frightened glance around, then stepped inside again, emerging almost immediately with an infant clutched in one arm, a toddler clinging to her other hand. David held his breath as two more youngsters crept out after her—a girl of perhaps nine years and a boy of six or seven, who leaned against the doorframe clutching a pair of slender sticks with crosspieces tied to the tops like toy swords. Oh God, surely the child didn't hope to fight off the mob with those pitiful toy weapons!

The infant gave a sudden, piercing wail. The mob surged toward the alley, spewing their hatred as they spotted the children. The youngsters stared back, apparently frozen in terror. Run, for God's sake run! David thought, his voice seemingly paralyzed as well.

The older girl snapped from her stupor, speaking urgently to the others, her words drowned by the mob's shrieks. Thrusting the infant into the arms of the second girl, she lifted the toddler onto her skinny hip and grabbed the arm of the boy. The second girl shifted the infant to clutch his other hand. The girls strained fruitlessly to run down the alley, dragging the boy between them.

A bottle flew from the crowd, striking the younger girl on the shoulder. She cried out and dropped the boy's hand. A second bottle sailed just above the children's heads, showering them with broken glass as it smashed at their feet. The older girl turned, her face contorted with desperation and terror. She loosed her own grip on the boy. The two girls fled, the babies bouncing and shrieking in their arms. A shot exploded. The bullet missed its mark, splintering the window frame of one of the shanties. The man who'd fired cursed as the girls reached the alley's end and darted out of sight.

The boy stood frozen where the girls had left him, leaning on the two sticks. Not toy swords, David realized in horror, but makeshift crutches. He could see plainly now how the youngster's right leg hung withered and useless.

The man with the revolver raised it again. A toothless woman next to him shoved his arm down. "Are ya that daft, then, to waste bullets on a nigger brat!" David exhaled, then gasped as the woman squatted, rising triumphantly grasping a,heavy pavingstone. The youngster's eyes dilated with fear. A thin whimpering sob escaped him.

More of the women grabbed up pavingstones. Men grasped bottles by their necks, made clubs of sticks and revolvers. David forced his eyes from the mob to the trembling child. Oh God, don't let them hurt him! Oh God, why didn't somebody stop them?l

The toothless woman broke into a furious chant. "Kill the damn little nigger." Other voices took it up. "Kill the damn nigger! Kill all the bloody niggers!" He could grab him. For God's sake, he could grab him up and run. He could at least give the kid a chance.

The angry howl rose. Move, goddamn it move! His legs felt like reeds, trembling and useless beneath him. Sharp elbows shoved him aside as the mob closed in on the crippled boy. Stones and pistol butts rose and fell, came up red and slimy, thudded down once again. David closed his eyes and clung to the edge of the shanty, trying not to listen to the thudding blows, the boy's high, piercing shrieks of pain.

The mob's cries rose into a victorious shout that slowly trailed off. David forced his eyes open. The last of the mob was disappearing down the alley. The boy sprawled motionless. He took a tentative step toward him. The child's skull was crushed, blood and brains oozing onto the dirt, his left eye torn from its bloody socket.

David stumbled away blindly. He tripped over the curb and fell heavily, pulled himself to his hands and knees, sank down on the curbstone. Finally he pulled a sheet of paper from his pocket, managed to unfold it. He stared down at the page, trying to visualize his drawing, then bent forward and retched, covering the paper, his hands, his trousers, with hot, bitter vomit.

After a long time he rose and staggered downtown toward *Leslie's*.

"I can still hear him screaming. Oh Jesus, God, Zach, I can still hear it." David lowered his head into his hands and shuddered. He'd stumbled back to the boardinghouse dazed and silent, but once he found Zach he hadn't been able to stop himself from pouring out the whole, terrible story. At last he'd quieted, drunk the brandy Zach had produced, let Zach urge him out of his soiled clothes into a clean nightshirt. And then the images had welled up anew and he'd started sobbing it out all over again.

"David, steady yourself. Try to put it out of your mind now." Zach pressed the brandy glass into his hand, steadied it till he finally gulped it down.

He looked up at Zach. "I just stood there. I just stood there and let them beat the kid to death. I didn't even try to stop them."

"You couldn't have done. You'd have been helpless against them."

"I could've tried. I might've gotten him out of there. But I was too damn scared to even try. I just stood there—"

"David, listen to me, they'd have served you the same way if you'd tried to thwart them."

David shook his head. "I didn't do anything. I didn't even try to help him."

A moment went by. "You set it down on paper for the world to see though."

"On paper— Christ, I don't even remember walking to the paper. I just found myself there drawing the whole thing right on the blocks. Leslie was pleased. God, pleased. He wants to put out an extra." He took another shuddering gulp of the brandy.

"And he should. When the public sees what's been done, they'll be bound to come to their senses and put an end to it."

"That's not gonna help that kid any." David closed his eyes, then opened them and looked at Zach so he wouldn't see the crushed skull, the ruined brains dribbling onto the brown skin. Zach was silent a moment. "Not that one, no."

"Oh God, he looked like Josh— He must've been the same age, he was of a size, and those big eyes— And I just stood there— Christ, what the hell kind of a man am I?"

"Hush, hush now. It's not your blame. Get some sleep now." Zach wrapped his arms around David and stroked his hair as if he were a frightened child in need of comfort. David drew in another gulping sob and let himself slump against him. Zach tightened his arms and held him, rocking him gently till he could no longer hold his eyes open against the brutal, bloody images.

Chapter 14 - 1863

"In the midst of life we are in death;
of whom may we seek for succor,
but of thee, oh Lord,
who for our sins art justly displeased?"

THE WORDS OF THE ANTHEM TRAILED OFF. Stones and sod dropped with a final grating clatter onto the lid of James Harrison's coffin. David shivered. He stepped back from the edge of the grave and took his father's arm. The service of committal sounded solemnly over their bowed heads. "In sure and certain hope of the resurrection to eternal life though our Lord Jesus Christ, we commend to Almighty God...."

The mourners dispersed. His uncle's body lay in the ground. And his soul? Hell, whatever his faults, Uncle James probably never knowingly sinned. Which is a damn sight more than I can say for myself.

David rubbed a few loose grains of sod from his palm onto his trousers and shuddered again. In the midst of life— How would he stand with the Almighty if he were to be overtaken by death right now? It was right there in First Corinthians: "Know ye not that the unrighteous shall not inherit the kingdom of God? ...neither fornicators...nor adulterers...nor abusers of themselves with mankind...."

It had been far too many months since he'd even attended Sunday worship. As soon as he returned to New York he'd see a priest, ask him to hear his confession. Though why wait? He could do it here just as well. The ritual phrases of penitence ran through his mind. "For these and all other sins... I am truly sorry. I pray God to have mercy on me. I firmly intend amendment of life...."

Christ. How many times over the past three years had he promised himself to amend his ways? What would it avail him to make the promise in confession if he fell into sin again the moment he found himself alone with Zach? He sighed. Since that terrible night of the draft riots two months ago he'd clung to Zach's company and comfort more than ever. He couldn't separate from him.

"I'm thankful you were able to reach home before James passed on. It meant a good deal to him to be reconciled with you his last years."

David gave a guilty start, wondering how many of his father's words he'd missed, lost in thought as he'd been ever since they'd left the graveyard of Christ Church. He took his father's arm. "I'm glad I was able to see him a last time."

George Carter nodded, his face growing slack with fatigue as they entered the house. He sank into his wing chair with a sigh and closed his eyes.

David looked at him with concern. He looks so old and worn out. And he must be five or six years older than Uncle James was.

"Are you all right, Dad?" he asked.

His father managed a tired smile. "I'm fine, son. It's just— Troubles seem to follow at one another's heels, don't they? Peter missing and then James passing. Crusty as he was, I miss him sitting there. The house seems empty without him."

"I wish I could stay with you longer, but I've got to get back to work." David drummed his fingers absently on the arm of his chair. "You've got Mike nearby though."

George Carter brightened. "Thank God! He was disappointed to be posted to a hospital in Washington City, instead of out by some field of battle, but I'm thankful for God's mercy in keeping him safe. Will you have time to see him on your way back to New York?"

"I thought I might." David slumped in his chair, thinking of his last visit with Mike, in Boston that May. I couldn't get Zach off my mind then either. And those damn advertisements— He closed his eyes, visualizing their horrors. Still, Mike is a doctor. He might know of some way. If I can bring myself to ask him. But what other choice is there? One of the doctors who sit and gossip over beer at Pfaff's? At least I can trust Mike. And I'm sure as hell not amending my life on my own.

He opened his eyes again. "Yeah, I can take time to see him, Dad."

Like Alexandria, Washington had become a city of military encampments and hospitals. David rode the horsecar to the last stop, then continued on foot down the muddy, rutted lane northwest toward Twelfth and R streets: the location of Freedman's Hospital, established by the government for the contrabands, those runaway slaves who'd slipped through the Union lines to freedom.

Hundreds of makeshift shanties stretched beyond the boundaries of the rickety wooden barracks that had been provided to house the contrabands. Half-naked children ran and shouted in the rapidly falling evening, women stirred pots of greens over smoky fires, men lounged together talking and laughing. Chickens and dogs roamed free, squawking and barking, their noise drowned out by the sound of hymns swelling from fire to fire. The smells of people crowded together, cooking pots and poorly drained outhouses hung over the area.

The hospital was a one-story frame building, in little better repair than the fugitives' barracks. A Negro man wearing the uniform of an army officer was entering the front door. David called him. "Mike! Hey Mike, wait a minute"

The man turned, startled, then hurried toward David. "Can I help you?" he asked.

David looked at him in embarrassment. From the front he didn't look much like Mike at all. The same mulatto coloring, but his features were sharper and Mike had never sported a handlebar mustache like that. "I was looking for a colored man who's a doctor," he managed.

"Well, you've found one, sir." The man smiled and held out his hand. "I'm Major Augusta. I have charge of this facility."

David extended his own hand. "I didn't realize—" He stopped, feeling foolish.

The major smiled again. "That there was more than one colored doctor serving in the army? I believe there's seven or eight of us stationed in Washington City. Who are you looking for?"

"Mike— Michael Mabaya. He's—"

"Yes, I know him. He's here. He should be going off duty about now." Augusta waved his hand in the direction of the doctors' quarters.

Mike smiled a greeting, leading the way to a bench outside the noisy barracks. David sank down next to him. He looked older, David thought. His frizzy black hair showed new patches of white at the temples. The same place Dad first started to gray—

David started, realizing he'd missed Mike's words of condolence on his uncle's death. Not that Mike could be very grieved, after the way Uncle James had dragged him back to slavery. "Do you see much of Dad?" he asked.

"When I get a chance. We're pretty well swamped here. The camp's full of smallpox, yellow fever." Mike closed his eyes a moment, rubbed them with the back of his hands. "He's been helping out at one of the hospitals in Alexandria a couple of times a week. At his age." He smiled tiredly.

"He didn't say." David paused. "I— I wanted to ask you—" He broke off. How could he bring himself to ask Mike for his help? They sat in silence a few minutes. Hell, he'd come all the way out here. "There's something I thought maybe you could tell me—"

"What?" Mike turned to look at him. "Sorry, I wasn't paying you much mind." He rubbed his eyes again. "I had my mind on Peter. Truth is, I haven't thought of much else all summer. God help me, sometimes I think it would be easier if I knew for sure he'd been killed."

Christ. He'd been so caught up in his own troubles he hadn't said a word to Mike about Peter. David stared down at his hands. To tell the truth he hadn't paid much attention to the scanty news stories, following on the heels of the draft riots, of the failed assault on Fort Wagner, spearheaded by the 54th Massachusetts. Nearly a fourth of the regiment had been lost on the flat stretch of sand dunes surrounding the fort or in hand to hand combat on the earthworks that formed its defenses. Colonel Shaw, struck down as he urged on his men, had been buried by the Confederates "in a common ditch with his niggers," news reports said.

Even when he'd gotten the news that Peter was missing in action, it had barely intruded on his own concerns. He looked back at Mike. "You haven't heard anything more?"

"Not a thing." Michael gave a deep, shuddering sigh. "Abigail found one of the boys in hospital, when she went to Beaufort to help with the nursing, who thought he'd seen Peter wounded inside the earthworks. He didn't know how badly. She was going to see if he could tell her more when he'd recovered a bit, but he died of his wounds before she got the chance."

David swallowed. "But if he was taken prisoner, surely they'd have put him in a hospital. It might take months to get news of him. You shouldn't give up hope yet."

"It's what I tell myself, what I write Rachel and the children. I can't make myself believe it though. Oh Lord, David, I'm so scared for him. I keep thinking—if he was captured by the Rebs he might be better off to have been killed outright."

"Christ, Mike, don't say that!" David looked at him in shock. "He couldn't be better off dead than to be a prisoner."

"The Confederates won't treat colored as prisoners of war. He could be sold into slavery. I keep thinking of him being chained up, whipped—hanged even, like the prisoners they took at Milliken's Bend."

Both the *Tribune* and *Times* that summer had carried stories of colored prisoners summarily put to death. "But since then," David argued, "Lincoln's warned the Secesh our government'll retaliate if they murder colored prisoners or try to enslave them. Anyway, it's the thought of arming slaves that troubles them. There's no reason for them to treat free colored any different than white."

"Free or slave won't matter. A nigger's a nigger to them." Mike's voice shook. "Those white boys are savages. Get a little liquor in them, there's no telling what they'll do. They're not gonna be stopped by any order from Lincoln."

It had grown too dark to see Mike's face but David could feel him tremble. I've never seen him so scared, he thought. He searched for words to dispel his fear. The memory of the draft riots rose vividly in his mind. It had taken the force of troops recalled fresh from the victory at Gettysburg to stop the mobs from their mindless violence. He shuddered and kept silent.

Christ. He couldn't just sit here. David reached out and put an arm around his brother's shoulders, held him tightly for a long moment. "It's too soon to give up hope," he said finally.

Mike drew a deep breath. "I know. Thanks. There's no use borrowing trouble." He managed a smile. "What was it you wanted to ask me?"

He couldn't ask him now. Mike had enough burdens as it was. "I don't remember. I— I guess it wasn't that important," David said.

He continued to cling to Zach's company through the fall, missing him even the few days Zach was in Pennsylvania, covering the dedication of the cemetery for the war dead at Gettysburg. He admitted as much to Zach on his return.

"And I you. I'd hoped we could travel there together. It's a shame Leslie decided to rely on photographs."

David grimaced. "I've been copying them all day. I have good news though. Mike's had word of Peter. He was taken prisoner. They're being held in the city jail in Charleston."

"That is good news."

"Yeah. Though he lost an arm in the fighting." David shuddered. "Mike wrote he's just thankful his life was spared. He was so frightened for him." David fell silent, musing on his visit with Mike and the help he hadn't brought himself to ask of him.

"Do you ever give thought to how we're imperiling our souls by lying together?" he asked abruptly.

"What brings that up all of a sudden?"

"I don't know. I guess it's been preying on my mind since Uncle James passed on."

Zach grew thoughtful. "I think I can answer you best in verse," he said, smiling at David.

"When he whom I love travels with me or sits a long
while holding me by the hand...
Then I am charged with untold and untellable wisdom,
I am silent, I require nothing further,
I cannot answer the question of appearances or that of
identity beyond the grave,
But I walk or sit indifferent, I am satisfied,
He ahold of my hand has completely satisfied me."

David smiled reluctantly. "More Whitman? But hell, Zach, that's not
enough."

"It's enough. I find it so, at any rate."

"I wish I did. But you know we'll have to answer for our sins in the
next life."

"Not every religion preaches hellfire and brimstone." Zach finished
unpacking and sank onto his chair. He pulled off his shoes, then
slumped back with a comfortable sigh. "I'd sooner spend Sunday
mornings other than listening to a sermon, but when I was younger I
sought out churches that taught God's love instead of His vengeance.
The Universalists, Unitarians. I'd not mind attending again if you'd
like."

"I don't think so."

"You might at least read a few modern religious thinkers. I know
you've read precious little of Emerson or—"

"Hell, Zach, just because someone sets down his notions in an essay
or poem doesn't make them so."

Zach's brows drew together in concentration, preparatory, David
knew, to pursuing his argument. David cast about for a change of
subject. "Where the hell is he anyhow?"

"Where is who?"

"Whitman. I haven't seen him around Pfaff's for months."

"Washington City. He's been helping tend the wounded there, I've
heard. Why do you ask?"

"I just wondered. He must have his hands full if he's helping care
for wounded. When I was home this fall it seemed half the houses in
town had been turned into hospitals. It's a wonder there's any men left
to go on fighting."

"Let's pray Lincoln can bring it to a speedy conclusion. When I gave
thought, at Gettysburg, to how many—" Zach halted himself. "There's
precious little point to such gloomy conversation. What do you say to
a glass or two of beer at Pfaff's?"

"I don't think so. It's late to go out. And I ought to finish my letter
to Mike." David took in Zach, still slumped in his chair, and smiled.

"Anyhow, by the looks of you, you'd do better to get a good night's sleep than go out drinking."

Zach's smile stretched into a yawn. "I daresay you're right. Once I've got my shoes off, I'm fairly well settled for the evening. Though I'll probably do a bit of reading before turning in. Speaking of which, why not take my copy of Emerson with you?"

"Maybe another time. I'm too tired to wade through Emerson this evening. Sleep well." David kissed him lightly on the brow and left the room.

David slid the completed letter into an envelope. He stood and stretched, walked restlessly around his room. It was still an hour before his accustomed bedtime.

He should've taken the essays, he thought, read a few pages. If nothing else, it would've pleased Zach. Well, he doubted Zach was asleep yet. He knocked softly, then pushed Zach's door to as he entered his room.

Zach was in his nightshirt, reading in bed, back propped against the pillow, legs stretched out atop his coverlet. David glanced at the clothes strewn across the chair, and sank onto the foot of the bed. Zach drew up his knees to make room for him. "I hope you're not about to suggest going out for a beer at this hour."

"Hardly. I came to borrow your book after all, but I'm not so sure I feel like reading either, to tell the truth." David leaned back against the wall, smiling at Zach's comfortably sprawled body. Zach's thick hair was already as disheveled as after a night of sleep, his rumpled nightshirt hiked up to his thighs, exposing the pink tip of his penis.

"You'll catch yourself a chill, sitting like that." David reached forward to tug the nightshirt down. His hand strayed to Zach's thigh, fingers twining themselves in the heavy pubic hair, his palm beginning to tingle as it moved in tiny, quickening circles. Zach gave a sigh of delight. His shirt fell back further, exposing the quickening excitement in his member.

David caught his breath as the tender, wrinkled skin swelled with life. His hand moved between Zach's thighs and encircled the hot throbbing flesh. God, he thought, all my talk about sin and I can't be in a room with him five minutes without— Zach's first moans of pleasure sounded softly in his ears, banishing his dismay. Zach stroked David's hair, murmuring his name in joyful gasps.

David bent forward and left a line of moist kisses on Zach's stomach and thighs. His lips brushed Zach's member, moved slowly up the shaft, parted to engulf it with hot rhythmic caresses. Zach's moans grew louder.

The door flew open simultaneous with a sharp knock. Elliot's breezy voice called, "Hey Zach, you got a match—" There was a moment of stunned silence. "My God!" Elliot breathed. "Holy Christ! Holy Mother of God!" An eternity of seconds went by till Elliot stepped from the rooms slamming the door behind him.

David flung himself from the bed. His legs trembled. He made his way to the window and stared blindly at the drawn curtains. In the sudden silence he could hear the creak of the bedsprings as Zach stood, the sounds of his bare feet walking toward him.

"I daresay that'll teach us a lesson about locking doors," Zach said at last.

"Christ, Zach—" David broke off, shaking. He leaned his forehead against the pane, the curtain clenched in his fist.

Zach put a hand on his shoulder. David jerked away. Zach stepped closer, gripping his shoulder. "David, listen to me. It's all right. I'll have a word with Elliot. He won't give us away."

"Have a word with him! God, how can you face him? How can you ever face him again?"

"David, I daresay I'm as embarrassed as you, but—"

"Embarrassed! Oh my God, Zach, did you see how he looked at us? How he saw us? A pair of disgusting perverts— Oh Jesus!"

"Elliot's no saint himself."

"Oh Christ, what does that matter? I— I've got to get out of here!"

Zach dropped his hand. "I daresay we'll both feel better after a night's sleep."

"David! Are you there, David?" Zach burst into his room as he opened the door. "I was afraid you might be taken ill. I thought you'd slept past breakfast, but when you failed to appear for supper as well—" Zach broke off and stared around the room at the empty bookshelves and bureau top, the packed carpet bag and boxes.

"Hell, Zach, you think I could just sit down to table with Elliot after what happened?" David drew a deep breath. "It was bad enough having to go past his drawing table to reach Leslie's office." He'd scurried past, sensing Elliot's stare on his back, not daring to meet the other man's eyes, picturing his look of scorn and disgust. "I can't stay here anymore."

Zach dropped onto the chair, still gazing at David's belongings. "I daresay you're right. There's precious little privacy in boardinghouse living," he said at last. "I've said more than once, we ought to seek lodgings together. If we pool our funds, I'll warrant we can find something more to our liking. A small house, even, if we were to venture as far afield as Brooklyn. It's not a bad trip on the ferry—"

"I can't stay in New York! I'd still see him every day at work. Leslie still needs artists with the troops. I told him I'd finally got fed up with copying. I'll be covering the Army of the Potomac as soon as I can get outfitted and get a pass from the War Department."

A long moment passed, punctuated by Zach's indrawn breath. "On your return, then," he said. "Surely the Rebs can't hold out much longer. I'll keep my eye out for a suitable place and—"

"Dammit, Zach! No!" David shoved his carpet bag aside and sat on the edge of his bed. "It's more than Elliot. Can't you see that?" He stared down at his hands, not wanting to see Zach's face. His fingers entwined, clenching together as if for comfort. "We can't go back to sinning. I mean to break myself of you once and for all."

"David, for— There's no sin in loving! David, listen to me—"

"I've made up my mind." David looked at Zach, looked down again. "I've made my mind up," he repeated.

"And our friendship counts for nothing with you? You've no concern for my affection for you?"

"You know how I feel—"

"I'm damned if I do!" Zach rose, strode the few feet to David, grabbed him by the shoulders, shook him hard. "You've precious little feeling for me, I daresay!"

"Zach, for God's sake." David caught hold of Zach's arms and pulled himself up. "Get a grip on yourself." Standing, his hands still gripping the tensed biceps, David could feel Zach's breath ragged on his face, the nearly imperceptible tremors shaking his body. Long seconds went by as they stood, locked in angry embrace.

Zach tightened his grasp, squeezing David's shoulders with painful intensity. "You've never given a tinker's damn for me, have you?" His voice broke. His arms went limp, fell to his sides.

"Oh God, Zach!" David shook. He moved a step closer, wrapped his arms around him. Zach gave a strangled sob, pressed his lips to David's. David closed his eyes. His lips parted. He felt Zach's arms start to encircle him with longing. Oh God, if he could just forget everything, pull him down to the bed— He pulled back and shoved Zach furiously from him.

Zach reeled backwards, grabbing at the bureau for balance.

"I love you! I love you, dammit! I've never said that to anyone else in my life. Now get out of here. Just get the hell out!"

Zach straightened. He sucked in his breath. His hand still gripped the edge of the bureau, the gray hairs standing out against his whitened knuckles. "Your love isn't worth a damn to me, David. Not a tinker's damn. You needn't worry *about breaking* yourself of me. Our friendship is a closed chapter in my life, so far as I'm concerned."

The door closed after him with soft finality.

Chapter 15 - 1863

"Fix yer signature to both copies and see you read this here through before you send anything out for publication." The Federal official shoved the papers at David and sent a stream of tobacco juice into the spittoon beside his desk before drawling, "Next."

David scrawled his name across the bottom of the parole and duplicate, attesting his loyalty to the Federal Government and his pledge to publish nothing detrimental to its interest. He stepped back, running his eyes down the closely printed paragraphs of the circular detailing contraband information, while fumbling for the kit he'd set behind him. His elbow hit a young man folding a similar pamphlet into his coat pocket.

"Sorry," David muttered.

"It's okay." The youth held out his hand. "Looks like we're on the same errand. I'm Al Matthews. With the *Missouri Republican*. I'll be covering General Meade and the Army of the Potomac."

David smiled. "I've the same assignment, for *Leslie's*. I'm David Carter," he added, following Matthews from the Army Intelligence office into the crowded corridors of the War Department.

The lawn fronting army headquarters was dotted with displays of captured weaponry. Blue-uniformed army aides and clusters of women clerks bustled across it. Matthews halted, turning to David. "Can you direct me to a livery stable? I just got off the train this morning and I've no idea where to get mounted. Fact is, I've no idea how to get around this town at all." He ran his fingers through a cap of closely cropped brown curls and grinned at David.

"There's one nearby," David assured him. "Behind Willard's Hotel.

I'm on my way there myself. My editor's made arrangements for a mount through our correspondent here." Matthews fell into step with David, darting curious glances around him as they walked the three blocks down Pennsylvania Avenue. His bright eyes topped a smooth cheeked, oval face and short, wiry frame that seemed swallowed up in a coat at least one size too big.

He's just a kid, David thought. Hasn't even started to shave yet, by the looks of him. He noticed Matthews' short, quick steps as he trotted alongside, and slowed his own long-legged stride. "That's newspaper row." David waved toward the bustling block of shabby buildings across from Willard's. "The livery's just beyond here."

David stowed his change of clothing and extra drawing supplies in the left-hand saddle bag and walked behind his rented horse to set his field glasses in the right. The animal shied. David jumped back, belatedly recalling long forgotten admonitions never to startle a horse by coming up behind it. From the corner of his eye he saw Matthews, already done dickering with the liveryman, leading his mount toward the stable door.

His own mount stared at him skittishly. The stable owner stepped over and patted the horse on the neck, with a grunt of amusement. He gathered up the reins and handed them to David. "She'll get used to you. Just talk to 'er a little, let 'er know who's boss." He watched, chuckling, as David gingerly led the horse outside.

Matthews, already mounted, watched David hoist himself awkwardly into the saddle. The younger man guided his mount around with one hand on the reins, patting the horse with easy affection and grinning at David. "Not much of a beast, is she? Reckon the cavalry's got hold of anything halfway decent by now, so there's nothing for it but to make do with these nags." He gave another grin and started down the street at a lively trot.

David nodded, with what he hoped was a nonchalant grin in return., His horse lurched after Matthews'. He caught his breath and leaned forward, clutching the reins, clumps of shaggy mane caught between his clenched fingers. The ground seemed impossibly far below. Matthews reined in, waiting for him. David caught up, clutching harder as the horse came to a jerking stop in response to his yank on the reins. "The Long Bridge is the best way from here," he said, willing himself to untangle his fingers from the mane to point out its direction.

"I'll follow your lead." Matthews hesitated. "You've not done much riding, have you?" he asked.

"Just a few times as a boy." David glanced at Matthews' easy posture. He must look ridiculous, he thought. He could feel his pants legs creeping out of his boots, his bare calves sweaty against the stirrup straps. "I'm afraid I never got the hang of it then either."

Matthews laughed. "I thought as much, the way you're riding on the neck. You want to sit up straight and stay in the middle of your saddle."

David inched backwards, trying to emulate Matthews' ease.

"That's the ticket." Matthews smiled encouragingly. "You look pretty athletic. It won't take you long to catch on."

"Well, I hope not." David managed a smile. "It's a long ride to Culpeper." Sit up, he told himself. You're not about to fall off. He breathed a small sigh of relief, nevertheless, as they drew rein for the pass checkpoint at the entrance to the bridge.

Matthews moved ahead of David, his hips moving in rhythm with his steed as its hoofs clattered on the wooden planks of Long Bridge. They were halted for a second pass inspection at the Virginia end. David paused after the guards had waved them through, gazing at the endless rows of tents and fortifications.

"Don't you know the way from here?"

"What? Oh, yeah. I was just— This is my hometown. My father still lives here. At least he's managed to hold on to his house. A lot of his neighbors wouldn't take the loyalty oath and had theirs confiscated. My uncle's home was taken for a hospital. He spent his last years living with Dad. Now that he's gone, Dad's pretty much obliged to offer his spare room to put up army officers."

"You're stopping for a visit then?" Matthews asked. His youthful tenor rose in sudden anxiety over the prospect of parting company.

David shook his head. "I've just spent a couple of weeks with him, actually. Said goodbye this morning." And none too soon, he thought. Two weeks of listening to Dad ask if I've taken leave of my senses to leave a safe post in New York for the front lines. How in the hell could I give him a reason that made sense? I could hardly tell him—

He tried to shake off his mood. "It's just coming on all these camps like this. I still find it startling. We'd best get going if we're to get any distance toward Culpeper before evening."

Matthews nodded with relief. He spurred his horse on ahead, then reluctantly reined in and waited for David. He grinned apologetically as David drew alongside him. "I'm used to a faster pace, I reckon. Not that there's much sense breaking our necks getting there. I'd hoped to reach the front lines in time for Meade's drive against Lee, but now that Lee's pushed him back again he'll be content to sit tight in camp till spring."

"I suppose. I can't say I mind though. I'm not eager to witness more bloodshed, to tell the truth."

"You've covered the front before then?"

"The home front, mainly. Though even there, with the draft riots—I've been drawing for Leslie's nearly ten years now. I finally got restless staying in New York."

"I know how you feel. I've been getting darn fed up myself reporting Sanitary Commission fairs and politicians' speeches when the real news is with the armies."

David smiled. "You hardly look old enough to have been reporting any news for very long."

"It's my size, I reckon. Folks always take me for younger than I am. I'm no kid though."

"Well, I meant no offense." No point pressing him; the army was full of youngsters from what he'd heard, some not even in their teens. "I thought the Western papers were relying on the Associated Press to cover the fighting here in the East. I didn't realize any Missouri papers had correspondents stationed with Meade."

"Don't reckon there's many." Matthews grinned. "I'm just a stringer. They're paying me by the dispatch. But I figure once I show them my worth, I'll be able to write my own ticket."

"Well, I wish you luck." David sat a little straighter in the saddle, looking at the brash young reporter with amused admiration.

They left the farmhouse where their Federal greenbacks had bought them a grudging night's shelter at dawn, pressing on toward Culpeper. David forgot his soreness, straining for a better view as they caught their first sight of the winter camp. The once pleasant countryside, stretching out toward the Blue Ridge mountains in the distance, lay stripped of trees and fences. Dirt paths ran through the sprawling array of log huts that had been erected in the few days since Meade's retreat. The rhythm of axes sounded a sharp counterpoint to the shouts of men, braying of mules and neighs of horses. A blue haze of campfire smoke hung over the site.

General Meade accepted their credentials with scant welcome. An aide directed them from the general's headquarters to the correspondents' quarters near Brandy Station: a ramshackle farmhouse abandoned by its fleeing owners. Two Negro servants, also abandoned by their former owners, took charge of their worn-out mounts and stowed their gear in a chilly attic bedroom. The coterie of newsmen lounging in the smoke-filled parlor greeted them with casual scrutiny. "Welcome to the Bohemian Brigade, gentlemen." Frank Chapman, of the New York *Herald*, gave a mock bow. David smiled, introducing Matthews to the other New York reporters while committing to memory the names and faces of men from Boston and Philadelphia papers.

The fair, strapping *Harper's* artist, Alf Waud, was recognizable by his
flowing beard, as well as his resemblance to his younger brother Bill—
who'd himself left Leslie's for *Harper's*. Waud sat on a battered couch
talking to Edwin Forbes, a young art student Leslie'd hired two years
earlier. David joined them. "I've been admiring your camp sketches,"
he told Forbes.

"I wish Leslie did as much. He keeps reminding me he's paying for
scenes of the war, not men taking their ease." Forbes smiled ruefully.
"When he took me on, I fully expected to be able to seat myself on a
hilltop and sketch battles at my leisure."

David nodded. "I'd been hoping the same myself."

"The reality's different, you'll find out. Still, you can pick up a good
bit of detail with field glasses without endangering yourself. You've
brought a good pair, I hope?"

"As good as I could find. I had to wait nearly two weeks till my pass
came through, so I had ample time to provision myself."

Forbes grinned. "If Leslie'd foreseen such a quick end to Meade's
assault at Mine Run, he'd have kept you in New York till spring."

"If Lincoln doesn't put Grant in Meade's place, he might as well
keep him there half a dozen springs," Waud put in.

There was a general murmur of agreement. The talk turned from
the likelihood of Grant's appointment to command the Union armies
to tales of besting rival correspondents and gossip about absent
colleagues. Newspapers rustled. A stocky *Philadelphia Inquirer* reporter shuffled cards with a riffling flourish as a trio of newsmen drew
up chairs for a game. Flasks and glasses were drained.

He might as well be back in Pfaff's. David stood restlessly and
nodded to the other men. "I guess I'll take a look at the camp before
dark."

Matthews walked with him as he left the room. They followed the
dirt paths from the outskirts of the camp, past the baggage wagons of
a Massachusetts regiment, their mules braying in their enclosure.

The log huts erected by the infantrymen for their winter quarters
were clustered in closely packed rows, separated by little more than the
space of their outdoor chimneys. Smoke curled from a hodgepodge
of chimney materials, from neatly laid masonry to open pork barrels,
stacked one above another. The chinked log shelters were roofed over
with small shelter tents, the two tent halves joined together at the peak.
Many of the white duck tents were boldly lettered with the names and
companies of their occupants, even decorated with stick drawings of
the men.

David paused, smiling at a sketch of two sparring pugilists. The two
men, P. Moran and C. Kelley, according to their lettered canvas roof,

sat on stumps by their doorsill, peacefully sucking on pipes, their
attention fixed on a poker game in front of the adjacent cabin.

A pair of rifles were propped up against the log wall, looking out of
place alongside a washboard and two tin buckets. Several pairs of socks
dripped from a line strung between two upended logs. A bearded man
stepped from the next hut and wrung some additional moisture from
the laundry, then sank onto his doorsill, leaning comfortably against
the frame. He pulled a boot off his bare foot, and began studiously
paring his toenails with a knife.

Zach could make himself comfortable anyplace like that, David
thought. He'd enjoy this scene, the split log huts, built for just a few
months use but fixed as cozy and homelike as the men could make
them, firewood stacked outside and walls papered with illustrated
pages showing through the open doors. He could write him that
evening, maybe enclose a small sketch of the decorated roofs—

No! Dammit, what was he thinking of? He'd come down here to
break himself of Zach. And Zach had let him know their friendship was
over, in any case.

"Is something wrong, Mr. Carter?" David started at Matthews' high,
youthful voice, suddenly aware of the young reporter standing anxiously at his elbow. He shook his head, glad to be distracted. Several
of the soldiers were staring at him with expressions of amused
curiosity.

"No, everything's fine." He managed a smile, nodded at the curious
soldiers. "I was just reminded of something. I guess we'd best be
getting back before it's too dark to see."

"Sure, if it ain't our Special Artist! Where's your chicken?"

"My what?" David stared back at the husky infantryman sitting in
front of the hut topped with the sketch of the prizefighters.

The soldier grinned. "Your chicken. The little feller who was here
with you the other night."

"He's— I don't know what you mean." David shifted his feet
nervously, clutching his sketchpad tighter under his arm.

"Pretty young lad like that. Ain't he your chicken?" Christ. He didn't
imagine— "I don't know what you're talking about. I just met him—"

"Hey, don't let Pete here rile you." A lanky redhead stepped from
the doorway, grinning at David from a face spattered with freckles.
"That's just army lingo. Now him and me's been tentin' together since
we joined up, so I call him my old woman, makin' me the old man. If
you're from Marblehead like us, your chum's your chicken, 'specially
if he's a young feller like that."

"Oh. He's gone to try and talk Meade into letting him ride along on a scout." David hesitated, then lowered himself onto a log. He rubbed his chin where the itchy stubble of a new beard was growing in. "How long since you enlisted?"

"Be three years come May." The redhead sat on the doorsill. "Five months and two days till we're mustered out. And then this here army won't see us for our dust. Ain't that right, old woman?" He nudged his partner with an elbow and grinned again.

"Damn right. Goddamn generals use up men like turkeys at a shootin' match and what in hell for? This here's the same ground we fought over back in May. Now they're sayin' Lincoln's gonna put Grant over us. Ain't gonna make a blame bit of diff'rence. He'll be the same as the others, hold the life of a private soldier 'bout as much account as one of the baggage mules. It's gettin' out I am while my hide's still in one piece."

"I don't blame you."

The soldier grunted. He clamped a pipe between yellow-stained teeth and shoved tobacco into the bowl with a thick forefinger. He groped in his pocket for a match, then removed the pipe a moment. "Saw you lookin' at our pitcher when you was here before. Might not look like much to an artist like you, but it suits us fine."

David smiled. "Were you prizefighters before you joined up?"

"Sure were." The redhead grinned. "Leastways, we had us a couple matches apiece. Pete here won us a five dollar gold piece once. We're sparring partners, see, ever since we were boys. So we made up our minds to keep helpin' each other out and split our winnings.

"Pete even got himself his name in the paper that time. Hey, how 'bout you drawing Pete and me for the illustrated? That's Pete Moran, and I'm Colin Kelley. Kelley with two e's." He grinned again, with a sudden hint of shyness. "I got a girl back home. I'd kinda like for her to see it."

"Sure." David flipped his pad open to a clean page, past sketches of infantrymen drilling, sutlers' wagons, camp barbers and mess call. "Only I don't know how many pictures of camp my editor'll be willing to print."

David stretched out on his cot, watching Al Matthews shave—mostly for show, David suspected. Still, Al never skipped a day. He wet his brush in the washbasin and began lathering up with his usual elaborate care. That water's probably freezing, David thought. He stroked his own new growth. "Why put yourself to all that bother out here in the middle of an army camp? Anyway, beards are the fashion now."

Al shrugged. "I'd sooner be clean shaven," he said mildly.

"Well, I guess it's none of my affair." David got up and walked over to Al, peered over his shoulder into the glass. His hair was still the dark blond it had been from boyhood, but the new growth of beard was coming in a soft, decided gray. He fingered it again, smiling ruefully. "I'm growing old," he said.

Al scraped the last bit of lather from his chin. "Nonsense. You don't look a bit old." He turned to examine David. "It's not gray, anyway. More of a silver. Let me see." He reached up and put a hand on David's cheek, ran his fingers down along his jawline. "Yeah, it's silver all right. I think you look very handsome bearded."

David flushed and pulled back. "Well, thanks. I—we'd best get downstairs before they drink up all the Christmas punch." He hurried down to the smoky parlor.

"Looks like we're about to have this celebration preserved for posterity," Ed Forbes said, winking at David. David turned. Alex Gardner, a one-time assistant to Brady, was setting up the cumbersome photographic equipment he lugged in his "what's-it" wagon.

"If you'll gather round the punch bowl, gentlemen," Gardner directed.

Ed grinned. "Might as well have another glass apiece while we're waiting." They stood watching Gardner group the correspondents, peering each time through his camera lens, then making minute adjustments to his tripod.

"Here, you from the *Herald*. Suppose you stand behind the bowl like this." Gardner waved the Boston reporter to a spot between the two solemn black servants. "And let's have the little fellow up front here." He tugged Al Matthews into place. "There. Now everyone stay put."

The *Herald* reporter raised his glass. "I propose a toast. To a swift and victorious conclusion to this noble struggle! And a swift, telegraphic route for all our dispatches!"

"Hear! Hear!" Glasses clinked. Gardner pressed his camera shutter, admonishing his subjects to hold still. Al came up to David and Ed Forbes. "An A-number-1 device, the camera. You ever worry the photographers will take the livelihood away from you artists?" As if he didn't have worries enough. "Not unless they can come up with a way to capture their subjects in motion," David said.

Ed grinned. "By that time I'll be earning my living from the sale of my paintings, which will hang in none but the finest galleries." He winked broadly and headed toward the punch bowl.

The posing correspondents broke into groups of twos and threes, returning to their usual pursuits of drinking, smoking, cards and gossip, reminding David once again of Pfaff's and the evenings spent there with Zach. He rose. "Colin Kelley and Pete Moran are stuck on guard duty," he told Al. "I guess I'll ride on out there, take them a drop of punch."

"Mind if I tag along? I'd like to get a look at the picket line."

David smiled. "Not if you give me a hand getting saddled."

They rode slowly, following the directions Colin'd given David, letting the horses pick their way in the gathering dusk till they came to the brush lean-to Union pickets had built against a fence. They tied the horses a few yards away.

Pete was stirring the contents of an iron kettle that simmered on a fire a few feet from the shelter. Al sniffed appreciatively. "Mmmn! Rabbit stew! You trap it out here?"

"Didn't have to. Bought it off of Johnny Reb for a week's coffee ration."

"You did what?" David asked.

Pete grinned. "Traded with the Reb pickets. One of them's a damn fine hunter. Sure and we've got ourselves a sight better Christmas dinner than the mess the camp cooks are dishing up."

"Good Lord!" David looked around apprehensively.

"It's nothin' to get rattled about," Colin said, stepping from the shelter. "They're in no more hurry to trade shots than me and my old woman here."

"Oh. Well, here." David pulled the flask of punch from his pocket. "Merry Christmas."

"Thanks. Hey, sit down and warm yourselves. Dinner's just 'bout ready."

"This puts me in mind of home," Al said as they dug into plates of the savory stew. "My oldest brother was always a good hand at bringing home rabbit meat. Ma used to fix it this way, too, with plenty of onions and salt."

David smiled. "Well, it's certainly a lot different from any Christmas I remember." He looked at the three other men sitting on logs pulled close to the fire. The quiet of the surrounding darkness was broken only by animal cries and the noises of the horses, though the Secesh pickets couldn't be far away. Colin handed him the flask. He took a long swallow and passed it to Al.

"It's nothing like Christmas at home. Or at my brother's house up in Boston either. Of course it's a lot different for his family this year too. Mike's an army doctor now; he's at a hospital in Washington City. And my nephew—his oldest son, that is—was captured by the Rebs. He's in a prison in South Carolina."

"Yeah? That's a shame," Pete said. "What's his regiment?"

"Fifty-Fourth Massachusetts."

"Fifty-Fourth! A nigger regiment!" The two Massachusetts soldiers stared at David in surprise. "He's an officer like his pa, huh?"

"An—" Hell, David thought. Of course they'd know the Fifty-Fourth. He doubted there was anyone in the state of Massachusetts who hadn't heard of the first regiment of colored volunteers. Or who didn't know that only whites served as commissioned officers in the colored regiments—doctors and chaplains excepted.

He was damned if he felt like explaining how he happened to have a colored half-brother. Well, Peter'd made sergeant before his capture. "Yeah, he's an officer."

"Then the Rebs'll treat him better than if he was just an enlisted man," Colin said. "Only thing, if he was leading nigger troops like that, they might be harder on him just to make an example—" Colin stopped. A flush spread over his freckles, visible even in the firelight. "Hey, listen. I shoot my mouth off too much. He'll be okay."

There was a long moment of silence. "Now Pete and me," Colin said at last, "we're used to roughing it for Christmas. This here's our third one since we joined up. But next year ain't gonna be like this. We'll be outta the army and back home. And my girl and me, Rosie, that's her name, we've been writin' each other regular and we're kinda thinkin' 'bout tying the knot." He gave an embarrassed grin.

"Anyways, next Christmas her and me'll be together. Course even if we do get hitched by then, I figger we'll have to live with her mother and father till I can put enough by for a place of our own, but...."

David's attention wandered as Colin talked of the Christmas dinner he and Rosie would share with her family. What would he be doing in a year's time? Well, if—God willing—the war was over by then, he'd like as not spend it with his father and Mike's family. He didn't have anyone else to go home to.

Hell, here he was feeling sorry for himself when he could be a lot worse off. Look at Zach. He hadn't seen his family in years. Who was he spending Christmas with? Still, Zach would be all right. He had enough old friends in New York. That Byron Roosa, for instance. They might even have rekindled—

Stop it! David told himself. He forced his thoughts back to the circle of firelight, listening as Colin shared his plans for the future. They mopped their empty plates with fresh cornbread and washed down the dinner with strong, hot coffee, parting with a final exchange of Christmas wishes.

"Reckon marriage is all right for him," Al said, after they'd ridden in silence a few minutes, "but I'm in no hurry to settle down. I aim to make a name for myself first. Though I wouldn't mind having a family after that. How about you?"

"What about me?"

"You're awful close-mouthed about yourself. Do you have any family besides your father and brother?"

"Some cousins. They didn't live too far from these parts, but I've lost track of them since the war started."

"No wife and children though?"

"Oh. No, I'm afraid I'm just an old bachelor."

"Not all that old. How come you never married?" David shrugged, then realized Al couldn't see him in the dark. "I don't know. I guess I just never had the inclination."

"Still, I don't see how you kept from it."

"What do you mean?"

"A good-looking man like you. You must've had to fight off the ladies."

"I—" David paused, startled by the teasing lilt in Al's voice. Hell, he thought, if he was a girl, I'd swear he was flirting with me. What in hell's wrong with me? What in God's name am I imagining? "I'm afraid I've never been much of a lady killer," he said at last.

Chapter 16 - 1864

The door to David's bedchamber creaked open. He turned over sleepily, smiling at the shuffle of Zach's footsteps as he picked his way softly across the floor. An anticipatory ripple of pleasure ran through him. "You're not still mad, Zach? God, I've missed you." He slid to the edge of the bed to make room. A thought surfaced: "Did you turn the lock? We don't want anyone surprising us."

"Beg pardon? I didn't mean to wake you."

David woke. He stared groggily at the blanket-wrapped figure across the dark attic room. "Al? I— I must've been dreaming." He shivered and pulled the covers tighter around his shoulders, marveling sleepily at the modesty that drove Al down two flights of stairs to an icy outhouse rather than use the chamberpot in the room.

Of course he'd been dreaming, confusing Al's footfalls with Zach's. God, what in hell had he said? "I guess I was talking in my sleep," he muttered.

"Reckon." Al's voice was muffled by the blanket he'd pulled over his head after sinking back onto his cot. He couldn't have made sense of what he'd heard, David assured himself. He sighed, wishing he could return to the dream. Forget it, he told himself. Anyhow, if Zach were in anyone's bed, it was likely to be Byron's.

He tried to thrust the thought from his mind. The room was too cold to return to sleep. His feet stuck out of the skimpy blanket; the chill crept through his long underwear. David drew up his knees, flexing his toes in an effort to warm them. He stared at the gray, predawn dimness, wishing it was time to get up. Sketching might keep his mind off—

123

"I'll be glad to see warmer weather," David said aloud. "My fingers are so damn stiff I can scarcely hold my pencil."

"You said it," Al replied. "I'll be darn glad to have done with this waiting for the war to start up again."

David shuddered. "I'm not eager for that. I'd sooner draw the men in camp than fighting." He gazed curiously in the direction of Al's cot. "Have you ever seen anyone die in battle?"

"Sort of. We've had skirmishes in Missouri since the war started; Independence isn't far from the Kansas border. One of our neighbors was hung by some of Quantrill's band last summer—after they raided Lawrence and burned the town. He'd called them a pack of murderers, not soldiers at all. I sent an account of it to the *Republican* and the editor printed it. It was pretty sad. His wife and kids found him in the morning. They were sobbing and carrying on. We had to cut him down, get him buried. I don't reckon on fainting or anything."

"It's not the— Well, I guess there's no sense dwelling on it now," David said. He sighed and shifted position, trying to keep the covers around him.

"Reckon what I'd do if I was in your shoes," Al said suddenly, "is go on home and visit a spell. Bound to be more comfortable than what this is."

"I suppose I could, though I already spent a week there, after New Year's. Dad wanted me to stay through the winter, but Alexandria's pretty grim since it's been occupied. I'd just as soon put up with the cold here in camp.

"Anyhow, there's not really room. My father's putting up two officers in my old bedroom. I had to share a bed with Dad when I was up there."

Al yawned. "Well, bunking down together's one way to keep warm, at any rate. Colin Kelley told me the soldiers do it all the time. Spread their rubber blankets underneath and lie together with double blankets on top, snug as a bug in a rug. I don't suppose—" He broke off abruptly, gave another mighty yawn. "I'm too tired to go on chatting like this. Reckon I'll go back to sleep."

David closed his eyes. God, it would be good to sleep that way. He opened them before Zach's image could tease him again and lay staring toward the ceiling. Al's breathing sounded with soft rhythm across the room. Maybe they should pull their cots together, David thought sleepily, huddle under the covers and share their warmth. He imagined Al's curly head resting against his shoulder, his breath warm against his neck. It wasn't a bad notion. It would be a lot less lonely way to pass the night, at any rate. Not like lying with Zach, but still—

Christ, had he taken leave of his senses? He lay still, willing himself to think of something else, smiling finally at the notion of Colin and Pete bunking together—and as like as not sparring away in their sleep.

January, February and the better part of March of 1864 had gone by, and the army was still in winter quarters. On March 9th, Ulysses S. Grant was appointed by Lincoln to the newly created rank of lieutenant general, and placed in command of the Union armies. A day later, General Grant reviewed the Army of the Potomac and promised to establish his headquarters in the field, near Culpeper Court House, rather than at the War Department in Washington City.

With the exception of an abortive raid aimed at freeing Union prisoners held in Richmond the last week of February, there'd been no military action since the army had gone into winter quarters. Drill took up the better part of the morning, but the rest of the day there was little for the men to do. The sutler's tent, with its stock-in-trade of tobacco, high-priced canned goods and sweets, became a daily meeting spot. Baseball games, wrestling, foot races and sharpshooting were organized to pass the time.

Pete and Colin had scratched out a rough boxing ring in the dirt clearing in front of their cabin, conducting daily sparring practice as preparation for an anticipated regiment-wide boxing match. A dozen or so soldiers lounged around the ring as David and Al strolled up. The two boxing enthusiasts had stripped to the waist, and stood jabbing at each other with quick, bare-handed blows.

"It's time you were giving someone else a chance." Patrick McFarland, the bearded man who bunked in the adjacent cabin stepped into the ring. Colin grinned and obligingly climbed over the clothes line serving as the boundary. He picked up a grimy towel from the stump at the corner and sank down next to David, wiping sweat from his neck and chest.

Patrick grunted as he and Pete traded blows. David watched with fascination, his eyes dropping to his pad just often enough to check his sketch. The rhythmic thud of flesh on flesh, the low cries of the watching men, even the sharp odor of fresh sweat, were oddly exhilarating.

"Hey Pat, don't drop your left arm that way!" Colin's call came a second too late. Pete's fist thudded into Patrick's jaw, knocking him heavily to the dirt. Pat stayed on the ground a few seconds, then shoved himself to his feet. He moved woozily as he walked from the ring, cursing his stupidity in a colorful monotone.

Bert Scanlon, Ezra Hollings and Jack Maroney followed him into the ring as Pete and Colin took turns sparring and yelling pointers. An hour or so went by. The onlookers began to drift away. "Hey, how 'bout you givin' it a try, David?" Colin offered. David started. "Me? I've never done any boxing."

"It's no reason for not trying," Pete put in. "You and Colin're nearly matched for size." He grinned slyly. "Sure and you could impress your chicken here."

Christ. David flushed and fixed his eyes on his pad. Did Pete actually suppose— He ran a hand through his hair, his fingers pausing at the site of his old injury. "I— I'd better not take a chance. I had a bad skull fracture a few years back. I don't want to—"

"Hey, I wasn't gonna hurt you," Colin said. "I know you ain't no boxer. I'll pull my punches. I was just thinkin' you might want to try it, maybe pick up a couple pointers for your pictures."

"Well..." David cast a sidelong glance at Pete's amused expression. "I guess in that case." He laid his jacket and vest on the log, slowly unfastened his shirt. The air chilled his back and shoulders as he stepped into the dirt square.

Colin looked him over. "You ain't badly muscled for a feller who just draws pictures," he said. David smiled, glad of the hours he'd spent in the gymnasium. "Now you hold your hands like this, see," Colin told him. "No, get the left one a little higher. You're right-handed, ain't you? Now get your chin down against your chest. Yeah, that's it."

David shadowboxed a few moments. Colin watched closely, correcting or praising each swing. The unaccustomed movements began to feel a trifle less awkward. "It's time you were tryin' a little sparring now," Colin said after a few more minutes.

Sparring with Colin was a hell of a lot harder than shadowboxing. Colin's fists slid easily past his guard, while his own blows landed uselessly on the redhead's blocking arms. If Colin hadn't kept his word to pull his punches he'd have knocked him out long ago, David thought ruefully. He threw a quick jab at Colin's chest. Colin blocked it effortlessly.

David's knuckles began to sting. He hadn't yet landed a single blow. Hell, surely he'd tried it long enough to call it quits.

Al rose, moved closer to the ring. "You're gettin' the hang of it, David!" he yelled. "Reckon all you need to do now is hit him before he can hit you."

Pete guffawed. "Like I said. Sure and you ain't gotta do much to impress your chicken here." David winced. He turned to confront Pete. Colin's fist sailed by his ear. Christ, he'd better keep his mind on what he was doing. He whirled back to face Colin, his left leg straightening to take his weight. His right arm shot out and smashed into Colin's face.

Colin's lip split. A bright trickle of blood started down his chin.

126

David stared at him, stunned. "Oh my God! I—Are you all right?"

"Yeah, sure." Colin managed a grin. He stepped over the rope and held the towel to the cut. "Hey, you did real good for the first time. If you was to keep at it, you might turn into a pretty fine prizefighter."

"You do catch on pretty quick," Al echoed him.

"Well, thanks." David smiled, suddenly feeling ridiculously pleased with himself. Pete turned on Al. "Well, now. It's your turn, sonny."

Al laughed and shook his head. "'Fraid not. One of you fellers would make two of me."

"You can take a turn with Sean here. He ain't got his growth yet, it's just goin' on sixteen he is. Sure and the two of you'd be a pretty even match."

Sean got to his feet eagerly, with a shy smile. Al shook his head again. "Reckon not. I don't much feel like it."

I wonder why not, David thought. He's usually so damn eager for a little excitement. Hell, he's been bitching all month about Meade's refusing to let him go along on that raid Kilpatrick tried on Richmond. He'd probably be pretty good at it, too. He can move fast. Look at the way he swings onto a horse. He looked at Al's stubbornly set face, his body swallowed up in his oversized coat.

What would he look like without all those clothes? David wondered. He imagined Al stripping down, exposing his lithe, strong, boy's body—

"What the hell you scared of, sonny boy?" Pete demanded.

"I ain't scared. I told you, I just don't want to." Al looked down, scuffled his feet in the dirt, his face reddening.

Hell, no reason he should be forced into it. David tapped Pete's shoulder, waited till he had his attention. "Forget Al. When are you all going to have the boxing match?" he asked him.

"Day after tomorrow if the weather holds. I'd sooner wait a couple weeks, have a bit more time for practice. Don't want our boys lookin' bad in front of the whole regiment. But we're after leaving for home on Monday."

David halted with one arm half in his shirt sleeve. "How come? I thought your enlistment wasn't up till May."

"It ain't," Pete said. "We're gettin' a month's furlough, account of it's another three-year hitch we've gone and signed up for."

"You have? But I thought— How come?"

"Cause we're a bunch of damn fools," Pete said shortly. He searched in his pocket for his pipe, busied himself lighting it.

"Hey, it makes sense!" Colin exclaimed. He pressed a new part of the towel to his lip, examined it to see if the bleeding had stopped, then wadded the dirty cloth in his hand. "It makes sense," he repeated. "First off, we get to go home right now, 'stead of waitin' for May. And have the whole month free of cares, so to speak. And then we get four hundred dollars in bounty money, plus what the state adds to that.

"Way I'm thinkin', it would take a hell of a long time to save up that much from wages. It's likely Rosie and me would be living with her family for years till we could afford a place of our own. But with this bounty we can get hitched while I'm home and buy a little cottage right off. And then she can save up a lot of my army pay, she's right fine at saving. Time the war's over, we'll be sittin' pretty."

"But still. To go into battle again. Even for hundreds of dollars—"

"Well Christ's sake, David, it's not just for the money. You seen the kinda recruits we've been gettin' lately: bunch of cowards and bounty jumpers. So we've been talkin' it over and made up our minds to see this thing through." Colin grinned, a faint flush of embarrassment spreading across his freckles. "'tis thinkin' we are that Uncle Sam's gonna need some good men stayin' in if we're ever to win this war."

Chapter 17 - 1864

The boxcar jolted along tracks that had been laid and torn up in successive advances and retreats; the rough road buffeted the riders. David sat crowded on the floor with the other passengers, soldiers on furlough for the most part. He shoved a hand into his pocket, fingered the telegraphed message from Mike that his father was suffering from chest pains, asking for him.

Mike had sent the telegram the previous afternoon, but the grinning young fugitive the telegraph operator had entrusted the message to hadn't found David till nearly noon. He'd caught the next train leaving Brandy Station. The sixty mile trip had taken the better part of the day. David listened uneasily as the soldiers debated whether the delays were due to operations of Confederate guerrillas. It was nighttime when the cars pulled up to the military railroad station at Duke and Fayette streets.

Alexandria was occupied by colored troops; the citizens left in town hurried by them with angry, averted eyes. David took little notice, covering the few blocks home at a near run. Mike was coming down the stairs as he yanked open the front door.

"Is Dad— He's not—" David gasped.

"No, he's much better, thank the Lord. Probably just a case of heartburn. Sorry I alarmed you for nothing. It's just, at his age—" Mike turned up his hands. "He's still awake. Go on up and see him."

"David?" His father stood on the second floor landing tying the cord on his dressing gown. "I thought I heard your voice. It's good to see you, son." He put his hand on the bannister, took a step forward.

A Different Sin

"Wait, Dad, I'll come up." David ran upstairs, Mike behind him. He reached his father and embraced him.

"I'm sorry to have brought you all the way home for a false alarm."

"Well I'm glad it was! How are you feeling?"

"A lot better than yesterday." Dr. Carter gave a rueful smile. "Michael tells me this is most likely due to indulging myself too freely on Phoebe's onion pie." David smiled his relief. His father doted on the housekeeper's savory pie. "I'm glad it's nothing worse than that."

"Just a molehill blown up into a mountain. I have a sound constitution."

"You still need your rest, sir," Mike said. He put an arm around his father's shoulders. "It's late, Pa. C'mon to bed. You'll have plenty of time to visit with David. You can stay on a few days, can't you?" he asked David.

"What? Oh, yeah, sure. I'll stay a while, Dad. Mike's right." Funny, David mused. I never heard Mike call him Pa before. At least he's never brought himself to call him anything but sir or Dr. Carter that I can remember. Well, Dad looks pleased enough about it.

He followed Mike and his father down the short hallway toward his father's bedroom. The bedroom door across the hall was suddenly pulled open. The Union captain David had met when he visited in January stepped into the hall. A second, unfamiliar Federal officer followed him. "Beg pardon, sir," he said. "We don't mean to intrude."

"Not at all." Dr. Carter beamed. "David, you've met Captain Schaefer. This is Lieutenant Todd. This is my older boy, Lieutenant. He rushed home to be with me when he heard I was under the weather."

"Sir." The lieutenant nodded shortly. "Delighted to see you back on your feet, Doctor. If you'll excuse us, gentlemen, we're on our way out."

The two officers hurried off. A fragment of whispered conversation rose up from the stairwell. "...must be in his dotage. Introducing his son in the same breath with his nigger bastard."

David stared down at the floor, sensed Mike stiffen beside him. If his father heard, he gave no sign. A moment passed; they moved silently to the bedroom.

"Have you had supper?" Mike asked David when they'd seen their father comfortably settled for the night. He hadn't. David foraged through the kitchen, found the fixings of a sandwich while Mike heated coffee and poured it into two thick mugs. They settled themselves at the old pine trestle table.

"Have you any word when Meade'll start advancing on Lee?" Mike asked.

130

"I'm afraid not," David said. "Though it's bound to be pretty soon. The officers' wives are starting to leave for home. And there's a lot of restlessness among the soldiers. The men are pleased Grant's made his headquarters in the field, but nobody knows quite what to make of him."

"Let's pray he can win the war for us."

"I was talking with Alf Waud from *Harper's* the other day. He's pretty knowledgeable, says Grant's a man who means business. At any rate, there's been a lot more drilling going on since he's taken charge."

"At least if there *was* an exchange of prisoners. The Charleston jail's right in the path of fire from our own batteries." Mike twisted his fingers together. "Well, it won't do Peter any good to dwell on it." A moment went by. Mike brightened. "Did you get the news yet in camp? The Senate passed the Constitutional amendment to abolish slavery, thank the Lord! Thirty-eight to six."

"Yeah, I saw it. It still needs to get through the House and the state legislatures though."

"They'll pass it. I'm sure they will." Mike drank a swallow of coffee. "I wish Mama could've lived to see the end of slavery. She used to tell me it was too late for her to hope for freedom in this life, but she prayed I'd be set free one day. I've always regretted she never knew I made it to the North."

David pictured Hetty moving around the room, stirring a pot of stew, stamping out biscuits with quick motions of her dark hands, scolding Mike and him for tracking in mud, then handing them each a biscuit hot from the oven. Sending Mike off to the corner pump for water, while he'd reluctantly started his lessons. He'd never have guessed she gave a thought to freedom. "You'd likely never have run off and left her if she'd been alive."

"No, maybe not," Mike said slowly. "I reckon you're right."

David looked around. Except for the cast iron sink, installed after the construction of the town water system, the kitchen looked as he remembered it from childhood. Pine boards worn with scrubbing, crockery and pewter tableware on the open shelves, wood canisters of flour and sugar. He smiled. "You know, sitting here like this makes me feel like a boy again."

"It's taken some getting used to, coming back to this house. I used to sleep in that storeroom." Mike waved at the small lean-to off the kitchen.

"But before that, when we were kids, you slept in my room. You'd lay your mattress out on the floor and we'd lie in the dark and talk. How did you come to move into that room anyway? It's hardly more than a shed."

"Lord, I don't know." Mike wrinkled his forehead in thought. "Probably so I could sneak in books without you telling on me. And you used to be so all-fired bossy." Mike smiled. "I remember now. You woke me up three times one night to hand you the chamberpot. Said I was supposed to do it because I was your slave. So I picked up my bedding and marched on down here."

"I did? God, I'd forgotten that. Well, I don't know how you put up with me."

Mike laughed. "I don't recollect that I did very often."

"No, I suppose not. I'm afraid I wasn't much of a brother though."

"You weren't so bad. All children are ugly to one another at times. If you had any, you'd know that. Anyhow, we were hardly brought up as brothers."

"Well, how could we have been? Hell, we didn't even know it."

"Oh c'mon, David. It was all over town. Boys were throwing it up to me far back as I can remember."

"I don't remember anyone—"

"I reckon I didn't want to admit it either. But Mama told me the truth herself, before she passed on. Well, no sense dwelling on it now. We oughta get some sleep. I've got to get back to the hospital first thing tomorrow. I'm glad you were able to come up and stay with— Pa for a bit. Lord. I'm just about too tired to move." Mike yawned, rested his head on his arms. He wore his shirt without its removable collar, the top button unfastened. A scar stretched across the back of his neck as he bent forward.

David stared at it; a memory nudged him. Christ, of course. The whipping the town magistrate had ordered after Mike and his friends had been caught breaking curfew, breaking the ban on blacks gathering in groups, worse yet, being caught with that damn geography book. Right after Nat Turner's uprising it had been. The whole state had been on edge, fearful of new slave revolts.

Dad wouldn't plead for Mike. Said he'd known better, would have to take his punishment. Though you could see how much it hurt him to see Mike cut like that. Mike wouldn't speak to Dad after. He sat at the table while Dad tended his wounds, as rigid as a trapped animal, his fists clenched in fury. At Dad, most of all.

Hell, you couldn't blame him. It must've hurt like hell. Mike didn't talk about it, but he screamed in his sleep for weeks afterward. He remembered Mike's shrieks catapulting him from sleep—high, piercing, pain-filled. You'd think Dad would hear— David ran downstairs, squatted beside Mike's pallet, shook him. "Mike, hey Mike, wake up!" The shrieks stopped. Mike moaned. "Wake up, Mike," David said once more. "You dreaming about being whipped again?"

"David?"

"You were screaming in your sleep again."

"Oh Lord, they had me tied to that post and kept cuttin' and cuttin'— Felt like it would cut right through me!" Mike sat up, clasped his knees with his hands. "Lord! Thanks for waking me."

"Yeah, sure." David sat next to him on the pallet. He put a hand on his shoulder, feeling ridges of scar tissue on the bare skin. He shuddered. "They never should've done that to you. Just for reading a book!"

"Can't let us learn nothin'. We might get to thinkin' we human bein's like them." Mike's voice quickened with the anger that had possessed him since the whipping. "Jesus, I hate bein' a slave!"

Christ. What could he say to him? They sat in silence a few minutes. "Maybe Dad'll give you your freedom when you're older," David said finally.

"He'll never give me nothin'. Wasn't nothin' to him to see me whipped. I hate him! He's my own father and he don't care no more 'bout it than if I was some mule he own!"

David started. "Dad is? Your father?!" It couldn't be!

"Mama told me 'fore she died. And he admitted it himself. But it don't mean nothin' to him." Mike's voice held nothing but quiet, bitter certainty.

Hell, if his precious mama had told him. And Dad had owned up to it, he said. Dad and Hetty— Christ. How could Dad bring himself to it? It didn't seem possible.

But look at Mike. As dark as Hetty had been, it stood to reason he'd been fathered by a white man. He'd known that. Bits of ignored gossip, overheard snickers began to surface in his mind. That explained Uncle James as well: how he couldn't stand Mike, why he'd overheard him yelling at Dad once, "It killed my sister when Hetty had him."

He supposed Mike was waiting for him to say something. "Yeah, I should've realized. I should've realized before this," David said at last. "You're right about Dad. He ought to treat you differently."

"Well." Mike sat up, running his fingers through his graying sideburns. "I'm pretty sure there's a cot in there somewhere. We can carry it up and—" David tried to bring his thoughts back to the present. "You used to be so angry at him and now— What?"

"At Dad. I mean—"

"Good Lord, David, that was years ago."

"I know. I was just thinking back. I wouldn't have imagined you'd ever come to terms with him."

"Why wouldn't I? The man's my father, same as he is yours."

"Well, I know that. I just meant—"

"I'm not sure I know what you're getting at," Mike said. "But I suppose even before I ran off, when there was so much hard feeling between us, I always hoped one day he'd—" He shrugged. "Be a father to me I guess. Acknowledge me as his son. I'm not saying matters have always been easy between us since he found me, but he's tried so damned hard. I'm surprised you can't see how much he's changed."

"Well, sure. Sure I can see." Hell, why shouldn't he have? David thought. I've always been pretty much of a disappointment to Dad. No wonder he couldn't get over how much Mike had made of himself. How he'd put himself through medical school, become respected as a doctor. You can't help but admire Mike for managing it. No wonder Dad was willing to admit Mike was his son, accept his kids as his grandchildren.

"Hell, you've both changed," he said.

"And that's how come your nephew was in a colored regiment." Al's face, brushed by shadows from the trees bordering the porch where they sat, was alive with interest. "Yeah, I'm afraid so," David said. He stretched out his legs, still cramped from the train ride back, wondering why he'd blurted out so much about Dad and Mike, when all Al'd asked him was how his father was doing.

At least Al didn't seem shocked or disgusted. David watched as Al peered into the tin mirror he'd propped on the porch rail and positioned the sewing shears with which he was cutting his hair. Al pulled on a curl and scissored it, grinned at David. "Sounds like your family's a sight more interesting than mine."

David smiled. "I don't know about that. A big family like you all had. It must've been fun for a kid."

"I reckon it was. It wasn't easy being the baby though. Seemed like I spent half my life trying to catch up with my big brothers, and just when I'd learn—oh, I don't know—how to shinny up a tree or saddle a horse, they'd've moved on to something new. And there I'd be tagging behind them all over again."

David laughed. "How many brothers do you have again?"

"Six. And Julie. She was the only other— She's my big sister. She and Ma were always trying to keep me from running wild like a savage Indian. That's how Ma always put it. I'm glad enough of it now though. At least she kept me at my schoolbooks so's I learned to write tolerable enough for the newspapers.

"Pa always had a hankering to move further West, though he did pretty well where we was, selling saddlery and gear. Independence is pretty much of a jumping-off point for wagon trains. The Santa Fe and Oregon trails start out there. Nearly every night Pa told us stories held heard 'bout gold out in California or land in Oregon. But Ma wouldn't budge. Most of my brothers headed West soon as they could though, all but Jimmy—he enlisted two years ago."

"I'm surprised you didn't head West yourself," David said. He picked up one of the brown curls from the porch floor, twisted it idly around his finger. It sprang back as he loosed it. Al must have taken advantage of the warm weather to wash his hair while he'd been gone, David thought, watching the sun glint off his curls. He opened his hand and let the strand slide softly to the floor.

"It never appealed to me that much. Anyhow, after Pa died, I was the only one to home besides Julie, so it wouldn't have been right to leave Ma. Everyone but me was pretty well grown by then. There's five years between Jimmy and me. We had two more brothers between us, but they died in the bad cholera epidemic back in '49.

"Reckon I'd still be home if Ma hadn't passed on. I stayed on with Julie and her husband a few months. Pa left his saddlery to them. I gave them a bit of a hand, wrote some for the paper. But it didn't satisfy me staying in Independence when the big story's here. I reckon this campaign's gonna make the difference in whether we beat the Rebs or not."

The farmhouse door opened and banged shut. Footsteps creaked the porch boards. Ed Forbes, in company with three or four other newsmen, strolled up to David and Al. "You fellows want to ride into Culpeper with us?" Ed asked. "Might be the last chance before we move on out." He gave them a wink. "Thought we'd see if the prospect of us leaving won't soften the heart of the fair rebels, win us a little lovemaking."

The others laughed. "I know a few whose hearts'll be softened quick enough by the prospect of a few greenbacks," said a short, dark Boston reporter.

There was another round of laughter. "How about it?"

"I—" David looked down. No reason he shouldn't, he told himself. Hell, it might do him good. He'd woken more than once tense with urgency for—For Zach. Memories of their lovemaking flooded through him. How could he lie with someone else after the kind of closeness they'd shared? "I guess not," he said. He looked up. Al was shaking his head.

"Reckon I'll stay and finish trimming my head, now I've started."

"You,ought to get one of the contrabands to do that," Ed said. "There's some of them are pretty good barbers and they'll give you a haircut for next to nothing."

Al shrugged. "Next to nothing's what I've got till I can send some dispatches to my editor. I'm just a stringer, remember. I haven't been paid for sitting in camp all winter like the rest of you fellows."

"Well, suit yourself." The reporters ambled off, joking and laughing, leaving David and Al in sudden, awkward silence.

"I reckon I'm not making too bad a job of being my own barber," Al said after a moment. "Only hard part's right here in back." The sun caught the rich highlights of his curls as he patted them briefly.

"I guess I could cut that part for you. It doesn't look that hard," David said. He touched a curl tentatively, let his hand linger on Al's head, ran his fingers through the soft, thick ringlets. Al turned, a little surprised, then smiled at David.

David drew his hand back a little, his fingertips still caressing the curls. I could lie with Al, he thought suddenly. Hold him the same as— Christ! David dropped his hand as if Al's hair had turned to fire, backed abruptly away. Oh Christ, not—

"Say, would you? I'd appreciate it." Al held out the shears with another smile, his voice fresh and innocent.

"Yeah, yeah sure." David reached for the scissors, managed to take them without brushing Al's hand. He gripped them hard a moment, steadied himself. Hell, it had just been a stray thought. Nothing was going to come of it. He wasn't perverted like— It was just with Zach that— He set to work snipping Al's ringlets, forcing his thoughts to remain focused on his task.

Sunlight flashed from the bayonets of marching Federal troops, glinted off the ripples and eddies of the Rapidan River and whitewashed the covers of the long train of baggage wagons. From the bluff overlooking the river, where Grant and his staff had halted, the columns of Union soldiers below stretched endlessly on both sides of the pontoon bridges. Newspaper correspondents clustered around the general and his officers with rapid-fire questions.

"General Grant, about how long will it take you to get to Richmond?" a reporter called.

"I will agree to be there in about four days—that is, if General Lee becomes a party to the agreement; if he objects, the trip will undoubtedly be prolonged."

David smiled. He scribbled a few words of description on his pad and gazed down at the scene he'd just sketched. Gusts of soft spring breezes carried the sounds of men and animals moving steadily across the twin pontoon bridges erected overnight by the 50th New York Engineers—stealing a march on Lee as they gained the southern bank of the Rapidan. A parallel column, led by General Hancock, was making the crossing at Ely's Ford, six miles below. Even through field glasses, the columns wound out of sight—an army of close to a hundred thousand men, supported by over four thousand baggage wagons. At the rear of the train, far out of sight, lumbered droves of beef cattle to be butchered as needed.

"Looks pretty formidable, doesn't it?" Al said, dropping down beside David at the edge of the porch fronting the deserted house commandeered as temporary headquarters.

David put down his field glasses. "I was just thinking the same thing," he said. "We certainly outnumber Lee, at any rate. Though he's on home ground. Here, you want to look through these?" He handed Al the glasses. Their fingers brushed. For a moment David felt the discomfiture that had plagued him around Al since that afternoon on the porch two weeks before.

But hell. The army was on the move. It couldn't be more than a matter of days till they engaged Lee's troops in battle. There were a hell of a lot more important things to concern himself with.

He got up, walked back and forth restlessly. Grant and his staff were heading into the old house for their noon meal. The reporters wandered to the edge of the bluff. The colored servant who traveled with the baggage wagon that served as field headquarters of the New York *Herald* passed plates and tankards to *Herald* reporters; other correspondents lunched catch-as-catch-can. David shared canned sardines and crackers with Al. The headquarters wagon arrived and orderlies began pitching tents for Grant and his staff.

David rose. "If Grant means to wait till Burnside gets here from Alexandria, I doubt there'll be much change the next few hours. I think I'll ride out a little ways, see how the crossing went at Ely's Ford, maybe see if I can find Colin and Pete's company."

Al rose, uninvited, to join him. They made their way with difficulty down Germanna Road, through the noisy stream of infantry and wagons, then bore east on the Orange Turnpike. Woods bordered the dirt road, pine and scrub oak, wildflowers blooming in the underbrush. Dust swirled under their horses' hooves, the afternoon sun sifting through the trees started rivulets of sweat down their backs. An occasional birdcall could be heard.

Hancock's corps were camping for the night in a sprawling line along the turnpike, not far from the field where the battle of Chancellorsville had been fought a year before. The sentry who inspected their passes gave them further directions.

They tied their mounts and made their way on foot to the clearing where the 19th Massachusetts was camped, walked through it till they found Colin and Pete seated around a fire with half a dozen other men from their company.

"Hey, look who's here," Colin hailed them. "Sit down and have some of these here beans and pork. They're pretty good." He grinned shyly. "Not like my Rosie cooked when we was home on furlough, but they ain't bad."

Al dug into the beans. "So you and Rosie got hitched while you were gone?" he asked, swallowing a mouthful. Colin gave another shy smile. "That we did. We'll be married three weeks come tomorrow."

"Come tomorrow, we'll be lucky to get out of these woods with our hides intact," Pete said abruptly. "This here's a damn fool place to stop. We coulda pressed on a helluva lot further. This ain't no place for a fight."

"How do you mean?" David asked.

"Use your head, David! You can't see worth shit in all this underbrush, and sure the Rebs know this ground a helluva lot better than we do. They'll be taking us by surprise, same as they did last year."

"But surely Grant—"

"Goddamn generals!" Pete spat. "Lot they care 'bout the enlisted man! Sure and it's right out here, what we're coming to. You're looking for something to fill up that pad of yours, I'll show you it." Pete rose and walked off. David followed, the others trailing along.

A few minutes walk took them to a field near the road where the artillery caissons were massed. Occasional broken limbed trees, scarred by bullets and shellfire, stood like wounded sentinels. Small groups of infantry and artillerymen clustered uneasily, talking in low tones and poking at the ground as they walked. "Sure and 'tis what we're heading for," Pete repeated with grim relish.

"Christ!" David breathed. Dozens of grinning white skulls lay scattered about the ground like abandoned marbles.

"Chancellorsville," Pete said. He jabbed his bayonet at a mound of earth where a long white armbone lay partly exposed. Grains of reddish dirt fell away, revealing the tattered cloth that still clung to the fleshless bone. Pete peered at it. "Goddamn uniform's too faded to tell if the poor bastard was Union or Reb."

David swallowed. The battlefield had become a graveyard of men buried where they'd fallen, in haste, so the earth now barely covered them. He drew a step closer to Al, felt him shudder involuntarily beside him, gazed at the solemn faces of the others. Pete grinned at them fiercely. "You lads scared of a few old bones?"

"I ain't scared." Sean's voice cracked. He grabbed up a skull and stared into the sightless eye sockets, quickly turned it over. Teeth rained onto his hand. "Holy Jesus!" Sean sprang back, the skull bouncing on the ground as he flung it from him.

Pete laughed. "It's what we're coming to, sonny boy, and some of us tomorrow."

"Christ, Pete, leave the boy alone," Patrick McFarland growled. "Is it tryin' to scare him to death you're after? And that before his first fight?" He turned his bearded visage to Sean. "Sure and you'll be fine."

"Hey, yeah," Colin seconded him. "Listen, Sean, we come through some pretty hard fights without a scratch. Just do like we do tomorrow. Now it's sleep we oughta be gettin' while we got the chance." Sean started back, followed by Patrick and most of the other men.

"The hell of it though," Colin said, still gazing at the unmarked graves, his voice barely audible, "is all these fellers laid down their lives for nothin'. Just so's Hooker could call a retreat, just turn tail and run right back across the river." Pete cuffed him lightly on the arm. "You said it." They stood in silence a moment.

"C'mon, old woman, it's gettin' dark," Colin said finally. He clapped his hand on Pete's shoulder. "Let's get on back. I wanna finish writin' Rosie tonight."

"Pretty sobering sight, ain't it," Al said to David after they'd hurried back to their horses and ridden a few miles in silence.

"I'm afraid you're right." David peered into the wilderness that pressed the roadway on both sides. The skeletons of fallen soldiers seemed to lie under every tree, gleaming white in campfires and moonlight. He drew even with Al, glad of his company on the lonely turnpike, riding close beside him as they hastened back to Union headquarters at Germanna Ford.

Chapter 18 - 1864

THE RUMBLE OF WAGON TRAINS AND INFANTRY crossing the wooden pontoons finally lulled David to sleep that night. He opened his eyes to see Al already rolling up his blankets beside him. The night had been warm enough that they hadn't bothered with their shelter tent; the cloudless sky promised another day of sunshine. The air was ripe with the smells of horses and crushed grasses. David watched the reflection of sunrise on the river below as the campground stirred to life. The half-buried skeletons seemed a fading nightmare in the light of day, a day more suited to a picnic or ball game than armed confrontation. The aroma of strong coffee drifted across the encampment.

By dawn, most of the army occupied positions on the southern side of the Rapidan. Grant lingered at table in the headquarters mess tent while General Meade moved south along the Germanna road. Not till the lead divisions of Burnside's troops were seen crossing the river did Grant rise. Followed by reporters, Grant and his staff trotted down the Germanna road.

They'd traveled perhaps a mile when a Union officer galloped up with Meade's message: Rebel troops were advancing down the Orange turnpike; Union divisions commanded by Warren and Sedgwick had been ordered into position to meet them. A battle would be fought that day. David swallowed, his hands sweaty on the reins.

A four mile gallop up the packed-earth road brought them to the crossroads of Germanna road and the turnpike, where he and Al had ridden the day before. General Meade awaited Grant near a tumbledown tavern, its yard gone to brush. The two generals climbed to the top of a cleared knoll, conferring in tones too low to be overheard. Reporters hovered in edgy clumps as Grant dispatched orders to his generals to move against the enemy.

The chief of the New York *Herald* correspondents, Sylvanus Cadwallader, handed out assignments to *Herald* reporters with the crisp efficiency of a commanding officer. Correspondents scattered like shot, heading in the direction of the musketry and artillery fire now exploding in the distance. David raised his field glasses, straining to see past the tangled growth of wilderness that lay beyond the low hill.

"You can't get any kind of view from here," Al said beside him. "Reckon I'll head on down, see what's going on." He paused, glancing expectantly at David.

David gripped the glasses. "I— I guess I'll stay here at headquarters a bit." He watched Al hurry excitedly away. I ought to go with him, he thought, get closer to the front. New bursts of shelling sounded as the sun rose higher overhead. Clouds of dark smoke hung over the tops of trees.

Hell, he told himself, this was headquarters for the Army of the Potomac. There'd be plenty going on here.

Grant had settled himself on the ground, back resting against a tree trunk, his shoulders stooped over a stick of wood that he whittled as couriers raced in from the front. David flipped open his pad, his fingers already outlining the first broad strokes of the general's figure. Grant whittled imperturbably, incongruous on the ground in the formal dress uniform he rarely bothered putting on. Despite the warm weather, he wore tan cloth gloves, leaving them on as he cut away at the twig.

He's got the weight of the whole army on his shoulders, David mused. He studied Grant's face, recalling Pete's fear of a battle in these woods, his avowal that the generals didn't give a damn for the enlisted men. If Grant was disturbed at not getting the army through the wilderness before meeting Lee in battle, he gave no sign.

David penciled in the details of Grant's hat and beard, the thin lips clamped on a cigar. Grant continued to whittle, the gloves he'd forgotten to remove snagging and shredding as they caught on the rough pine sticks he shaved away.

He turned to a clean page, listening as couriers brought news of the conflict: Warren's Fifth Corps faced troops led by the Confederate general Ewell across one of the few open fields adjacent to the turnpike; divisions of Hancock's Second Corps had been ordered to throw up breastworks at the crossing of Plank and Brock roads, where fighting had raged since morning. David finished a sketch of Grant handing a scrawled message to a waiting courier, moved to another angle. But hell, he was wasting his time here. He knew Leslie well enough to know his editor would expect him to forward battle scenes, not portraits of Grant. Ed Forbes, for all his talk of covering battles in safety through his field glasses, had long since headed toward the lines of skirmish. At any rate, you couldn't see a damn thing that was going on through field glasses today.

Reluctantly he started down the knoll. Musketry sounded in staccato rolls, mingling with a frenzied undercurrent of shouts and cries. Zach's warning over a year ago sounded in David's mind: in order to sketch the conflict he'd have to come under fire as much as if he were a soldier himself. He swallowed, slowing to a standstill.

But he'd asked Leslie to send him here; he could carry out his assignment as well as his fellow correspondents. He'd just stay to the rear of the action. Ed had told him he'd ride east in the direction of Hancock's corps. David mounted, made his way to the turnpike and turned west. A dense scrub growth of pines, oak and chinquapin closed in on the narrow road. Half a mile down the road, in the fields of the plantation house commandeered for Warren's Fifth Corps headquarters, caissons lay parked, the artillerymen unable to bring them into play in the overgrown wilderness. The din of musketry and hoarse cries rose as he rode.

Union breastworks of logs and earth had been thrown up a half mile farther down, where a second cleared field opened out on either side of the turnpike. A line of Federal troops stretched out behind them across the perimeter of the clearing. David tied his mount well behind the Union line, edged cautiously forward.

Between the Union and Rebel lines lay a quarter mile of open field, dusty earth divided by rows of trampled corn stubble. A gully ran the length of the field. A low, tense murmur ran through the troops as the buglers raised their instruments to sound the signal for a charge. The first line of troops poured over the breastworks, shouting hurrahs as they raced across the field with fixed bayonets.

Gunfire spattered with fierce intensity. David climbed a stump and raised his glasses. Small clouds of dust boiled up from the field as bullets landed on the dry earth like skipping stones on a river. Men screamed and fell, lay twitching in the gully. David held his breath as the remainder of the infantrymen continued their charge and gained the shelter of the woods. The cries of fierce fighting sounded from across the field. "Let's help them boys!" a Union officer yelled. The second Union line charged. David watched in stunned admiration as men ran past the bodies of wounded and dead soldiers, pressing on through the hail of Rebel bullets. The cries, screams and shrill cheers swelled, then slowly moved farther away. David strained to see through the field glasses, caught an occasional glimpse of a blue uniform, flashes of musket fire. The Union charge was driving the Rebs back from their breastworks, as far as he could make out through the trees and powder smoke.

The dusty cornfield was quiet, except for the moans of the wounded. Here and there, men struggled painfully to their feet, began limping back in search of the field hospital, their faces dazed and anguished.

The skirmish line had moved out of sight, into the wilderness. David felt startled by the sudden fascination drawing him toward the struggling men. He let the now useless glasses dangle on their strap, set out gingerly across the field.

Dust swirled around his feet. Pieces of dry corn stubble blew into his face on the warm breeze. His mouth was dry. A shiver ran down his spine, despite the heat of the sun, as he neared the scores of bodies that littered the field and piled up in the ravine. Wounded men too weak to walk lay waiting for aid, gazing blankly upward from bloodless faces. Here and there men ripped aside blood-soaked uniforms to stare at their torn flesh with numbed horror or grunt with relief at discovering a wound less serious than they'd feared.

A hand clutched at David's leg. "You got water, mister?" The wounded infantryman, a husky blond boy of eighteen or so, spoke in a halting whisper he had to strain to hear.

"Yeah, sure." David pulled his canteen from his belt, knelt and held it to the soldier's mouth. The boy took several deep gulping swallows, then fell back with a low moan, eyes closing, his breath coming in shallow gasps. Blood dampened the front of his uniform in a slowly growing circle. A half dozen greedily buzzing flies landed on the wet cloth, walked stickily over the oozing wound.

David shuddered again, broke into a run as he covered the remaining distance across the field. The Confederate entrenchments, abandoned now, stretched along the edge of the woods. The ground was littered with odd bits of gear, trampled slouch hats, scraps of cartridge paper, a half filled cartridge belt. More bodies lay on the ground. The roar of musketry, frantic shouts, an occasional shrill rebel yell sounded from farther within the woods. David plunged into the underbrush in the direction of the sounds.

Thick brush impeded his way, honeysuckle vines and Virginia creeper tangled around his ankles, sharp blackberry thorns caught his clothes and scratched his skin. He pushed his way through a clump of briers, nearly losing his footing as he skidded down the side of a small ravine, stopped to get his bearings once he climbed the other side. Thickets of interlaced branches of scrub pine, clumps of saplings, tangled vines blocked his view. Thick, acrid smoke hung over every-thing like a morning fog. He couldn't have worked his way more than a few hundred feet into the woods, but he could no longer spot the clearing he'd crossed, was uncertain even of its direction.

He pressed on toward the noise of the battle. The rattle of musketry grew into a deafening roar. Twigs and small branches rained to the ground ahead of him. He edged on a little farther, stumbling suddenly on a half dozen blue-uniformed soldiers. Other infantrymen could be seen dimly, stretched every few yards in a ragged line, standing or kneeling for shelter behind the larger trees. David edged over to the nearest of the soldiers. "Could you tell me how to find the battle?" he asked him.

The man gaped. "Where the hell you think you're at?" He turned back, blazed away with his rifle, then ran in a low crouch to a tree several yards away.

"Christ!" David looked wildly around. The explosion of rifles around him was answered by a volley from a short distance off. Men fired without bothering to aim. David peered at an indistinct line of butternut-clad soldiers, barely visible through the smoke and trees. He raised his glasses for a better view. A bullet thudded into a tree a few feet away. A large branch crashed in front of him. He flung himself to the ground behind a large oak, lay trembling, afraid to raise his head from the ground.

Bullets flew by, smacking into trees or tearing with a dull, sickening splatter into living flesh. My God, he thought, how could he have been so stupid as to blunder into this? A cry of agony sounded a few feet away. David peered over. The man who'd spoken to him was clutching his hands to his groin, blood spurting between his fingers and sinking into the dry ground.

An eternity seemed to pass by. Fierce shouts sounded on either side of David. He raised his head an inch. Unbelievably, men were moving toward the Rebs, firing swiftly, dodging from tree to tree, closing the gap on a retreating Confederate line. The ground around him was littered with dead and wounded. He rose gingerly to his knees, brushed dirt from his face. He'd been clutching his sketchpad to his chest, gripping it so tightly his fingers had stiffened around it. He flexed his hands, got to his feet, freezing in momentary panic as dry twigs cracked underfoot, terrified of drawing a sharpshooter's bullet.

He took a deep breath, choking on acrid smoke, cast wildly about, desperate to retrace his steps. He stumbled past the man with the shattered groin, now mercifully unconscious, past the body of a redheaded youth, arms outstretched, mouth gaping and blood-filled. An undercurrent of moans sounded under the steady roar of the gunfire that had been sounding so constantly he'd almost ceased to hear it.

A few yards away, a bearded man sat on the ground, cutting a blanket into strips with the edge of his bayonet and wrapping them around his bleeding upper arm. He checked his rough bandaging, grunted in apparent satisfaction, then stood unsteadily, a look of fierce determination on his face as he headed into the underbrush. David stumbled after him.

"Help me outta here, mister! I gotta git to a hospital!" David halted. The infantryman who'd called to him sat on the ground, back against a tree, legs outstretched, eyes burning in a pale, smoke-grimed face. David stared at him, slowly taking in the boy's broken left shinbone, the white bone showing through his bloody pants. Christ, he thought, it's all I can do to get out of here myself. How the hell am I gonna drag him along? He looked down at the soldier again, started to shake his head, took in the panic in the thin face, white from pain and loss of blood beneath the coating of dirt, the downy attempt at a mustache. Hell, he's just a kid, he told himself. What kind of a man would leave him here?

He knelt, put an arm around the boy, managed to heave him from the ground. The boy threw his arm around David's neck, his face drawn with the effort of keeping his damaged leg from touching the ground. His weight, surprisingly more than he'd expected, pulled down on David. David grabbed hold of his wrist, tightened his free arm around the boy's waist, straining his muscles in the effort to support him as he walked. They moved forward with painful slowness. Briers and interwoven tree limbs closed in on them. There was no landmark in any direction.

They inched forward a few minutes, stopped to rest, fought through the thickets, stopped to rest once more. The clamor of gunfire was growing louder, coming closer. David looked back, caught sight of musket flashes in the woods behind them. "Christ, we'd better hurry," he muttered.

They struggled on again. David looked over his shoulder. Blue-clad troops were streaming toward them, crashing through thickets in disorderly retreat from pursuing Confederates. The firing grew in intensity. An occasional bullet swept past them. He saw the young infantryman's quick fearful glance behind them. "You gotta carry me!"

Hell, he should've thought of it. He could manage his weight, probably move a hell of a lot faster. He grabbed the boy up as a bullet tore into a tree a few feet behind them, moved forward at a stumbling run. A second bullet whizzed by his ear, so close David could feel its passage. He gasped, froze with panic. "I— I can't— I— I'm sorry, oh

Christ I'm sorry!" He laid the boy on the ground behind the scanty shelter of a tree, crashed blindly through thickets, tripping over vines and roots, stumbling to his feet and running till the whistling of bullets died out behind him.

He stopped, gasping for breath. His hands were ripped by scratches from thorns he hadn't felt. He leaned weakly against an oak, too limp with relief to move. His field glasses still dangled from their strap around his neck. He raised them, looked back. The haze of smoke was too thick to make out the line of skirmish he'd fled from, but the flashes of muskets made pulsating sparks in the smoky fog.

Sparks flared and grew as he watched, joined together into candles of reddish flames. Christ! he thought. Fire! These damn dry woods— They'll go up like kindling. Just like Chancellorsville last year. Oh my God, oh Christ, I left that kid to that!

He fell forward, smoke-blackened vomit spewing from his mouth, racked by waves of shame. Long moments went by. Finally he rinsed his mouth with water from his canteen, got shakily to his feet. He couldn't go back. He'd best find his way out of this wilderness before he was trapped as well.

The regiments he'd followed had been somewhere near the right flank of the Union lines. If he headed north— Hell, no telling which way it was. He stumbled on again, away from the fires. The ground grew marshy and sucked at his feet. His body ached with exhaustion. Rivulets of sooty sweat ran down his face and plastered his clothes to his body.

He stumbled up the side of a ravine onto dry ground, sucked in his breath as he heard the sudden ringing of axes. He worked his way slowly forward, weak with relief as he emerged to a line of Union soldiers frantically throwing up breastworks. Men surrounded him, asking what the hell he was doing there, demanded to know the number of Reb troops they faced before he'd half finished explaining.

David shook his head in helpless ignorance.

Men spat in disgust.

"Shit, no one can see in this Godforsaken place. Can't hardly tell what regiment you're fightin' with," a grizzled sergeant told him. "Onliest way we know where they're at is hearin' them work on their fort'ications same as us. You listen good. They're throwin' up breast-works, right the other side of this here low area."

"Christ!" David listened, heard the sound of Reb axes on the opposite bank of the ravine, an occasional burst of gunfire from invisible gray lines. God, he was damn lucky not to have blundered the other way, walked right into the Reb lines and ended up in Libby Prison the rest of the war. Or worse yet, been trapped between the lines. He shuddered. "How do I get out of here?"

The sergeant snorted. "You expectin' a road map?" He fished a compass from his pocket, held it close to his face. "Danged if I know if this thing's still workin', but that way should bring you somewheres close to the turnpike."

Swelling volleys of musketry, the fierce opening cries of a charge gave new strength to David's legs as he fought his way through the wilderness, taking care to stay well behind what he could see of the Union lines. He crossed one of the narrow mining roads that wound through the region, kept on through a section of woods where the debris of earlier skirmishing lay strewn. He pushed through a patch of thorn bushes and stared down at a worn-leather boot that lay discarded in his path.

You'd think someone would miss that in all these briers. He stooped, picked it up. "Oh my God!" The jagged remains of a white ankle bone protruded from the boot; drops of partially congealed blood oozed onto David's wrist as he stood, horror-struck. He could feel its stickiness on his skin long after he'd let the boot slip from his grasp, even after he'd rubbed his hand on his pants over and over as he ran away.

He skirted more corpses, stopped twice to offer the last trickles from his canteen to weakly pleading wounded men. The marshy area was well behind him now. Dry pine needles lay thickly underfoot. The cloud of smoke seemed thicker than ever, clotting in his throat as he breathed. The acrid smell intensified. He could see flames shoot up through the haze.

The moans of wounded men changed to sudden, agonized screams. A new, sickly sweet smell spread through the thickets. David breathed in, gagged in sudden horrified recognition of the odor of burning flesh. Flames ran toward him, leaping from bush to bush, then turned and raced in the other direction with a change in the wind, like wily children playing tag.

Men screamed shrilly for help. Some fifty feet from David, a bearded man huddled under a tree, crying out. Despite bloody bandages wrapped around both legs, he held tightly to his rifle. David gasped in sudden realization of his intent. He took a tentative step toward him. A gust of wind sent a wall of flame between them that sped toward the wounded man on the twining branches of dead pines. His rifle exploded. Blood and brains spattered from the back of his skull, mixing into a dirty pink stream that trickled slowly down into the flames.

David fled. Ahead of him he saw soldiers hurrying frantically about, supporting injured men able to walk with help, bending to lift the more seriously wounded onto stretchers improvised of blankets and sticks. A wave of relief overwhelmed him at the realization that he'd made his way out of the wilderness, succeeded by a sudden wave of shame. How could he be thinking only of his safety when all around him—

He made his way to the rescuers, took hold of one end of a makeshift stretcher and emerged from the woods at the edge of a blackened clearing. Charred stubble smoldered here and there. Numerous lumps of blackened material lay on the ground and massed together in a narrow gully. He'd helped maneuver the stretcher halfway around the clearing before he jerked to a stop, drew in his breath with sick recognition of the field he'd crossed just hours ago, the heaped bodies of the charging infantrymen, now burned beyond any hope of recognition.

The turnpike swarmed with men and wagons, couriers carrying messages from the front lines, ambulance drivers trying to maneuver through crowds of walking wounded. David stood staring back at the clearing, still unable to take in the fact that only an afternoon had passed since he'd tied up his mount to take a look at the battle. His horse was nowhere in sight; he bestirred himself, walked slowly down the road.

A clump of newsmen had gathered near a muddy creek, not far from Grant's headquarters. David walked over as they hailed him and slumped to the ground, not returning their greetings. He yanked off his smoke-grimed shirt, soaked it in the stream and doused water over himself, washing layers of soot from his face and hair, scrubbing as if he could wipe away the images of the day. One of the reporters handed him a whiskey flask. He gulped deeply, still not speaking.

Ed Forbes sat alongside him, soberly and mechanically adding crosshatching to a sketch of rescuers carrying wounded from the flame-threatened wilderness. The correspondents compared notes, trying to piece together a coherent account of the day's battles, arguing over mistakes in strategy. David sat on, unable to care which flank had been left unsupported, which generals were found wanting in strategy. He reached for the flask and drank again.

Alf Waud raised his head from his sketchpad, looked at him with concern. "You all right, old chap? Better buck up now. You look as down in the mouth as your chum here."

David started, for the first time noticing Al, sitting a little ways off from the other men, his head down on his knees, shaking. Al looked up. "I didn't know it would be like this," he said, his voice tremulous.

"Hell, kid," one of the *Herald* men asked, "you think you came out here to cover a picnic?"

"Shut up, dammit!" David told him. "Leave him be." He looked back at Al's dazed face, his eyes about to swim over with tears. He got up, walked over to him. "No sense sitting here rehashing things. Let's get away from here."

Al nodded gratefully. They walked aimlessly, following the creek, till they were out of sight of the reporters, sank down finally in a leafy hollow away from the road. Al gave a deep sobbing breath. "I just never thought how it would be, I never pictured it, all those boys like my brother Jimmy, he's a soldier you know. One minute they're cussing and joking, and next thing you know they're laying there screaming with their guts hanging out." He struggled to overcome sobs again. "Reckon you think I'm pretty chickenhearted."

"Christ, no!" David said, searching fruitlessly for words to console him. Al put his head on his knees, his shoulders trembling. David reached out a hand, stroked his hair. "I know how you feel," he said.

Al's body shook with strangled sobs. Hell, David told himself, he couldn't just sit there, he had to comfort him somehow. He put an arm around Al's shoulders, held him tightly. "I know just how you feel," he said again.

Al gave a choking sob, drew closer to David, nestled against him, threw an arm around his neck. He cried on, his tears hot against David's chest. David stroked his hair, wrapped his other arm around him, rocked him gently. God, he wished he could rid himself of his own memories of the day. That kid he left— Most likely burned to death by now. He shuddered, held Al tighter. Christ, he needed comfort as much as Al.

The roar of musketry in the distance died away as darkness fell. Al's sobs quieted. He pulled back a few inches, rubbed his sleeve across his face. "Sorry. I didn't mean to make a such a fool of myself."

"You didn't," David said. He moved his hand from Al's hair and stroked his face, brushing off tears with his fingers.

"Well, thanks. I reckon I feel a little better now." Al sighed and slumped back against David, leaning into the circle of his arm.

"Reckon we'd better get on back," Al said at last.

"I suppose," David said. He didn't move, suddenly wishing he could just go on clinging to Al, forget everything but Al, warm and alive in his arms.

"Reckon I've gone and cried all over you," Al said. He gave a tremulous smile, ran his hand over David's chest. His fingers sent tingling shocks along David's bare skin. David smiled down at him and caressed his face again. He could feel Al's breath, warm and moist, coming in short, ragged bursts against his neck. He drew in his own breath, leaned down a little to kiss Al, his lips gently brushing the corner of Al's mouth.

Al gave a start of surprise.

David jerked back, filled with sudden, painful awareness. My God, he thought, what in hell was he going to say to Al? Then Al reached up, his arms encircling David's neck as he returned his kiss. David gasped, drew Al closer, held on to him with helpless longing. Al gave a contented sigh as they finally drew apart. "I was afraid you'd found me out. Reckon I half wanted you to."

"I—" David shook, unable to answer, unable to stop himself from running his fingers through Al's cap of curly hair, stroking his back. Unable to stop himself from inevitable sin. Hell, he thought. What could God have in store for them any worse than the hell he'd witnessed today? "I guess I did," he answered.

He gathered Al into his arms again, covering his face and neck with kisses, letting his hands slide down his back to caress his slim hips, trembling now with pent up eagerness. God, it was good to lie here like this after all those lonely nights—holding someone in your arms, sharing increasingly passionate caresses, feeling strong and alive with desire.

"Wait just a second," Al murmured. "Let me get rid of these trappings." He unbuttoned his shirt and undid a cloth band wound tightly around his chest, caught David's hand and pressed it to a woman's warm, velvet-soft breast.

David, drew in his breath. "Oh my God, my God—"

"I knew you'd guessed," Al whispered again. "I—" David drew back his hand. He lay stunned, feeling the touch of Al's body, warm and yielding, next to his, her hands caressing him with gentle eagerness. His desire vanished. For a second he trembled with near revulsion. Oh Christ, he couldn't let her know.

He closed his eyes, letting himself recall the excitement of the nights he'd lain pressed close to Zach in lovemaking. Zach's voice filled his ears, his body pressed David's in remembered frenzy. Zach's tongue teased David's lips, his strong arms held him as he stroked Al's breasts, took her in his arms and managed to complete the act.

Chapter 19 - 1864

Bursts of gunfire forced David from a troubled sleep. It was barely light. Al was sitting on the ground bent over the notebook on her lap, writing with fierce, jabbing strokes of her pencil. He watched her numbly. "Al— What—"

"Writing up my dispatch. I was too upset yesterday to set anything down." She glanced at him, looked quickly down at the paper again.

"My God, Al— You shouldn't— What's your name? That can't be your name."

She managed a quick smile. "It's Alice. I just shortened it a tad."

"Alice. What in hell— I'm sorry— I didn't mean to swear. I mean—"

"It's all right. I've been listening to you cuss all winter." She smiled again. "Reckon I owe you an explanation. 'Course I never intended to let on. Not till I'd made some kind of name for myself anyway. Showed a woman can do as good as a man.

"Anyhow, there's not all that much to explain. I always signed the dispatches I sent the *Republican* with my first initial. Figured it would be easier to get them printed if the editor didn't know I was a woman. So there was no trouble getting him to take me on as a stringer. And I told my sister I was heading East to get a job as a government clerk, now they're willing to take on women, sent her a letter when I got to Washington City. We've never been close. I figure she has her hands too full to worry over me.

"But you can't— I mean, hell, Al— Alice. I'm sorry. But a woman— Well, I guess you realize that now. You've got to let Grant know. He ought to be able to arrange some kind of escort back to Washington."

She shook her head. "I've been sitting here a couple hours mulling it over. I reckon now I'm here I'll stay on and do what I set out to. Reckon the folks back home oughta know what it's like for the soldiers." She paused. "Now I know what to expect, I figure I won't lose my grip again."

"But— Oh God, Alice. I— I'm sorry. I mean— About last night."

It was light enough now that he could see her flush. "Reckon you oughta keep on calling me Al. It's all right, David. You didn't take advantage of me against my will."

Nancy, David told himself. Nothing but a damned nancy. Goddamned nancy pervert. He sat slumped on the ground, his head in his hands, a little ways off from Grant and his staff, ignoring the furor of the command post, the steady roll of musketry that had resumed with new ferocity at daybreak. The events of the night before played themselves over in his mind.

He'd lain with Al's head pillowed on his shoulder after his charade of lovemaking, envying her exhausted collapse into sleep, wincing at the rhythmic rise and fall of her breasts. He'd reached over and covered her with her discarded shirt, hiding the soft, mocking contours of her figure. Small, delicately swelling breasts where he'd expected a boy's firm strength.

At least Al hadn't sensed how he felt, hadn't seen behind his mumbled apologies, his promises never to repeat his act. As if he had any desire to lie with her, now that he knew the truth.

The truth about himself.

A pervert. Nothing but a damned pervert.

A pervert and a liar. Christ, all those infuriated protestations he'd made to Zach that his desire for him was nothing more than an overblown flowering of their friendship. His refusal, just days ago, to ride into town with the other reporters. He couldn't enjoy the pleasures of a prostitute's body after his closeness to Zach, he'd told himself.

But he'd grown close to Al during their months in camp together. Close enough that he hadn't given a thought to Zach while he was lusting after Al. Hell, he still cared about her despite his discovery.

A discovery that would excite the envy of any man in camp. Anyone but a damn nancy like him. A discovery that shriveled his lust at its core.

No wonder Zach had sought him out. Images rose in front of him. The same damning images that had come to him when he'd at last sunk gratefully to sleep. Men's bodies: half-naked, glistening with sweat, moving easily in the proud, casual knowledge of strength. Rippling muscles propelling a skiff swiftly upriver. Lean black men hefting loads onto barges with back muscles knotted. Weightlifters poised in the gymnasium, muscles bulging before that final burst of effort. And himself, sketchbook in hand, gazing with mute, transfixed admiration.

Right back to boyhood. That first visit to a bawdy house with his college friend, John Eustis. There in the parlor where the whores had posed, waiting to be chosen. He'd kept his eyes on John, told himself it was nervousness, embarrassment at his inexperience that riveted his eyes to his friend, to his laughing, handsome face, his broad, muscular shoulders. Till one of the painted women had taken his hand, led him toward the staircase. And upstairs, when he'd finally lain with a woman for the first time, he'd still— Christ! He dug the heels of his hands into his eyes, trying to dispel the memories.

"Hey, Carter!"

David jerked to attention, looked up into the grinning face of the *Herald* chief, Sylvanus Cadwallader. "You asleep there? You're in luck. I found your nag—that spotted brown mare with the bad swayback, right? Saw her over by Warren's headquarters when I was riding back to check the action on Plank Road. I tied her up for you at the bottom of the hill."

"Thanks," David managed.

"Sure." Cadwallader stared down at him with curiosity. "You been here all morning? What's the news from Hancock's lines?"

David shook his head numbly. Cadwallader gave him another curious glance and a brief wave of farewell. He's not much past thirty, David thought, watching him ride off, and in charge of that whole *Herald* crowd. Riding up and down skirmish lines without a thought for his safety. While I sit here like a coward—

Of course, he's not a damned nancy.

No wonder I deserted that poor kid yesterday. It's what you'd expect from a nancy. Damn perverted nancy. Oh Christ!

I ought to at least see to the horse. He stumbled to his feet, fed and watered the animal. The mare nuzzled him, then shied skittishly as artillery thundered. David climbed back up the hill. No use even pretending he had the guts to ride toward the skirmish lines. He reached the cleared top, looked over toward the turnpike. The battle had surged toward the command post; Warren's rear lines straggled back toward headquarters. Shells crashed onto the knoll.

David stood stunned, staring at Grant as the general calmly puffed on a cigar, then raced down the back of the hill again, grabbed the mare's reins and flung himself on her back. They crossed Germanna Road, well away from the battle, before he pulled up and dismounted, sank panting to the ground.

Rounds of musketry, wild yells and cheers sounded in the distance, an echo of the day before. He stared down at his hands, cursing his cowardice. Damn cowardly pervert. Unclothed men flexed their muscles, advanced on him with knowing, wanting grins.

Dammit, no!

He'd managed to hold onto his sketchpad. He looked down at its blank pages. Hell, he could still draw, still give Leslie what he was paying him for. He willed away the taunting images, closed his eyes till he saw Union troops charging fiercely across the meadow, branches lopped off by bullets, men writhing in agony, stretcher bearers staggering from the woods, a soldier blowing his brains out seconds ahead of approaching flames, that boy he'd left— He dug a pencil from his pocket and began to sketch.

Cadwallader sat his horse with obvious impatience, stuffing reporters' dispatches into his saddlebags. Two days of heavy fighting had petered out to sporadic skirmishes by the third day, the seventh of May. With communication by rail and telegraph disrupted, the *Herald* chief had announced he would ride to Washington City with the accounts of *Herald* correspondents and casualty lists compiled from field hospital records. "Eight to nine thousand on our hospital books," his voice boomed out to another reporter. "I'd put it at an equal number dead and prisoners. Maybe half that many for the Rebs."

"My God," David breathed softly. He stood at the edge of a cluster of reporters from rival papers, who milled around uneasily, arguing the advisability of accompanying Cadwallader.

"And no better than a standoff," Alf Waud said disgustedly. "The talk in the regiments is that Grant and Meade will hightail it back over the Rapidan like Hooker before them."

David nodded silently. Ed Forbes touched his shoulder. "We oughta make up our minds which one of us is going with him. Leslie's liable to blow his stack if we let *Harper's* or *Leggett's Illustrated* beat us out."

"I suppose," David said. His thoughts came with difficulty, as if he still stumbled through wilderness thickets. Ed wasn't eager to leave the army with Grant's next move still unrevealed, he realized. He should offer to go. Hell, he ought to leave for good, run back to New York like the coward he was. Only how could he face— "I'll take them for you. You and Ed both." David started, looked into Al's determined face. "I'm going with them. Reckon that's the best way to get my dispatch telegraphed to my editor."

"Say, would you? Thanks, we'd appreciate it." Ed dug into his knapsack, pulling out a carefully wrapped bundle of sketches.

"It's liable to be dangerous," David protested, trying to recall the scraps of information he'd just overheard. "Grant can't control the Reb guerrillas between here and Washington. And you're likely to run into Confederate troops on Germanna Road."

Al shrugged. "Cadwallader's planning to cut over to Ely's Ford to avoid them. He says once we've crossed the river, we can catch a ride to Washington on a hospital train. They'll be under escort all the way."

"But still, for a—" David stopped himself. He couldn't give her away in front of Ed and the half dozen other reporters within earshot. Everyone knew they'd been bunking together all winter; he couldn't expose her without ruining her reputation. Well, hell, she'd be in as much danger with the army. If only she'd come to her senses and stay in Washington once she got there! "Watch out for yourself," he muttered, holding out his sketches.

"I reckon I'll be all right," Al assured him. "I expect I'll see you again in four, five days." She gave him a quick smile and reached out for his drawings; her fingers pressed his a moment as she took them.

Cadwallader's party trotted off. The rest broke up into aimlessly chatting groups, or took advantage of the late afternoon lull to grab a few hours rest. David lay on his blanket and waited tensely for sleep. Memories mocked him, as they had the night before.

The hell with it, he thought, rolling the blanket up again. He didn't need to be alone with his thoughts right now. He sipped black coffee, listening halfheartedly as reporters second-guessed Grant's strategy, finally decided to see how Pete and Colin were doing while he had the chance.

He saddled the mare and headed down Brock Road. The Second Corps was stretched out along the road behind breastworks whose logs were charred and blackened. Men sprawled in sleep or sat in numb exhaustion, watching him with dulled, smoke-streaked faces. The stench of smoke hung over the wilderness; saplings split jaggedly in two by cannon balls rose from the blackened forest floor. It seemed impossible that only three days had passed since he'd ridden with Al through woods sprinkled with dogwood and wildflowers.

All that time he'd spent with Al. He'd sensed Al's interest in him. And his own, damning response. But he'd managed to deny it, explain it away. Till he could no longer avoid facing the fact of his perversion. No wonder Pete had ragged him with taunts about his chicken. He'd probably seen through him all along. David stiffened, anticipating Pete's mocking greeting. He ought to turn back.

He'd come within sight of their regimental colors though. It would look pretty odd, riding this far and then not even stopping by. He dismounted, searched out their company, hailed them as he walked up.

Colin glanced up at David, gave him a cursory nod. Sean sat slumped against him, breathing noisily in his sleep. The others lay on the ground, rifles at their sides, or sat in exhausted silence, washing hardtack down with coffee, pulling on tightly gripped pipes. David sank to his haunches, taking in their drawn, dirt-smeared faces. Hell, he thought, abashed, they have a lot more on their minds than my sins.

He looked around again, aware now of how their circle had shrunk. He wet his lips. Bert was there and— "Where's Pat McFarland?" he asked.

Pete looked at him indifferently, took his pipe from his mouth. "Pat's turned up his toes."

"He did what?"

"You heard me." Pete replaced his pipe, drew smoke in fiercely.

Sean sat up. "Pat got a bullet right through his eye," he said. "It was running all down his face. He kept clawing at it and twitching till he—" He broke off, his face contorted. Colin clapped a hand on his shoulder. "Don't be goin' to pieces now, kid," he said softly.

"Christ!" David breathed. "I'm sorry." They looked at him, not answering.

"This here march tonight," Pete said finally. "Would you be knowing if Grant means to run back 'cross the river?" David spread his hands helplessly. "I've heard talk, but—"

Pete grunted, lapsed back into silence. Darkness began to fall. He ought to start back to headquarters, David thought. He stood, then snapped to alertness at the sound of a commotion a little ways down the road. The others got up, straining to see.

David peered through his field glasses. Grant, his short figure dwarfed by his big bay, was trotting placidly south, his staff officers following. Waves of wild cheering swelled as the entourage rode into view.

Colin thumped Pete on the back, yelling, "Hey, old woman! Hey! He's headin' towards Richmond! He means to fight!"

A grin spread slowly over Pete's face. "Sure, it's about time." He pummeled Colin's arm, his grin broadening. "About time, old man!"

Sean whooped, tossed his cap into the air. Men threw off their fatigue to rush up to Grant as his party neared, reaching hands out to touch him, screaming their approval, ignoring staff officers' warnings to quiet the noise before the enemy was alerted. Wildly yelling soldiers buffeted David as he stood alone in dazed incomprehension, as the men cheered and cheered the prospect of more of the bloody fighting they had just endured.

Chapter 20—1864

Rain drummed on the slanting walls of the shelter tent, seeped damply through the canvas. David hunched over his sketchpad, ignoring the clamminess of the damp flannel shirt against his skin, filling in details and instructions to engravers with grim care. His back and shoulders ached. He set down his pencil and massaged his cramped fingers, wondering dully if exhaustion would grant him a few hours sleep. His candle flickered over the oilcloth-covered stack of drawings he'd completed since the night march six days before: the record of a week of unrelenting horror, a record he'd made compulsively, reworking his sketches with a fierce concentration that served only partially to keep his anguished self-knowledge at bay.

Leslie should be pleased, at any rate. He'd be forwarding him enough stirring scenes of battle. David stared down at his pad, memory coloring in the images of frenzied pain and death so inadequately conveyed by pencil and paper. He thought back to the soldiers cheering Grant's decision to carry on the fight. The incomprehension he'd felt then had only deepened. How in hell could anyone find anything stirring in these scenes of slaughter? Or call taking some damn piece of ground worth all those deaths?

Zach might be able to make some sense of it, he thought suddenly. God, how he wished he could talk to him right now! Well, he'd write him. He'd heard there'd be a chance to send out mail in a day or two. He grabbed his pencil, flipped to a clean sheet of paper.

No, dammit no! What in hell was he thinking of? He'd broken himself of Zach! And Zach had made it pretty damn clear he wanted nothing further to do with him. Even if he did respond, writing each other now would be like pus festering in an amputation.

Though Zach had been right about him all along. He could still—Goddamn it, no! Just because he'd found out what he was didn't mean he had to give in to perversion.

The tent flap flew open to a gust of rain. Al scrambled in, raindrops flying from her curls. More droplets cascaded from the rubber blanket she let slide from her shoulders. She grinned at him. "Sorry. I didn't mean to shake water over you like an old hound dog."

David smiled with unexpected pleasure. "That's all right. I'm glad to see you. I thought you'd be back a day or two ago. Though I'd hoped—"

"Reckon we would've," Al interrupted. "Only we got caught by a party of Rebs while we were still heading to Washington City."

"What! My God! What happened? How did you—"

Al laughed. "Whoa! Give me a chance to tell you." She dropped down next to him. "Well, we got 'cross the river at Ely's Ford okay. Only there weren't any trains fixing to go. So Sylvanus thought we oughta ride on to Rappahannock Station. There wasn't any moon that night, so we were pretty much picking our way down the road when 'fore we knew what was happening we were surrounded by cavalry pointing their revolvers at us and yelling `Surrender!'"

"My God! You must've been scared to death."

"Well, it was sorta scary. They got hold of all those casualty lists Sylvanus was carrying and that fancy rig of his, and figured him for a colonel 'stead of a correspondent. So they took us into custody, kept us under guard all night. It looked like we'd end up in Libby Prison for sure, and I was starting to wonder what I oughta do. Well, next morning we started riding toward the Confederate lines—still under guard, of course—and darned if we didn't run right into a bunch of Sheridan's pickets. Them and the Rebs started in skirmishing, so while their mind was off of us, we skeddadled on out of there and made our way to Washington. So it was lucky I hadn't given myself away.

"Anyhow, the Rebs took all the papers they found on us, so we had to write our dispatches over from memory 'fore we could send them. Sylvanus' paper was real pleased with him though. They made him chief correspondent here; he was only acting chief before. Only the Rebs got a bunch of the sketches I was carrying for you. I managed to fold some of them real small 'fore they could see, and hide them under my clothes. I left them with *Leslie's* Washington bureau. I'm sorry 'bout the others though."

"Never mind them," David said. "I'm just glad you're safe."

"I reckon we weren't really in that much danger," Al said. "Though I'm darn glad we got away when we did. I hear I missed a big battle here yesterday."

"Thank God you missed it! You can't imagine— There's been fighting ever since you left. Wounded men stretched out all along the road, just lying there waiting for the doctors to get to them. And the battle yesterday— The part I saw— It was through my field glasses, but still the Confederate troops and ours were pressed up on opposite sides of the breastworks, just standing there slaughtering each other. Jabbing their bayonets into men's guts through chinks in the logs. Firing canister point-blank right through them. And more and more fresh troops sent in, piling on top of men lying there bleeding in the mud. Hell, I saw men climb right over their bodies to get atop the breastworks, shoot down into the opposite side. Even club men down like wild animals."

"Well, reckon I'm glad I didn't see that."

"Hell, Alice— Sorry. But you ought to have stayed in Washington once you made it there. This is no place for a woman."

She shrugged. "Reckon it ain't much fun for anyone. But I told you, I still mean to do what I set out to. Anyhow, I thought you'd be glad to see me."

"I am. Only—"

"I reckon you weren't cut out for a war correspondent yourself," Al said. "You look downright awful. You've got terrible circles under your eyes." Her fingers stroked his face a moment as if to smooth them away, pulled lightly through his beard. "You oughtn't to set up drawing this late." She smiled, then reached up to kiss him.

David pulled abruptly away.

Al drew back and looked at him a moment, looked away flushing. "I reckon you're right," she said in a small voice. "Next thing you know we'd be at it again.

"David. You know, even upset as I was— I'm not some camp follower. I wouldn't— wouldn't have— if I wasn't awfully fond of you." She blushed furiously, twisted the tail of her shirt around her fingers.

"I know," David said. He sat numbly searching for words, staring at her boyish crop of curls. Hell, he was fond enough of her. If only he could bring himself to respond to her the way any other man would.

She wasn't like any woman he'd met, that was damn sure. Maybe it would be possible. She'd made her feelings for him pretty plain. Maybe he needn't be doomed to a life of loneliness after all.

Christ, she was sitting there waiting for some response. He put an arm around her shoulders. "Hell, I know that, Alice," he said softly.

The rains continued, churning fields and roads to mud through a second week of intermittent fighting. On May 20th, after repulsing a

Confederate attack, Grant ordered the army to march from Spotsylvania Courthouse southeast toward Richmond.

Sunshine was drying the road as Grant and his staff moved along the route taken by Hancock's advance corps a day earlier. The bright sunlight after days of rain and mud was a tonic. Here and there men broke into a few bars of song, trudging along in time to "John Brown's Body" or "The Girl I Left Behind Me." David felt his spirits lift. He smiled at Al riding alongside him.

Al grinned back. "Seems like everyone's glad to get shut of those darn woods, get out into some open country," she said, waving her hand at the cleared farmland around them.

"And to leave those bloody Reb entrenchments behind," Alf Waud put in, riding up alongside them. "It's what Grant's after, to force Lee to fight him in the open field."

"I suppose," David said, wishing he could forget the war a while. In the two weeks since crossing the Rapidan, casualty figures had climbed to over 30,000 Union soldiers killed or wounded. The road to Fredericksburg was clogged with ambulances struggling to move along the muddy ruts. The memory of men applauding Grant's decision flashed through his mind. At least Colin, Pete and young Sean were unhurt. He'd caught a quick glimpse of them as they marched out ahead of Grant's command a day ago. Though others of their company— Ezra Hollings had lost a leg and— David sighed, tried to fix his attention on the rolling farms, still sown with corn and tobacco despite the war.

Lee's Army of Northern Virginia also headed south, paralleling the Yankees in a desperate race toward Richmond. By the end of a week of skirmishing and night marches, the soldiers' momentarily buoyant spirits had vanished; men sank to the ground to sleep dressed in the mud-caked garments they'd worn since leaving the wilderness, stumbling to their feet again with fatigue barely lessened.

Grant's efforts to force Lee onto open ground were thwarted as the Confederate general outmaneuvered the invading Union army. Entrenched Rebel troops met Federal corps at the North Anna River. After brief skirmishing Grant withdrew his forces to the north shore of the river, dismantling pontoon bridges before daylight on the 27th of May.

"So what he's bound to try now," Alf Waud told some half dozen other reporters that morning, "is to outflank Lee, make some diversionary thrust while the main body of the army circles south toward the Pamunkey." Waud drew in the dirt with a pointed stick as he spoke, outlining the Confederate defenses, drawing a circle around Lee's right flank.

160

David stared into his coffee mug, listening halfheartedly to the newsmen argue strategy as they gulped their breakfast. Christ, he thought, all those maneuvers, diversionary thrusts, flanking movements, all of them aimed at more of the killing they'd seen so goddamn much of. Hell, the Peace Democrats were right in their demands for a negotiated peace.

Not that he'd voice his opinion and be labeled a Copperhead traitor, probably lose his press pass with the army to boot. Have to hightail it home in disgrace. The way he'd hightailed it down here in the first place. David gripped the tin mug tighter, cradling its warm comfort in his fingers. He was no Reb sympathizer. That wasn't his flaw. He knew damn well why he couldn't share the other men's enthusiasm for pressing the war. What else could you expect from a damn nancy?

The mare's hooves churned up clouds of yellowish-brown dust. David coughed, wiped his handkerchief over a face grimy with sweat-streaked dirt. It seemed a hell of a lot longer than four days since they'd crossed back to the north bank of the North Anna River. As Waud predicted, the army had circled south, crossing the Pamunkey May 28, only to find the Rebs already entrenched behind Totopotomy Creek, less than ten miles northeast of Richmond. Grant ordered still another flanking movement in the drive to get between Lee and Richmond. David climbed gratefully from his saddle as they returned to the general headquarters. Hell, he thought, I'm too old to be riding in this heat like a boy.

Still, at least he had a horse. Look at the infantrymen, making forced night marches. They must be dead on their feet. Look at Al, for that matter. You wouldn't think a woman would have the stamina to keep up like this, spending damn near every day covering another skirmish, up half the night writing dispatches.

Crazy as her scheme was, you had to admire her. He glanced over at her, caught her quick grin, drew in his breath in a resurgence of the hope he'd felt that dismal night at Spotsylvania.

A commotion rose among the staff officers as couriers dashed up with news. Sheridan's cavalry had taken the crossroads of Cold Harbor, less than a day's march from Richmond; a counterassault by Confederate forces had been delayed by the onset of darkness; Sleepless men waited tensely for Wright's Sixth Corps, making a night march to reinforce Sheridan's forces, then cheered exultantly as the Confederate infantrymen were driven from the crossroads after a day's fierce fighting.

A Different Sin

An all-out attack on the Rebs seemed imminent. If Grant could take Richmond, David thought, there'd be an end to the war. For once he was as caught up in the war talk as the other men: Grant had run out of room to maneuver; any further flanking moves would drive the Rebels into their Richmond fortifications. The ordered shift of Hancock's men from the extreme right to left of the army would give Grant the strength to attack before the Confederates could fully entrench.

Anticipation slowly died as Hancock's corps stumbled into their new positions well past daybreak, exhausted and desperately in need of rest, at the end of a twelve-mile night march. The scheduled dawn attack was postponed twenty-four hours, giving, men and officers knew, the Confederates ample time to strengthen their breastworks.

"They've bloody well entrenched six miles," Waud reported, "with their flanks protected by the Totopotomy and Chickahominy. But it's unlikely Grant'll back off from a frontal assault now. He's got his back to the wall. It's my guess he'll go ahead whatever the cost."

"Christ," David breathed. He watched Waud and the others disperse. He ought to take advantage of the delay to find a position to view the battle tomorrow, he told himself grimly. He rode slowly behind the Union lines, checking for elevations that would give a clear view of the assault, once or twice dismounting to do a quick sketch of sprawled infantrymen. He worked his way to the left flank and stood debating a moment whether to look for Pete and Colin. He looked around him at the tired, dispirited men. Hell, even if he found them in the growing darkness, they'd hardly be in a mood for visiting.

He prepared to mount.

"Wait a minute, mister!" David halted. The soldier who'd called him pointed at his sketchpad. "Can you spare me a sheet of that?" he demanded.

"I guess so." David tore a page from his pad, watched, startled, as the infantryman tore it in two, then tore the halves, handing the scraps to nearby soldiers. "You won't fit much of a letter on that," David blurted.

"Ain't writing one." The man pulled the stub of a pencil from his pocket and began printing his name and home address. Around him the others did the same. Finished, the soldier stripped off his uniform jacket and fastened the paper carefully to its back with a few bent pins.

"Ain't writing a letter," he repeated. "I just don't relish the notion of gettin' killed tomorrow and my folks never knowing for certain how I ended up."

Rain fell in wild bursts that halted shortly before dawn. The sky was barely light as the signal for attack sounded at half-past-four on June 3rd. The line of Union infantrymen scrambled from shallow rifle pits they'd thrown up the night before and advanced across open ground toward Rebel trenches a few hundred yards away. Musketry and artillery exploded from Confederate works dug in intricate, zigzag designs into a low chain of ridges, raking the Union soldiers with cross-fire. The blue-clad soldiers were mowed down like wheat before a scythe.

David gripped his glasses, his gaze riveted to the small portion of the battle he could see, his breath catching in his throat. Those soldiers who still stood were flinging themselves to the ground, their attempt to assault the Confederate lines ended. Less than half an hour had passed since the order to advance.

Seven thousand blue-clad men, wounded or dead, lay on the field between the Union and Confederate lines. Union soldiers obeyed orders to entrench where they lay, digging in along the thwarted lines of attack. Heavy firing continued, making any attempt to rescue the wounded a suicidal mission.

The cries and pleas of wounded men, sprawled among five acres of corpses, carried past the lines, resounding through the night. Grant declined to request a temporary truce. David shuddered in horror, trying not to imagine the torment of men trapped out on that field without help, without food or water. "Why in hell won't he ask for a few hours to get them out of there?" he demanded.

For once, the circle of reporters was silent. daresay he'd consider it an admission of defeat," Waud said finally, his face set.

By the third day, the cries of the wounded had died away. The nauseating stench of unburied bodies drifted over the camp. A six-hour truce to bury the dead and rescue the wounded was at last arranged.

David stood, simultaneously drawn and repelled, watching the work detail head to the field. Hell, he told himself, Leslie's not going to want pictures of Union dead. But he could be of some use if any of the wounded were still alive, at the least offer a drink of water. He could be man enough for that. He filled his canteen and Al's, thankful that for once she had the sense to shrink back from horror, and walked doggedly out past the Union entrenchments.

The ground was strewn with corpses, blackened and swelling in the heat. David stumbled through them, trying desperately not to gag, finding no one left alive.

Along the Union picket line, groups of Union and Confederate soldiers stood chatting in apparent friendship, trading sacks of coffee and sugar for tobacco. David stared at them in dulled amazement and plodded on. He skirted a swampy patch of ground and stopped to get his bearings. Hell, there was nothing he could do out here. He'd head on back, he thought with relief.

A few yards away, at the edge of a burial detail, a heavyset Union infantryman, his right hand bound in a blood darkened bandage, jabbed a spade at the ground. He swayed weakly, leaned on the spade a moment, then dug into the earth again with grim determination. David started, then hurried toward him. "Pete! What are you doing here? Where's— For God's sake, you're hurt! You've got to get to a field hospital!"

"Not till I see him laid to rest proper. Down far enough so's no animals'll be clawing him up."

David followed Pete's gaze. Colin's body, recognizable only by the shock of red hair, was as bloated and darkened as the others, his maggoty intestines protruding through a gaping rent in his stomach.

"Oh my God!" David squeezed his eyes shut, forced himself to open them and turn to Pete. "I— Here, give me that." He took the shovel and started digging, back muscles straining as he thrust into the ground, fiercely grateful that the awkwardness of the unfamiliar labor helped fix his mind on the task at hand. They lowered Colin into the new grave, covered his body with earth.

Pete swayed again. David took in the pallor of his face, the bloody bandage. "Come on," he told him. "There's nothing else we can do. I'll help you get back to the doctors."

Pete stood unmoving, staring down at the grave. "Pete." David laid a hand on his shoulder. "You can't stay here."

The infantryman shrugged off David's hand. "What in Jesus' name do you know? Ain't nothin' to do—" His voice was a ragged whisper. "I could've— I got these here fingers blowed off, but I still could've— Sure and I didn't give a damn for nothin' but my own skin. Didn't try goin' after him when it's knowing I was that he was layin' here all these days." He clenched his good fist, a shudder running through his body.

Oh Christ! David thought, what can I say to him? Hell, Pete hadn't intended his words for him. But he couldn't just stand there. "Pete, he'd never have pulled through with a wound like that. You'd have just gotten yourself killed as well."

Pete turned on him. "Sure, I know what you're thinkin'! It should've been me 'stead of him."

"Christ Pete, I didn't— I— Let me help you back," he said finally.

"I'm not needin' help! No, wait. You wanna— Here." Pete pulled a dirty sheet of paper from his pocket. "It ain't your place to, but I can't write no letter with my fingers gone. I took this off his body before—

Here, send this to his Rosie and write her— You write and let her know." He pushed the folded paper into David's hand and moved unsteadily away.

"My Dear Wife Rosie, We have been marching all night to get to this place, Coal Harbor, where we are laying up resting, so I take this opertunity to write you, my Dearest Wife. There seems no peeple left in this part of the Country, only our men and Johnny Reb. The rebs has dug their Rifle pits in front of us, but our Officers beleeve we are suficent strong to take them. We are laying now in the rain which don't bother us none as this Country is so hot you would not beleeve. Some of the men has taken sick with the Diarear but I remain healthy as a horse so don't give yourself any Uneasiness about me. Where we are camped now is so near to Richmond I have hopes we may bring a Close to the war this summer which I Pray for as I know you do too, my Dear Rosie. To bring an end to all this terrible Sufering and that we will be united again as God intended for Man and Wife to live. But I will write you more particulers after the Battle. Till then I remain your afectionate Husband, Colin."

David dropped Colin's letter, wishing he'd never unfolded the sheet of paper Pete had handed him. "Christ," he burst out. "What did he have to reenlist for!"

"Reckon he thought it was the right thing to do," Al said soberly. She rubbed her eyes. Shadows from the candle flickered on her face.

"I'm sorry," David told her. "I didn't mean to keep you awake. It's just, I can't find the words to tell her."

"That's all right. I wish I could help you out. It's plumb awful, isn't it, them just married and all."

"God. He was so happy, going on about the cottage they'd have and now—" David slumped in exhaustion, rubbed his own eyes. Colin's freckled face formed behind his lids, grinning in half-embarrassment as he talked. The image disappeared, replaced by the bloated, stinking corpse they'd buried that afternoon. He shuddered, stared at the blank writing paper. "She'll be looking forward to hearing from him and then— My God, what can I say to her?"

"I reckon it might be easier to think of the proper words in the morning," Al said. "We can put our heads together. There's no way to send mail out now, anyhow."

"I suppose." David set aside the paper, blew out the candle, closed his eyes. Once more he gazed through his field glasses at the doomed assault on the Reb trenches. The glasses grew heavier as he watched the battlefield. He stared at them, suddenly realizing he held a rifle, awkwardly gripped between his hands. The bayonet waved wildly at the sky.

"Hey, move your hands a little farther apart on the barrel. That's it. You're gettin' the hang of it!"

David started at Colin's voice, moved his hands as he directed. Pete grunted in amused approval on his other side. He stared around him at the rest of their company, the exposed, muddy field ahead. Christ, he didn't belong here with them. He ought to run for the rear. But he couldn't show himself a coward in front of them. He bent over like the others, moved forward at a stumbling half run. Thunder crashed around him. He gasped, screamed. "My God, we'll be hit!"

"Calm yourself now, David. Just follow my lead." Pete's voice boomed out with unwonted warmth and reassurance. David turned toward him. Not Pete, but— "Zach! Oh my God, Zach! What are you doing here?" David dropped the rifle, ran to him, unheeding of anything but his growing joy. Lead pelted down like hailstones. Blood spurted from Zach's mouth as David reached him. His face darkened, bloated. Maggots crawled toward his eyes.

"No! No! No! No! My God! My God! No!" He couldn't disentangle himself from Zach's fierce embrace, as Zach shook him, crying from his blood-filled mouth, "You've never given a tinker's damn for me!"

Zach gave him another fierce shake. David opened his eyes, dimly made out Al's concerned face, inches above his, as she shook him awake. "Al, thank God!" David wrapped his arms around her, pulled her down next to him, his body shaking with tremors.

"Are you all right, David? You were screaming something awful. I had the hardest time waking you."

"Oh God, I—" He gave a strangled sob.

Al pulled him closer, pillowed his head on her breast. "It's all right now. What were you dreaming about?"

"I— I can't—" David drew a deep breath, clinging to her, pressing his face against her warm breasts as they rose and fell in quiet rhythm. "Just a crazy nightmare— I don't— Oh God, Al. Hold me. Please. Just hold me."

After twelve days at Cold Harbor, Grant ordered the Army of the Potomac to withdraw from their positions. Stealing from under Confederate noses, the troops abandoned their trenches during the night of June 12, heading toward Charles City Courthouse, near the James River, where hastily massed ships waited to ferry them to the southern bank. If Grant couldn't take Richmond by frontal assault, he would try the back door: an attack on the Confederate rail center at Petersburg, twenty-two miles below Richmond and a vital supply link to Lee's army.

By the evening of June 13, Union infantry were streaming up to the north bank of the James, while army engineers raced to complete a massive pontoon bridge for the train of supply wagons and cavalry. David headed toward the riverbank to sketch the engineers before darkness fell, leaving Al scribbling her dispatch in their tent.

He finished his sketch and sauntered along the riverbank toward the steamboats. Infantrymen camped for the night thronged the shoreline, plunging into the river with the glee of schoolboys given an unexpected holiday. Men pulled off uniforms that were little more than dirt-encrusted rags after two weeks confined to trenches, whooping and calling as they splashed one another.

David reached for a pencil, then stayed his hand, content just to watch the scene. Water streamed down men's backs and arms as they scrubbed and splashed, droplets beaded on wiry, hardened muscles, reflected the fading daylight from taut, powerful flanks.

A stocky, grinning soldier hoisted another man to his shoulders, pranced around like a good-natured bear, then tossed the other into waist-deep water with a powerful heave. The second man came up sputtering and laughing, wrestled with the first in mock anger. Their bare thighs strained together as they struggled for a hold. David raised his field glasses, stared through them greedily.

The stockier man pushed the other down, released him with a broad grin. He looks a bit like Zach, David thought. Those shoulders and the way his chest and back are covered with hair. Only younger. Like Zach must've looked before I met him. The man stepped from the water. David's eyes followed him, moved down his body, drinking in the firmly muscled thighs, water dripping from his pubic hair.

Christ! What am I doing?! David turned away, shame-faced, hurried to the bluff over the river and his tent. He shoved open the flap, stumbled into the dimness inside.

Al smiled at him. "I was just wondering if you weren't getting hungry," she said. "I'm about starved. Though I wish we had something besides these darn sardines. Well, I finished my dispatch, at any rate, so at least I won't have to strain my eyes none working by candlelight. From when we skedaddled out of Cold Harbor without Lee being any the wiser right up to coming here. Even though we can't send anything out till after the battle, of course."

"I'd sooner never see another battle," David said. "I was watching the men swim out there, without a care in the world, and then to think a few days from now—"

"No sense getting in a fret ahead of time," Al said. "Though I wish I could peel off my clothes and jump in with them. I feel grubby as an old hog that's been wallowing in the barnyard. I must look a sight!"

"You look fine. Well, we've all gotten a little dusty from the road." Al laughed.

"No, you do." David sank down next to her. "There's nothing wrong with your looks." He reached out and ran his fingers through her curls. "If you let your hair grow out and put on a dress, you'd be a fine looking woman."

"Well, I reckon I'll do that sooner or later. I don't mean to live as a man forever, David." She looked at him, her face suddenly serious.

"I should hope not." David stared back at her. Hell, she'd probably turn heads. With that pretty face. And that hair. And a tidy little figure under that disguise. There's not many men wouldn't want her. I can see it. Why in hell can't I feel it? Christ, I can at least make the effort. We get along. And to have someone. Have her there to hold in the night.

"After the war's over— He faltered, unable to continue. Al looked at him expectantly. The moment of silence lengthened. David took her face in his hands, let his fingers slide through her ringlets. Oh Christ, if he could just feel the way he did about—

"David." Al's voice was a whisper of happiness. Her arms encircled him.

David closed his eyes and drew her into a closer embrace, clinging to her like a lifeline.

Chapter 21 - 1864

THE GENERAL HEADQUARTERS AT CITY POINT, where the waters of the James joined the Appomattox, seemed a city in fact. Steamboat traffic ran daily to Washington City, newly constructed wharves and storehouses served the supply base. Hospitals were built and manned with the assistance of the civilian Sanitary Commission. On a high bluff overlooking the rivers, reached by a wooden staircase, stood the tents of Grant and his staff. Outside the guardline, the plateau was covered with the shanties and tents of civilians: volunteers and employees of the Sanitary and Christian Commissions, sutlers, curiosity and favor-seekers, proprietors of eateries.

From the edge of the bluff, where David sat with Al, the waters below reflected the last rays of sunlight, the bustling wharves grew still with evening. The neighs of cavalry horses carried through the still, hot air.

Al glanced around, then took David's hand, her fingers twining with his. He smiled, brushed her lips in a quick kiss. Hell, he told himself, as he must've done a hundred times since they'd watched the army cross the James a week earlier, he could be happy with her. They could make a life together after the war.

Not that an end to war appeared imminent. A Union victory, seemingly within reach days ago, had slipped from grasp, the advantage Grant had gained by his brilliant, stealthy maneuver lost. On June 15th, with Lee ignorant of the Army of the Potomac's whereabouts, a division of colored troops, commanded by General William F. Smith, broke through a portion of the Petersburg defenses, taking two artillery batteries and several hundred prisoners. But Smith awaited the arrival of reinforcements to press his attack further; the delay gave Confederates the time they needed to strengthen Petersburg's thinly manned defenses.

Supporting strikes in the Shenandoah Valley by Union troops were rebuffed. The assault on Petersburg faltered and ground to a halt. Uncoordinated Union attacks on the 16th and 17th broke through Rebel lines, but the brief successes were not followed up. By June 18, when Grant and Meade issued orders for an all-out Union assault, Lee's Army of Northern Virginia had arrived, entrenching in a tightly drawn line around the city of Petersburg.

Union troops were repulsed with heavy losses. Inexperienced regiments were mowed down by Confederate fire while veteran Union infantrymen lay prone, refusing to make an assault against earthworks as formidable as those of Cold Harbor.

And who could blame them, David thought, tightening his grip on Al's hand. Who the hell could blame them?

At any rate, Grant had accepted Meade's assessment that nothing could be accomplished by further attacks, and ordered the troops to entrench and settle down to a siege.

"City Point, June 21, '64, Dear Mike, Our General Head Quarters and the men in the Front Lines were enlivened by a surprise visit from President Lincoln today." David paused, sifting through the pictures in his mind for words to describe the spectacle: Abraham Lincoln, his black frock coat and high silk hat silted with thick yellow dust from the road, sitting his horse like a countryman ill at ease in Sunday clothes as he accompanied Grant to view the Union entrenchments, his gaunt, lined face lighting with a smile as battle-weary veterans crowded around to catch a glimpse of him.

"On the return to City Point, the President's party passed the encampment of negro troops under Smith's command who captured a part of the Reb breastworks last week. I have forwarded Leslie an illustration, which you will see if he chooses it for print. Mere words can barely describe the fervor of these men, jostling and shoving to catch sight of the President, kissing his hands, shouting and praising him as their Emancipator, Father Abraham. The President in his turn appeared sincerely moved, removing his hat and thanking them while tears welled up in his eyes.

"The situation here otherwise stays a Stalemate and seems pretty likely to remain so for the summer. Give my best to all your family when you write them, and when you see Dad next, let me know how he is getting on. Affectionately, David."

David read his letter over, sealed the envelope and worked a postage stamp loose from the gummed mass.

He ought to write Zach about Lincoln's visit. As much as Zach admired the man, he'd surely relish-The thought came unbidden into David's mind. He closed his eyes, visualizing Zach's surprised pleasure as he opened the envelope, the way his forehead would wrinkle in concentration as he read. It wouldn't hurt to write him, let Zach know he still thought of him from time to time, still counted him a friend. Hell, he'd been in his thoughts more than just occasionally for that matter, nearly every day since they'd crossed the James.

Since— Self-disgust flooded through David as he recalled how he'd trembled with perverted lust as he watched the men swim. Well, he'd faced up to what he was. Zach had been right—

David clenched his fists, forced himself to turn his thoughts from the familiar, tormenting litany. Anyway, he reminded himself fiercely, he intended to overcome his perversion. He shoved the writing supplies into his knapsack, grabbed his letter to Mike, and hurried to catch the daily mailboat.

The sun that blazed down on City Point seemed twice as hot in the entrenchments, eight miles distant. The red clay walls of the dugouts baked and cracked in the heat. Soldiers squatted or sat in ankle-deep dust, passing the time with desultory card games or letters home. The stench of souring food, open latrines and unwashed bodies struck David as he and Al emerged from the narrow trench leading to the rear. The rattle of sporadic firing sounded up and down the lines.

The card players looked up at them with dulled interest. David gazed around the stifling enclosure, trying to imagine it duplicated over and over along the five mile front: the cramped earthen trench, buttressed by earth and log walls topped with sandbags, the cave-like bombproofs dug into the ground for protection against shelling. Like rats in a hole, he thought. He sat on the edge of the packed earth firing-step and opened his sketchpad, while Al approached the men with an eager series of questions.

The gunner on duty stepped heavily from the fire-step, dipped a tin cup into a bucket of water, scattering a cloud of flies from its surface, and drank deeply. Al looked up at the man who had taken his place. "Reckon I could take a quick look through the firing slit?" she asked him.

"Sure, sonny, be my guest. Get you a mighty fine view of Petersburg from here. If you don't mind chancing a bullet in the face, that is," he added, chuckling, as Al moved to climb onto the step.

There was an answering round of laughter from the slumped soldiers. The gunner who'd come off duty glanced at Al's startled, disbelieving face. "Mebbe you gotta be showed, kid," he said. He snatched Al's cap, dropped it onto the point of his bayonet, and hoisted it slowly in the air till the cap waved just above the top of the sandbags. Rifle fire exploded from the Confederate lines. The soldier lowered it, handing the bullet-riddled hat back to Al with a triumphant grin.

"God, Alice, you should've stayed at City Point. You don't belong out here," David said to her when they'd made their way back to the rear and were preparing to mount.

"You told me that already." Al sprang lightly onto her horse. "You sound like my Ma. She used to say I was too headstrong for my own good. But I can't hardly write a dispatch about the siege without ever seeing the trenches. 'Sides, if I was to stay put where I belonged, reckon I'd still be back in Independence helping my sister mind her babies."

"But still—"

Al prodded her horse into a sudden gallop, raising a cloud of thick, yellow dust. She reined in, grinning at David as he caught up, wiped the dust from her face as she waited for his answering smile. "Anyways, David, if I had stayed to home, then you and me would never have met up."

The muffled thud of picks sounded with steady rhythm from under the ground. Working with the stealth of moles, a regiment of Union infantrymen burrowed stubbornly into the earth, laboriously carting out dirt in wooden cracker boxes, excavating a shaft that was—according to whom you talked—either a brainless expenditure of time and energy or a brilliant subterfuge that would break through the Confederate defenses.

Hell, David thought, it was worth a try. With five days yet lacking till the end of June, casualty tolls were mounting from dysentery as well as the sniping of sharpshooters. Summer stretched ahead in an apparently endless stalemate. Why not give Pleasants' 48th Pennsylvania a chance?

He walked over to the opening of the shaft, peering at it through the darkness. Hell, Colonel Pleasants' men had mined most of their lives. If they were convinced they could dig a tunnel from the rear of their own lines—a hundred yards from the Reb defenses—underneath the Confederate fortifications, they probably knew what they were talking about, despite the naysayers in the engineers corps.

They had Meade's grudging approval at any rate, as well as that of General Burnside, the Ninth Corps commander. David stood watching a while longer, listening to the comments of the handful of curious reporters present. For a moment he wondered whether Al would regret having missed the start of work on the shaft in favor of trying to telegraph her story on life in the entrenchments to the *Missouri Republican*. Though he had to admit the fascination lay more in the daring of the scheme than in the steady, monotonous labor of the miners.

Anyhow, even if the miners' scheme worked as they hoped, it would take them weeks to extend the tunnel underneath the Reb breastworks, perhaps a month or more till they could set a charge to blow a hole in the Southern defenses. David tried to imagine it—a trench full of men like the one they'd visited the day before blown sky-high in a sudden, violent explosion.

Like so much else he'd witnessed, it didn't bear dwelling on.

Two or three dozen infantrymen, enjoying a forty-eight hour rotation to the rear, had gathered around the opening of the shaft, calling out comments and encouragement as the 48th Pennsylvania doggedly carried out box after box of earth, concealing them from possible Confederate view under piles of brush. Three weeks of work had extended the tunnel five hundred feet, ending squarely under the Reb fortifications, and work had begun on a transverse shaft where the charges of powder would be laid.

"Them lunkheaded engineers'll have to eat their words!" The wiry, dirt-covered miner, just come off his shift of digging, smacked a fist into his left hand and grinned at Al. "You get that down in that notepad, kid? We got her dug, shored up and ven-ti-lated, and soon's we finish the cross tunnel we'll be set to blow them Johnnies to Kingdom Come."

"That so? Well, seein' is believin'." The voice of a tall, comfortably slouched infantryman sounded with lazy belligerence.

The miner bristled. "I got a buck right here says we done our part an' done it right." He pulled a wrinkled, stained greenback from his pocket, waved it at the other. "Put up your money or else dry up about—"

"*I'll lie in de grave and stretch out my arms; Lay dis body down.*" The plaintive line of song, carried by a hundred deep, rich voices, drifted across the evening. The men fell silent, listening. David looked up from the sketch he'd been trying to complete before dark. A swarthy infantryman spat, the spray landing wetly on David's cheek. "You hear that?!" the soldier demanded. "That's those damn black baboons Burnside's gonna send in to charge the Rebs after you boys work your asses off to blow a hole in their breastworks!"

"That's no skin off my nose," the tall soldier drawled. "I'm willin' to let Sambo stop a bullet 'stead of me." Half a dozen men laughed appreciatively. "Go on and laugh, you damn fools! But Johnny Reb ain't takin' bringing in nigger troops lying down. Or ain't none of you noticed how much more firepower they been throwin' against us since Burnside brought in his niggers?"

"Sure we noticed. Think we're blind?" the miner retorted. "But Burnside knows what he's doing. Them niggers been held to guard duty since they been in this army. They ain't worn out from fighting like the rest of us. Soon's we get this charge set off, Johnny's gonna find the tables turned."

"Burnside ain't thinking worth shit!" The swarthy soldier spat again. "There ain't a nigger alive'll stand up to white men. It's a damn disgrace to call them soldiers! First round the Rebs fire, those baboons'll turn tail and run halfway back to the jungle."

"You can say that again, mister!"

"Hold on a minute—"

David grabbed Al's arm and pulled her away, as men joined the argument with boredom-fueled eagerness.

"Wait a second, David, I was getting that down."

"Hell, Al, you don't want to find yourself in the middle of a brawl."

"I don't suppose they were fixing to come to blows. You needn't keep worrying on my account." Al shrugged off her annoyance, gave him a quick smile. "You reckon they'll fight? Those colored soldiers, I mean."

"I don't see why not. The regiment my nephew's in, the 54th Massachusetts— Of course most of them were free, not escaped slaves like these troops here, but still— The battle Peter was taken prisoner in, they made a frontal attack on Fort Wagner across an open stretch of beach, lost a fourth of the regiment."

"Maybe you should've told that soldier about them."

David winced. "I doubt it would've changed his mind." He quickened his steps, walking in silence. An uneasy memory assailed him, brought to mind by Al's implied reproach. Someone else taking him to task for not shouting down some bigot— When in hell— Of course. Zach. After they'd viewed Brady's photographs of Antietam. He'd nearly gotten himself into a brawl defending freedom for the slaves, then turned on David demanding to know what he found worth standing up for, when his own brother— Though why Zach had gotten so damned riled up about it—

Forget it, he told himself. "Anyhow," he said to Al abruptly, as he untied his horse, climbed into the saddle, "I suppose if these troops stand up to the Rebs then he'll see for himself."

"My army cross over; we'll cross de River Jordan ..." A rhythmic strain, half song, half chant, drifted through the evening once again. David

reined in, listening, glad for the distraction from his memories. "Hetty used to sing that," he said. "I remember from when I was a boy. Stirring the kettle and singing half under her breath. it must be years since I heard it."

Al nodded. "You know, they're camped less than a quarter of a mile from here. It wouldn't be much out of our way to stop off and talk to them."

"I suppose not."

They led the horses through the sandy pine woods to the nearest campfire of colored troops, walked to the rear of the swaying circle of men. None of the white commissioned officers was in evidence. A husky, ebony-skinned sergeant sang out a line of the spiritual in a deep, bass voice; a chorus of voices swelled the refrain.

A thin, light-skinned boy at the far side of the fire looked up, stared at David and Al in surprise, then nudged his nearest neighbors. The men, one by one, fell silent, eyeing them warily. A moment went by. The sergeant cleared his throat. "Evenin', massas," he said.

David nodded awkwardly. "I— We're reporters. We write about the soldiers for the newspapers. Well, I mostly draw pictures. We didn't mean to interrupt your singing."

"You all's welcome to set down and lissen," the sergeant said. "Here, you, slide over, make some room fo' these genelmens."

The silence seemed to deepen as they found seats on logs drawn around the campfire. "We understand General Burnside's picked the colored regiments to spearhead—uh, to lead—the attack on the Rebs once the mine's exploded," David said finally.

A few cautious smiles broke out, then broadened across the dark faces. "Yassuh," the sergeant said proudly. "We's spearheadin' it, sho enuf. Been trainin' every day, so's we be sho enuf ready when the day come."

Al scribbled a few words, looked up with interest. "And you'll be going into battle for the first time?"

"Yassuh." The sergeant nodded solemnly. "This be the firs' time. We been back guardin' the wagon trains befo'. Ah reckons we ready though, massa." The thin, light-complexioned boy suddenly spoke, his eyes shining. "We gonna march right into Petersburg 'fore summer be out."

"I should think you'd sooner stay on guard duty," David blurted. "You'd be a hell of a lot safer."

The circle of men turned as one to stare at him in amazement. "Yassuh," the sergeant said. "But that ain't why we jined up, suh." He paused, searching for words. "We be askin' ourselfs who we be if we don' fight fo' our own freedoms. And what we be tellin' our chillens we done fo' our own African race? And now we gots us the chance, got we the chance to show we stands up for our ownselfs same as any other mens."

"Amen, brudder!"

"You speakin' de truth!"

David nodded slowly as the chorus of approval seconded the sergeant's words. The memory of Zach's voice, loudly arguing that, "I warrant you the niggers would fight for their own freedom if they were but given leave!" once more came painfully to mind. He stood abruptly. "It's grown late. We'd best be getting back."

Forget that damn argument with Zach, he told himself, when they'd reached their tent and stretched out for the night. It was no use. His mind kept stubbornly turning it over, like a tongue probing an aching tooth: his own refusal to enter the dispute, Zach's short but bitter anger.

It wasn't his not standing up for the colored that had gotten Zach so hot. It was Roosa. That damn Byron Roosa. Stepping from the gallery and forestalling the brawl in that gracious, so-cultivated voice of his. The same low tones as when he'd murmured his invitation to David to join him in his perverted pleasures. He'd walked off on Roosa outside Brady's gallery, the same as he had that other time. That's what had angered Zach so.

Hell, when you looked back—as he couldn't stop doing now—nearly every damn quarrel he'd had with Zach had started over Roosa. Well, Zach and Roosa had been lovers. He knew that. Zach still counted Roosa a friend, even if they no longer— For that matter, for all he knew Zach and Roosa had rekindled their affection. He had a momentary vision of them embracing, Roosa moving those soft, elegant hands down Zach's body— David dug his nails into his palms. Stop it! he told himself. You don't know— Anyhow, he'd broken off with Zach. He ought to be glad for Zach if he'd found happiness with Roosa in his place.

In his place. A wave of longing engulfed him. To hold Zach in lovemaking again, fall asleep in his arms, feel the tickle of Zach's whiskers against his face, his beloved, familiar breathing in his ears. Oh Christ! Christ, forget it! His throat felt choked with yearning, his eyeballs burned.

"David? Are you all right?" Al's voice was filled with sleepy concern. "Seems like you've been tossing and turning half the night."

"I— I guess I've— I was having a little trouble falling asleep," he stammered.

"You sound awfully upset. What's the matter?"

Oh God, what could he tell her? He sought frantically for a lie. "I guess seeing those colored soldiers tonight got me kind of worried about Peter—my nephew. Mike just had word of him once since he was captured, and then it was that the Reb surgeon had to amputate his arm."

Al moved next to him, threw an arm around him. "I reckon he's all right. It's awful hard for prisoners to send letters home, you know. You oughtn't to worry so much."

"I—"

"Hush now, David. Here, let me rub your neck. Ma always used to do Pa this way when he was troubled. It did him a heap of good." Her hands reached around him, moved in a firm, soothing rhythm. David drew a deep breath, tried to calm himself.

"You feeling a little bit better?" she whispered after a few moments.

"I— Yeah. Yeah, thanks."

"It's okay, David." Al ran her fingers through his hair and kissed him gently on the mouth. He let his arms encircle her, returned her kiss.

"David. Oh David." Al held him closer, her lips parting, her tongue shyly seeking his. David could feel her unbound breasts pressed against him, her nipples hardening. He moved his hands automatically down the soft curves of her body, feeling the numbing emptiness of his response. He quickened his caresses, summoned his memories of Zach.

Of Zach joined with him in eager, unnatural union. Zach storming at him in sudden fury, forcing him to confront their mirrored images, his fingers digging painfully into David's arm, his low, angry voice crying, "I see two perverts here if that's what you choose to call us!"

Well, Zach had a right to be angry, the way he'd belittled Roosa for his perversion, all the while denying he was every bit as much a nancy.

"David."

He jerked back to awareness. "Seemed like you were a million miles away," Al murmured.

"Sorry." Forget Zach, dammit! David told himself fiercely. He ran his fingers gently through Al's hair, kissed her again, a soft, chaste meeting of the lips. Desire stayed mockingly out of reach. Christ, he thought bitterly, he'd felt desire enough back at the James, barely able to tear himself away from the cavorting, nude infantrymen. The scene replayed itself in his mind: the taut, hardened men's bodies, water streaming from hairy chests and thighs, muscles rippling as they wrestled with a careless, joyful spending of strength. He drew a quick breath, his body suddenly tense with urgency. He pulled Al closer, intensifying his caresses, the men's images vivid before him as she responded with quickening excitement.

guess seeing those colored soldiers tonight got me kind of worried about Peter— my nephew. Mike just had word of him once since he was captured, and then it was that the Reb surgeon had to amputate his arm."

Al moved next to him, threw an arm around him. "I reckon he's all right. It's awful hard for prisoners to send letters home, you know. You oughtn't to worry so much."

"I—"

"Hush now, David. Here, let me rub your neck. Ma always used to do Pa this way when he was troubled. It did him a heap of good." Her hands reached around him, moved in a firm, soothing rhythm. David drew a deep breath, tried to calm himself.

"You feeling a little bit better?" she whispered after a few moments.

"I— Yeah. Yeah, thanks."

"It's okay, David." Al ran her fingers through his hair and kissed him gently on the mouth. He let his arms encircle her, returned her kiss.

"David. Oh David." Al held him closer, her lips parting, her tongue shyly seeking his. David could feel her unbound breasts pressed against him, her nipples hardening. He moved his hands automatically down the soft curves of her body, feeling the numbing emptiness of his response. He quickened his caresses, summoned his memories of Zach.

Of Zach joined with him in eager, unnatural union. Zach storming at him in sudden fury, forcing him to confront their mirrored images, his fingers digging painfully into David's arm, his low, angry voice crying, "I see two perverts here if that's what you choose to call us!"

Well, Zach had a right to be angry, the way he'd belittled Roosa for his perversion, all the while denying he was every bit as much a nancy.

"David."

He jerked back to awareness. "Seemed like you were a million miles away," Al murmured.

"Sorry." Forget Zach, dammit! David told himself fiercely. He ran his fingers gently through Al's hair, kissed her again, a soft, chaste meeting of the lips. Desire stayed mockingly out of reach. Christ, he thought bitterly, he'd felt desire enough back at the James, barely able to tear himself away from the cavorting, nude infantrymen. The scene replayed itself in his mind: the taut, hardened men's bodies, water streaming from hairy chests and thighs, muscles rippling as they wrestled with a careless, joyful spending of strength. He drew a quick breath, his body suddenly tense with urgency. He pulled Al closer, intensifying his caresses, the men's images vivid before him as she responded with quickening excitement.

"David." She whispered his name like another gentle caress. "You know I love you, don't you, David?"

"I—" My God! Oh my God, he thought, what in God's name am I doing? Shame flooded through him in hot, sickening waves. My God, what had he been dreaming of? Spending the rest of his years with Al when he couldn't even take her in his arms without calling up his perverted lusts?

Christ, she deserved better, a damn sweet kid like her. He shuddered, pulled abruptly away.

"David?" Al reached for him. "It's all right to. With us planning on marrying and all." His throat felt clogged with thick, hot vomit he had to choke back before he could get his words out. "I— I can't— I shouldn't have—I'm sorry. I've been leading you on. Taking advantage of you."

Al gave a gasp of surprise and dismay. "But— I thought you cared for me."

"I do, oh God, Alice, I do. But I can't— I can't marry you." He faltered, searched desperately for some sort of explanation. "There's someone— Someone in New York. We quarreled. It's why I left, why I asked Leslie to assign me here. I thought I could forget, but—"

"Oh!" She gasped again, sharply, as if she'd been slapped. "You ought to've told me before this!"

"I know. I'm— I'm sorry, Alice." He felt her start to shake with sobs beside him, put his arm tentatively around her shoulders. She jerked away, sliding out of reach to the far side of the tent. David lay numbly, listening helplessly as she cried in stifled, choking spasms.

An endless time seemed to pass till her sobs diminished. She spoke, suddenly, her voice still thick with tears. "If you're still— still so in love after all these months, David, then I reckon you ought to go back to her."

Chapter 22 - 1864

"I RECKON YOU OUGHT TO GO BACK TO HER."

If he could just get Al's words out of his mind! Her tear-choked advice taunted him, followed him to the front where he'd fled at daybreak, mumbling his apologies over and over, ashamed to look her in the eyes, eyes still red with crying over him.

She wouldn't waste tears on him if she knew what he really was. Knew the truth of his perverted longing. Knew—

"I see two perverts here if that's what you choose to call us!" David closed his eyes against the mocking image as Zach grabbed him and pulled him toward the mirror, clamped his fists over his ears, useless defenses against Zach's damning accusation. Zach shook him fiercely.

"You tryin' to get killed!" David surfaced to awareness of the trench where he'd been sitting since noon. The shouting infantryman yanked him from his seat on the fire-step, jerked him toward the bombproof. The whistling fuse of a shell filled the air. David fell forward into the opening of the dugout, landed heavily on top of his rescuer. The noise of the explosion surrounded them; the ground rocked as if hit by an earthquake.

There was a second of profound hush. Then men crept cautiously to the opening of the bombproof, surveyed the sky, joking in tones loud with relief. "Johnny can't hit the side of a barn tonight!" a young voice sang out.

The soldier who'd grabbed David stared at him angrily. "Lissen, you wanna cover the front, watch out for yourself! You can't expect people to look out for you! Now you see a shell veer off to the side it ain't gonna hit you, but you gotta watch those bastards when they climb up in the sky like that."

A Different Sin

"Uh, yeah. Yeah, thanks," David mumbled.

"Mister, I was you I'd get the hell out of here. The Rebs're mad as hornets 'bout Burnside gettin' ready to throw those damn niggers against them. They ain't been a lull in their firin' long enough to take a good shit since Johnny learned 'bout those darkies."

David nodded. He stepped from the shelter, surveyed the debris left by the mortar. *If that fellow hadn't grabbed me I could've been dead by now.* The thought left him oddly untouched. Hell, it might've been for the best.

He stared at the sandbagged walls, the infantrymen scrambling to repair the damage. A portion of the wall by the nearest firing slit had crumbled; sandbags and wood chunks lay strewn on the firing-step. *Tall as I am, all I'd have to do is step up on one of those bags; it'd all be ended in a few seconds.* David took a tentative step forward.

"Get outta the way, will ya!" David started, gave a shudder at what he'd just contemplated. Hell, suicide was a sin too.

The mare lifted her head and nuzzled him as he stumbled up to her. David flung an arm around her neck, trembling with fear and relief. Christ, he told himself, get a grip on yourself. Keep your mind on your job, for God's sake.

Though there'd be precious little to cover till the mine explosion was set off. David looked up at the darkening sky. He'd best find a spot to unroll his blanket for the night. He couldn't face Al, share a tent with her again. He mounted, searched desultorily for a place to camp. The singing of the Negro troops swelled, a little ways off. Well, Leslie might be interested in a sketch or two of them.

The colored soldiers looked at him with only slightly diminished wariness, but made room for him without breaking off their song. David sank down next to the light-skinned boy who'd spotted him the night before, tried to fix his attention on the music. The mournful spirituals had given way to a robust, defiant tune. "No more peck of corn for me, no more, no more, No more peck of corn for me, Many thousand gone. No more driver's lash for me, Many thousand gone." The men's voices swelled on the refrain as if they hoped their words would carry to the Reb lines. David turned to the boy as the song ended. "Did you all make that up?"

"Reckon someone must of." The boy shrugged. "Ain't none of us start it though." He gave David a sudden grin. "We made us a new song though, massa. Been singin' it 'bout every night since we picked to head the attack. Thass it Sergeant Jackson lining out now."

David listened. The sergeant trumpeted, "We looks like men amarching on," his deep bass voice evoking the sound of a thousand marching footsteps. "We looks like men of war," the men responded in martial rhythm. The simple tune rose to a crescendo; the sergeant repeated his line, the men responding over and over, with unflagging enthusiasm.

"Thass it, suh," the boy said eagerly. "Men of war. Thass what we be now, massa."

Like Zach predicted, David thought. Christ. Stop thinking about— He forced his thoughts back to the circle of dark soldiers, the grinning boy next to him.

"Why do you keep calling me that, then?" he asked him.

"What you mean, suh?"

"You all ran off from slavery, didn't you? Why do you keep saying master?"

The boy frowned in thought. "Don' know, suh. Reckon we just be useta callin' white mens that. Don' mean we gonna let no man be massa over us no more," he added solemnly, his eyes fixed on David. "What you wanna be called? What you name, suh?"

David smiled. "It's Carter. David Carter."

"Yassuh, Mista Carter. I'm Amos. Amos Johnson, that be my last name."

"And did you run off to join the army?" David asked him.

"Yassuh, Mista Carter. Them Union soldiers come marching by our plantation and all our peoples what wasn't too old or crippled up to walk just follow 'long after them."

"Then your family all left with you?"

"No suh. My grandma be too cripple with rheumatiz, she still back on the plantation. I sho hated to leave her, cause she raised me from a lap baby after my mama sold away, but granny tell me take the chance while I got it."

"Oh. Is that all the family you have? How about your father? Was he sold away too?" Amos colored. "Don' know nothin' 'bout him," he mumbled sullenly.

David stared at him, surprised at his sudden change of tone, then flushed himself. Hell, he'd like as not been fathered by his owner. He certainly looked it, lighter even than Mike, more of a high yellow. No doubt it was nothing he was proud of. "Sorry," he said. "I didn't mean to pry."

"Yassuh," Amos said, looking startled in turn at David's apology. He smiled. "Granny's all the family I got left. After the war be over, I aims to go back for her, carry her up North where I kin take care of her. I ain't never gonna live on no plantation again. My ol' massa, he set me to learnin' carpentry, and I aim to find me work in some big city, big as Charleston maybe, and learn me how to build fine houses like those I seen there once."

A Different Sin

David smiled, enjoying the boy's enthusiasm. He was a bit like Mike had been at that age, maybe fifteen or so, he mused. Mike had had that same quick smile, displayed that same eagerness to tackle life despite the roadblocks in his path, on the few occasions he'd confided his dreams to David. Well, it ought to be possible for this boy to build some kind of future if he was a skilled carpenter. Assuming, that was, he lived through the war at all.

"Course first we gotta lick the Rebs 'fore any of that come to pass," Amos said, as if he'd read David's mind.

"I'm afraid so," David said, his dark mood returning. Get a grip on yourself, he warned himself again. He'd best concentrate on finding a place to sleep and some better fodder for his poor mare than the sparse grasses she'd found in these pine woods.

He ought to be able to purchase a little forage from one of the commissioned officers or his servant. He rode through the encampment till he found the officers' tents, made arrangements for the mare and accepted an offer to share in the officers' mess from a sober-faced young lieutenant.

The lieutenant, Christopher Pennell, served as aide to Colonel Henry Thomas, one of the two brigade commanders in the Army of the Potomac's only colored division—the Fourth Division of Burnside's Ninth Corps, under the command of Brigadier-General Edward Ferrero. David sat listening as the officers' talk ranged from the unending heat spell to the next day's drill. Colonel Thomas turned to David. "I hear you've been observing our infantrymen. Come to see for yourself, have you, if darkies can be turned into soldiers?"

"Well, not exactly—"

"Oh, they make good soldiers all right." Thomas pushed away from the table and brushed a stray crumb from his beard. "Drill from morning to night without complaint. Desertion's just about unheard of."

David nodded. "I've heard talk among the other troops though, sir. They're afraid your men won't stand up to their former owners in battle."

"Oh, they'll fight. Have you heard that martial air they've composed? They've sung it to the virtual exclusion of their whole repertoire of hymns since they learned we're to spearhead the assault."

"If I might be permitted to add a word, Colonel." Lieutenant Pennell turned to David, his face flushed with fervor. "I'm a Massachusetts man, Mr. Carter. I don't know if you're familiar with the record of the 54th Massachusetts the regiment of free colored volunteers, but—"

"Yes, I know," David said. "I mean, I know about their attack on Fort

Wagner."

"Then, you know what colored troops are capable of," Thomas said easily. "And since the atrocity at Fort Pillow, our men have redoubled their determination."

"You're familiar with Fort Pillow?" Pennell demanded. "I'm afraid so," David said.

"An atrocity," Pennell said, as if David hadn't spoken. "Sheer butchery on the part of the Rebs. Over three hundred men slaughtered in the act of surrender, for the offense of being of sable hue. Nathan Bedford Forrest bragged that the water of the Mississippi was dyed with the blood of the slaughtered."

"I know," David said. "I read the complete account when it was published in April." It must've been going on right while I was sitting and talking with Mike. I remember he didn't write a word about anything else his next letter, not even Dad's health. No wonder, with Peter in the hands of the Rebs— "It was a terrible thing. But wouldn't it serve to make the colored troops more fearful of the Rebs?"

"To the contrary," Pennell answered. "The response of our sable troops has been to fight with renewed ardor. With `Remember Fort Pillow' as their battle cry."

David nodded uncertainly. "I just meant—" He paused, trying to marshal his thoughts, wondering why in hell he was bothering to argue the question with these officers. He knew the answer to that though.

Anything was better than being alone with his memories.

The continuing bleakness of David's mood went unnoticed as work on the mine shaft was completed, just shy of a month from its beginning. Christopher Pennell, who'd offered David sleeping space in his tent, spent long minutes on his knees each night, praying for the strength not to falter in his mission; Colonel Thomas' easygoing manner grew edgier with each day that passed without orders for an assault.

The Confederates—rumors flew—had learned of the Union mine and were sinking shafts of their own in an effort to discover its location; Hancock's corps made a diversionary feint against Richmond, while Colonel Pleasants' miners lugged eight thousand pounds of powder down the long tunnel.

The colored troops awaited the assault with nothing but patient, unwavering faith, so far as David could see, a patience that turned to joyous anticipation as orders were given to be ready to attack at half-past three in the morning of July 30, immediately following the explosion of the mine. The infantrymen were tense with sleepless excitement as they lay on their arms the night before, just behind the covered way leading to the shaft.

A Different Sin

Christopher Pennell clasped his hands around his knees, eager as any man in his command as he awaited Colonel Thomas' return with Burnside's final orders to the brigade. "We're ready," Pennell told David. "Men and officers both. With God's help we'll prove to the world what our sable brethren are capable of." David winced at the echo of Zach's words. He forced himself to listen to the young lieutenant review Burnside's plan of attack, as much for his own benefit as David's. If nothing else, David told himself, he'd managed to position himself well to capture the start of the assault for Leslie.

Pennell broke off his explanation of how the attacking troops would sweep to the right and left of the crater formed by the explosion, driving the Rebs from their trenches and lessening the danger of flank attacks. David followed his gaze. Colonel Thomas strode toward them, his face a grim mask, and informed his regimental commanders that Meade and Grant had overridden Burnside's orders: The plan of attack had been changed. A white division would lead in place of the colored. David approached Thomas for further information on the last minute change. "I've unburdened myself of all the knowledge I have," Thomas snapped, "All I can add is that I fear the morrow is most apt to bring disaster."

He'd best look elsewhere for more information. David worked his way toward the breastworks nearest the Confederate lines, finally stumbling on a hill overlooking the field where most of the contingent of newsmen waited the explosion in murmuring, anxious groups. David joined them, nodded to Al with painful stiffness and found himself a spot well away from her.

Alf Waud gave him a broad grin. "We missed you the past couple of weeks, old chap. You intending to steal a march on the rest of us, moving down to the front?"

Christ, if he only knew— David managed a strained smile. "I'm afraid I've no more idea than you what's going on."

"Between you, me and the gatepost," Waud said, "Meade's interested in covering his arse if things go wrong. He doesn't want to be accused of using the darkies for cannon fodder, got Grant to back him up. I daresay Burnside was bloody well miffed. He didn't choose a new division commander to lead the assault, let his generals draw straws for the honor. Ledlie drew the short one," he added parenthetically.

Waud pulled his watch from his pocket. He lit a match, shielding its flame from view, and peered at his timepiece. "Three-twenty," he announced. "Ten minutes to go."

Conversations died. A silent tension stretched through the thousands of massed troops, strained near the breaking point as the moment came and went without sight or sound of the promised explosion.

Four o'clock came. Anxiety heightened. Daylight approached. The scheme was a failure, men whispered in agonized disappointment. The sight of the massed divisions, clearly visible from the Reb lines once day arrived, would be a dead giveaway of the Union purpose.

Two *Herald* reporters who'd made their way to the mouth of the shaft returned with news: the rope fuse had gone out at a splice somewhere along its ninety-foot length; two of Pleasants' miners had volunteered to enter the tunnel to relight the match. David breathed his admiration of the men's daring. Four-fifteen passed. Four-thirty.

With a suddenness that startled even the expectant onlookers, the ground heaved. The earth along the Reb lines erupted, spewing out a massive cloud of flame-shot smoke, dirt, sandbags, guns and the mangled bodies of men, rising on a pole of fire as if the flames of hell had burst forth into the living world. The cloud spread outward like a swollen, rotting mushroom. Rocks, timbers, severed limbs and clay hung suspended an instant, the space of an indrawn breath, then almost slowly fell back to earth. The rumble of the explosion was drowned out by the roar of cannon, thundering from the line of Union artillery like the war cry of a thousand vengeful devils.

Chapter 23 - 1864

Debris rained back to earth, chunks of clay falling as far as the lead troops of Ledlie's division. The first two Union lines scattered in panic. Through the cloud of settling dirt and smoke David made out the raw wound of the bomb crater. He stared through his field glasses, transfixed by the destruction.

"Mind if I take a look through those?" David jumped at Al's approach, handed her the glasses with a wordless nod, stood in awkward silence as she raised them to her eyes. Al lowered the glasses and turned to David. "Aren't you even gonna say howdy? Seems to me by rights I'm the one who oughta be mad."

"Oh God, Al, I'm not mad at you! It was all my fault. I just—"

"Never mind, David. This is the hardly the time to stand around jawing about it anyways." She focused the glasses on the crater, peered through them, then handed them back with a look of disappointment. "You can't hardly see what it's like, even with these glasses of yours. A couple of the *Herald* reporters are heading over to have a better look at it. I reckon the best thing to do is join them."

Shock jerked him from his silent embarrassment. "For God's sake, Al, have you gone crazy? It's bad enough you're here at all. At least have the sense to stay behind our lines!"

"I don't reckon you've any business telling me what to do! Anyways, it's not so crazy. It's gonna take a while for the Rebs to recover. It won't be dangerous to go out for a quick look."

David looked back toward the Reb works. The line of trenches surrounding the crater appeared empty, deserted by their terrified Reb defenders. No return fire met the fierce barrage of Union artillery. Yet he'd thought it safe to venture out after the Union charge in the wilderness, and damn near got himself trapped when the tide of battle turned. He said nothing. Neither of them, he was certain, wanted to dwell on that day.

"Anyway," Al persisted, "I suppose those *Herald* reporters know what they're doing."

"Dammit Alice, they're not women! This is no place—"

"Hush, David! Folks'll hear you."

"Let them," he said, startling both of them. He took a deep breath, looked at her stubbornly set face. "I mean it, Alice. You're not going out there."

"David." Al looked anxiously around, gave a sigh of relief as she saw the other newsmen preoccupied, Cadwallader snapping instructions to *Herald* reporters, Alf Waud and Ed Forbes already busy sketching with the aid of their glasses. "I told you, it's none of your business anymore what I do. I aim to write the best dispatch I can and—"

Christ, at least he could be man enough to keep her from running headlong into danger. He owed her that much. A lot more than that, if truth be told, after the way he'd led her on, compromised her virtue. He took another breath.

"It's still my business if you get yourself shot. I'll go out with Ledlie's division and take a look around, tell you everything I saw. You can write it up the same as if you were out there and still see the assault from up here."

"David, I told you—"

"Alice. I don't want to have to give you away. Look, tell Ed I'll get a quick sketch of the inside of the pit, will you?" He turned before she could answer and rushed toward the entrenchments.

Officers shouted and swore as they regrouped the panicked infantrymen. The Union breastworks formed a barricade to the advance of their own soldiers. Men clambered clumsily over the log and earth walls, jabbed bayonets into chinks to serve as make-shift ladders, climbed over piled up sandbags. David fell into the line of infantrymen; waiting hands hoisted him over the wall.

He followed the ragged line of soldiers as they fought their way through the further defenses of thorn abatis laid in front of the breastworks, emerged suddenly onto the open field. For an instant he felt the panicky exposure of nightmare. He fought it down and stumbled toward the bomb pit with the disorganized wave of infantrymen.

A wall of earth, thrown up by the explosion surrounded the crater. Men jerked to a stop at the rim, staring down in awe. David halted with them, gaping in astonished trepidation at the still smoking pit. More

Union soldiers raced up, pressed the front ranks forward. An officer barked an order to advance. The infantrymen began clambering over the debris, chunks of unearthed clay and bleeding Confederate bodies. David was shoved violently forward. He stumbled and slid down the slanting side of the crater, landing painfully on his hands and knees.

He struggled to his feet, clutched instinctively at his sketchpad and gingerly brushed tiny, sharp-edged stones from his palms. His left knee throbbed. He limped a little ways to his right, trying to stay out of the path of the shoving troops, and stared around.

Awe distracted him from his discomforts. The raw pit stretched nearly two hundred feet along the Reb line and sixty feet wide. The sides, nearly sheer, rose thirty feet above him. Acrid smoke drifted from crevices in the ground over a mass of splintered caissons, projecting timbers and huge red chunks of clay tossed about like toppled children's blocks. Corpses lay crumpled like rag dolls; the protruding limbs of men buried alive by debris twitched feebly. The groans of the wounded sounded weakly under the continuing thunder of Union artillery.

The Union troops milled about uncertainly in the bowl of the crater, awaiting further orders. Small groups of infantrymen began digging out the half-buried Southerners. David hastened to assist the nearest rescue effort, clawing up handfuls of loose dirt till a dazed young second lieutenant was pulled free. He opened his pad and did a quick sketch of the man as he gulped deep, grateful breaths of air.

A few more Confederate prisoners were taken. A Union officer supervised a squad of his men as they unearthed a couple of half-buried cannon, dragged them toward the far rim of the crater.

Union troops still poured into the pit, divisions intermingling in a disorganized mass. Line officers bellowed commands. "Go for the crest! Go ahead! Move out, goddamn it!" The leading brigade clambered with difficulty up the steep slope. Cheers rang out as they planted the colors of the 14th New York Artillery on Confederate fortifications ringing the far side of the pit and continued their advance through the labyrinth of abandoned Reb trenches toward the crest of Cemetery Hill, which overlooked Petersburg some four hundred yards to the rear of the Rebel line.

Gunfire spat without warning from breastworks flanking the advancing Union troops, raking their rear. Their line broke. Men struggled frenziedly back to the shelter of the crater as the Confederate counter-attack intensified. Blue-clad soldiers making a dash for the edge pitched forward, propelled by sharpshooters' bullets, toppled headlong into the crater.

David clenched the pencil in his fist, his sketch forgotten. Christ, he'd best get the hell out of here, get back to the Union lines! He scrambled frantically up the side of the crater, sliding backward every few feet as handholds of loose dirt disintegrated under his grip. The bulky field glasses on their neckstrap banged and jabbed into his chest. Chunks of clay, wood and metal rained down on him.

The thunder of artillery increased to near deafening pitch, with the ferocity of a sudden storm. David froze in terror. That wasn't just Union artillery! By the sound of it, the Rebs had brought up a battery, were sweeping the crest of the crater with canister, perhaps even the field between the lines. It could be worth his life to try to return to the Union lines. But if the Rebs had turned the assault around, were pursuing the Union brigades back into the crater— David scrabbled with his fingernails for a hold on the clay, flattened himself against the sloping wall.

Particles of dirt filled his nostrils as he clung to the slope. He was too petrified to move, unable to see either the field above or the pit behind him. Finally the uncertainty became too great to bear. He grabbed for the support of a protruding timber and edged carefully around, digging his heels into the earth for footing and maintaining his balance in an ungainly squat.

On the other side of the crater retreating Union troops were still scrambling down the slopes. There was no sign of Rebel pursuit. He drew a deep breath, tried to calm the pounding of his heart. Hell, the Rebs would have their hands full defending their rear lines, now that their defenses had been breached. As badly outnumbered as the Southerners were, they'd most likely pull back, tighten their defenses in preparation for assault by the Union divisions still massed behind their breastworks. This was nothing but a temporary setback. His best bet was to sit tight, take refuge in the pit out of the reach of cross-fire.

He slid gingerly back to the floor of the crater. Under the din of artillery the yells of officers struggling to regroup their commands sounded a weak interruption. A handful of troops attempted to reach the crest once more, scrambling up the crater wall braced to fire on Reb gunners starting to ring the pit. Despairing curses rose as the men fell back, raked by Confederate cross-fire.

Christ! David thought. We'll be trapped in this damn hole! What in hell had happened to Burnside's plan to throw troops to the right and left of the crater, drive the enemy from their entrenchments? He focused his glasses on the flanking breastworks, let his breath out in a rush as he caught a glimpse of blue-clad infantrymen fanned out in the captured works, pressing painfully forward through a maze of Reb rifle pits and trenches.

A Different Sin

A red-faced colonel mounted a block of clay a few yards from David and bellowed an order to the milling infantrymen to regroup and move against the Reb batteries on the crater's lip. "Move out, dammit!" He mopped his brow with a bandanna, then waved it like a flag. "You gonna let Willcox and Potter's men do your fighting for you?! Get over the side for chrissake!" His voice barely carried through the din.

A handful of men of varied brigades moved forward at his summons. David took a step toward the shouting officer, opened his pad. If he was stuck down here he could at least do his job as a newsman. Better than just standing, shaking in his boots.

A mortar shell shrilled. The colonel's sweating face vanished, spattering the men around him with bits of bleeding flesh. For a second the body remained upright, arm still raised in appeal, blood spurting from the severed jugular, then pitched forward with a dull thud.

David threw himself under the shelter of an overturned gun carriage. Vomit rose violently in his throat, spewing from him as he struggled to worm his way further under its scanty protection. Men fell atop him, clawing and shoving, as they struggled for cover.

The suffocating press of men finally lifted. David groped his way from under the carriage, wiped his face numbly. His sketchpad lay where he'd dropped it, trampled, bloody, spattered with dirt and vomit. He let it lie. The colonel's mutilated body sprawled on the crater floor, oozing blood that formed a vivid red pool on the hard clay.

David stared at it with sickened fascination. If that shell'd fallen a few feet different, that could've been him lying there. When he thought how a few days earlier he'd toyed with the idea of inviting just such a death—to be cut down like that, never to put pencil to paper again or see his loved ones— He slumped to the ground, beseeching God to let him survive this battle.

Reb artillery tore into the Union troops in the flanking trenches now. The men fell back in panic, took cover under the remains of bombproofs or poured in chaotic flight into the adjoining crater. The Confederates pressed forward, reoccupying the works as Union infantrymen fled.

The soldiers pouring into the crater pressed together in suffocating closeness, all semblance of military order vanished. A few line officers still called commands, relaying orders to advance from the pit in listless tones that betrayed no expectation of obedience. "Damned if I will," a soldier pinned next to David growled. "Goddamn generals issue orders to take the crest while they're settin' pretty behind the lines without no idea what we're up against. Heard it from one of Ledlie's men for a fact. Ledlie and Ferrero's holed up in a bombproof

190

together, expectin' us to throw our lives away assaultin' Reb guns."

"Christ," David breathed. He worked his watch out of his pocket, stared at it in dulled amazement. A quarter hour still lacked till seven o'clock. The air in the pit was stifling, the heat noontime fierce. Days seemed to have passed since he'd let himself be trapped in this hellhole, barely able to move, expecting to breathe his last at each shriek of a shell.

There was a sudden commotion from the men around him, a scattering of weak cheers. David raised his head in breathless hope. The colored troops had moved out from the Union lines, were advancing under heavy Reb fire along the rim of the crater. Several officers sprang to their feet with renewed vigor, urging their men to move out in support of the Negroes' assault.

"C'mon, we got us a chance!" the man who'd sat next to David cried. He rose, waving his bayonet like an officer's sword, his voice booming over the uneven lines of men slowly falling into formation. A babble of voices clashed angrily.

"Damn right! Let's move out and show Johnny!"

"I'll be damned if I follow after any pack of niggers!"

David got to his feet, straining to see what was happening. The leading colored brigades were struggling through the maze of trenches that connected with the right rim of the crater, their way slowed by the mass of Union troops still crowded into the section not retaken by the Rebs. A fierce barrage of rifle fire raked their right flank, from Confederates at close enough range to bayonet the nearest of the colored infantrymen. The left ranks of Negroes were forced from the rim into the crater, where they pressed doggedly through the throngs of milling white troops.

Canister poured into the pit. David shrank back against the steep earth slope, willing his body to stop trembling as he followed the passage of the colored soldiers. He gave a start of recognition as he spotted the company of men he'd visited over the past week among the intent, dark faces, raised his glasses to make certain. The colored men scrambled up the opposite side of the crater into a hail of artillery and sharpshooters' bullets. A slender, brown-skinned fellow ducked back from the crest, crouched for cover under a few jagged sticks of timber. A muscled, bare ebony arm yanked him mercilessly from his hiding place, hoisted him over the rim of the pit. David focused, recognized the barrel-chested sergeant who'd lined out songs for the company, stripped to his waist now under the hot sun as he leaped fiercely over the edge.

The leading brigades had already fought their way through the works rimming the crater. David clawed his way up the slope till he was

191

high enough to make out the Confederate-held ground on the opposite side of the pit.

A cheer went up among the men clinging to the crater wall around him as the first wave of colored troops swept over enemy-held entrenchments, attacking with bayonets and rifle butts, capturing a squad of Confederate prisoners in hand-to-hand fighting and retaking a captured Union standard.

Some twenty minutes passed in tense waiting, the Union troops half hidden from view by the zigzag walls of the trenches. A small party of officers and men leaped from the last of the Reb breastworks then to make a rush for the crest of Cemetery Hill. A storm of cross-fire swept them, drove those still standing back to the trenches.

A Union officer jumped to the parapet, his figure commanding even at a distance, sword arm upraised and flag flying from his left hand. David gasped as he recognized the young lieutenant, Christopher Pennell, who'd shared his tent with him for the days just past. Pennell paused an instant to urge on his men, then sprang forward, greeted by fire so fierce his body seemed torn to fragments even before he fell.

David lowered the glasses, stunned and dispirited, not bothering to watch as the men around him shouted out news of a second rush from the breastworks, a second storm of Reb artillery fire from a ravine out of range of Union guns. A Reb countercharge poured from the ravine. The colored soldiers and those white troops who'd followed them broke in retreat, streaming wildly back into the crater.

There was no longer any hope of Union success, had not been since the rout of the colored soldiers hours earlier. The likelihood of leaving the crater alive was the only question occupying the men still trapped in the bomb pit under a blazing sun that now sat directly overhead.

General Burnside had accepted the inevitable, issued orders for a Union retreat shortly after nine, but the Confederate artillery spewing canister on the field between the lines made withdrawal a death-defying gamble. The bodies of Union soldiers lay so thickly strewn on the field it was difficult to cross to the Union lines without setting foot on human flesh, a courier to the rear-based command reported back in horror.

The crater floor too was strewn with the jumbled bodies of dead and wounded, the litter of severed limbs. The few patches of bare ground were stained red with blood. The moans of wounded men begging for water rose to David's ears during lulls in the firing. The stench of dead flesh and opened bowels clogged his nostrils even on the side of the slope where he still clung in desperation.

Like a vision out of hell, he thought with numb horror. Dante's Inferno or— Christ, keep your wits about you! he told himself. Thinking had become a strain. His head swam from the noise and heat. His mouth was parched. What few drops of water he'd been husbanding had been snatched from him over an hour ago, by two soldiers who struggled fiercely over his canteen till the precious liquid spilled out on the ground.

He strained to make sense of the scene around him. The infantry-men were jammed into the pit chaotically, colored and white regiments mixed together. A handful of soldiers at the base of the slope dug their bayonets into the loose dirt, scraping out the beginnings of a shaft through which they hoped to cross the field protected from Confederate fire. David stared in wonder. It had taken weeks to hack out the tunnel for the mine! But still, the courier who'd made it to the general command reported Burnside was setting men to work cutting a similar shaft from the Union lines. There was always a chance, he supposed.

Hell, he'd lend them a hand. Better than crouching here helplessly. David made his way down the slope, looked about for something to dig with. More of the men were gathering around the newly begun shaft now. David gave a start as he spotted Amos, the young colored boy who'd reminded him so of Mike, in a cluster of approaching Negro soldiers. Amos stared back in surprise, as David headed toward him.

The simultaneous explosion of hundreds of muskets shattered the brief lull; Reb soldiers swarmed over the crest in a fierce hand-to-hand charge on the trapped Union troops. David threw himself to the ground, crawled under the wreckage of a caisson.

Frenzied cries and firing raged over his head while he lay shaking, possessed by raw terror. He raised his head at last as the noise of the battle died down. The Rebs had been driven back to the rim, though any fool must know they were merely reforming for a stronger assault. The Union troops couldn't hold out much longer; already the bodies of dozens more dead and wounded had tumbled in grisly heaps into the pit. David searched with his eyes till he found Amos, fiercely glad to see the youngster still alive and uninjured.

Though how much longer could any of them count on living? God, what a fool he'd been to venture out beyond their lines! For that matter, Zach had been right from the first to warn him off. If only he'd listened to him!

My God, he thought, I'll never see Zach again, never be able to tell him—

He sobbed, closed his eyes on burning tears. This must be God's judgment for his sin. Zach's face swam up in front of his closed eyes, his look filled with loving scorn. "I daresay there's worse sins than loving, David." But then Zach never did worry about the life beyond. What was it he'd said that last day they'd had together? Something by that poet. When he whom I love holds my hand, something like that. I am satisfied. That was it. "I cannot answer the question...of identity beyond the grave, but I walk or sit indifferent... He ahold of my hand has completely satisfied me."

Oh God, Zach, Zach!

Shouts started, the din of renewed Reb assault. David snapped from his reverie, huddled further under the caisson. God, he had to get a grip on himself! It was hopeless to think of making a run for it to the Union lines. Just sit tight, keep under the cover of the caisson, then surrender first chance he got. Better to be in Libby prison than dead.

"Hell, only a fool would tangle with them Johnnies again! Ain't no chance of fightin' our way outta here!"

"Damn right! Only chance we got is to throw down our arms."

David jumped at the echo of his thoughts. He peered cautiously out. Around him, other men were taking shelter, some dozen or so jammed up by the opening of the escape shaft, displaying no intention of trying to beat back the assault.

"Shit! We ain't got a fuckin' chance even so!" The voice of the third speaker shrilled in near hysteria. "I been listenin' to a feller made it out of the trenches this mornin' one step ahead of them Reb bayonets. Way he tells it, them Johnnies charge yellin', `Death to the niggers! No quarter!' Now what the hell you reckon them Rebs gonna do they come on us fightin' cheek by jowl with them stinkin' darkies?!"

"Hell, ain't by no doin' of ours."

"You gonna stop and 'splain that to Johnny?!"

"I'll be damned if you ain't talkin' horse sense. What we oughta do—" The hoarse voice dropped too low for David to hear. More voices joined in an inaudible murmur.

"Hell yeah!" the shrill voice rose. "We kill them darkies ourselves, oughta prove to Johnny we ain't no lousy nigger-lovers!"

David gasped in shock and horror, scrambled from under the caisson. A line of six or seven men, bayonets at the ready, were quietly closing the distance to where Amos and two other Negro boys stood huddled, their eyes riveted to the wave of Reb troops pouring down the opposite slope. David jerked to his feet, stumbled after the men, screaming hoarsely, "Amos! Amos, look out!"

His yells went unheard. He ran faster, his field glasses banging his chest. He yanked them off, clutched the leather strap in his fist. The soldier nearest to Amos prepared to plunge the bayonet into his back. David sprinted. "Amos! Amos! Leave him alone! Leave him alone, you goddamn bastard! Amos!!" he shrieked.

Amos leaped aside as his assailant lunged. David swung the field glasses on their strap. The heavy glasses smashed into the side of the white infantryman's face. Blood streamed from his ear and nose. The soldier next to him spun in disbelief, started furiously toward David. He swung the glasses wildly at the man, heard the sickening snap of bone, pulled his arm back to strike again when a searing blow struck the back of his head, sent him reeling to the ground.

He rocked dizzily on his hands and knees, barely taking in the sounds of struggle raging above him or the more distant yells of the Reb troops streaming into the crater. He felt himself yanked to his feet then, dragged toward the slope by Amos and a second, unfamiliar black soldier, pulled roughly up the crater side, pelted by loose dirt and debris.

Then they had clawed their way to the top and Amos' wiry arms jerked him over the rim. David stumbled blindly across the expanse of field, clinging to the two boys with desperate strength, only dimly aware of the blue-clad mob streaming by in a single-minded, frenzied dash for the Union lines. The crash of artillery sounded in his ears like distant thunder. The Union breastworks swam up before him and consciousness fell away.

Chapter 24 - 1864

GRINNING VICIOUSLY, DEMONS CAME AT HIM WITH BAYONETS. He shrank back into the horde of dead men around him. The devils shrieked with laughter, swung their weapons with gleeful abandon, lopping off legs and arms and pitching them into the smoking pit that yawned behind them. David struggled to flee; the mob of screaming, moaning men pinned him where he stood. The bloody bayonets flashed toward him. He closed his eyes, screaming, felt a hand grab his. "It's all right now." The voice was firm, warmly familiar.

"Zach? Oh God, Zach, did they get you too?"

"It's all right, David," the voice repeated. "There's nothing to fear. I've got hold of your hand." Zach's body bulked against him reassuringly. The demons drew back in dismay.

David drew a breath of incredible relief. "Oh God, Zach! Thank God!"

"It's all right, David. Are you awake now?"

He opened his eyes. Wounded men lay all around him on the hard clay ground, bodies bound in bloody bandages, some moaning or crying out, others still with shock. A heap of discarded limbs was tossed on the ground outside the surgeons' tent, a swarm of flies buzzing above them. The stench of gore hung over everything. Above him a cloudless sky soared to infinity. "I'm still alive," he murmured.

"How do you feel?" Al asked him. Her hand gripped his. He turned toward her. The motion filled his head with throbbing pain. Nausea assailed him. The sensations were unimportant next to his growing joy at having survived. He smiled at her weakly. "I've a pretty fierce headache, but—"

"No wonder," Al interrupted. "Reckon you got a pretty hard knock on the head. You'll be all right though. I got one of the doctors to take a look at you. He said there's no sign of skull fracture, just a flesh wound." She paused. "That colored boy told me you saved him."

"They were going to kill him," he said slowly, half under his breath. "Just stab him in cold blood to save their own skins. God, Zach was right. There are worse sins."

"What?"

He shook his head, bringing on a new wave of pain. "Never mind." Al gave him a quick smile. "You never let on you were so brave."

"Oh God, Al, I'm not brave. I didn't— I just—"

"Still and all, you could of got yourself killed. I was plumb scared to death when I first saw you, matter of fact. Thought I'd be writing your pa like we had to Colin's wife. But the doctor says scalp wounds always bleed like a stuck pig."

He closed his eyes, pictured his father's face on receiving such a missive. At least he'd have had Mike nearby to turn to. He wasn't alone in the world the way Zach was, for all his acquaintances. Hell, she'd never have known to write Zach. He'd have had no idea— Though he supposed Leslie would have mentioned it in print. He envisioned Zach coming on the item unawares, as he sat after supper in the boarding-house parlor. Or would Elliot have rushed to inform him, waiting slyly for his reaction? Not that Zach would've been unduly distressed, he supposed. He'd made it pretty plain he was through caring for him. David opened his eyes, gazed unseeing at the blue of the sky, remembering the loving pressure of Zach's hand on his.

Don't be a damn fool, he told himself then. You don't stop caring just like that. Hell, he hadn't stopped caring for Zach. Not for a minute. He made a weak effort to sit up. His head swam. "I'm going back to New York," he said.

"Don't try and sit up now!" Al pushed him gently back down. "You can't go traveling anywhere till you get that cut on your head stitched up. The doctor that examined you couldn't take time to do it with so many boys worse off. Told me just to keep this cloth pressed against it to stop the bleeding."

Now that he'd made up his mind, a delay of even a few hours seemed impossible to bear. David fingered the makeshift bandage gingerly. "It's stopped bleeding, I'm pretty sure. I can—"

"Don't be headstrong, David. The doctors'll get to you 'fore too much longer."

David looked at the gruesome spectacle around him, winced at the steadily growing pile of arms and legs. "Overnight at least. It could even be a day or two more. I've got to get away from here. And you

A Different Sin

ought to do the same. Hell, we're still within range of a shell. If you can get me a spot in one of the ambulance cars—

"No, wait! Listen to me, Al. It won't hurt me to ride in the car. It's only a few miles. And from there I can get on one of the steamers taking men north from the City Point hospital, stretch out on the deck the same as if I was lying here, be in Alexandria in a day. I'll stop and rest at my father's house, I promise. Remember, he's a doctor. I'd sooner trust him to take care of me than one of the surgeons here, anyway."

The airless freight car was laid with straw bedding to cushion the ride along the spur of uneven track laid from the front to City Point. Even so, the short trip was worse than he'd anticipated. David stumbled dizzily off the medical transport, clutching at Al. She looked up at him with quick concern. "I'm okay, Al. I—" He tried to marshal his thoughts. "I guess if you could ask Ed Forbes to take charge of my horse. If the poor thing hasn't wandered off or been stolen by now. Though I suppose whoever Leslie finds to take my place will—"

"Hush now, David. I'll see to it. Don't worry over it." She paused. "Reckon you might write me a few words once you get home, let me know you made it okay."

"I will. I promise. And you be careful, hear? I— Oh God, Alice, I don't know how to thank you. I'm— I'm sorry. I mean—"

"It's all right, David. I reckon there was never meant to be any great romance between you and me." She gave him a faint smile, reached up and brushed a bit of straw from his beard. "You go on back to New York and make up that quarrel. I reckon as eager as you are to get back to her, that sweetheart of yours must be a plumb special lady."

"I fail to understand your hurry," Dr. Carter said testily, settling himself more comfortably in the wing chair. "You've already played the part of a fool, dashing up here from the front lines without getting your wound attended to and now—"

"I've got to get back to New York, Dad. I told you. I feel well enough to travel. Better, probably, than if I'd waited for some army sawbones when I could get better doctoring from my own father."

His father smiled. "I guess my skills aren't as rusty as I'd feared. But I don't mind telling you, son, when you stumbled in here yesterday my heart was in my mouth. I just thank the Lord you weren't hit on the site of your old concussion. Another inch or two and—"

"I know, Dad," David crossed his legs restlessly, recrossed them the other way. His father had insisted on cleaning the cut with stinging carbolic acid before suturing it with hands he kept from trembling by sheer force of will, his face tense with strain. David smiled at him

198

affectionately. "I expect you're right. I should've—"

"What's done is done," Dr. Carter said firmly. "Thank God, it's worked out for the best. But now you're here—"

David glanced at the mantel clock. "I really have to go, Dad. If I wait any longer I'll never make the train."

"I can't believe you're going to rush off after less than twenty-four hours. Setting aside the question of your stamina, I should think a simple respect for your father's wishes— It's not as if we got a chance to visit with any frequency these days."

"I'll come back for a longer visit. I promise. In a month or two. Three at the very most."

"David. I'm seventy-seven years old. In two or three months I could be dead and buried. And the only thing on your mind, apparently, is trying to please that editor of yours. Is he more important to you than your own father?"

"It has nothing to do with Leslie."

"Mail him your pictures. Or send them by courier, if it is that urgent. You've just come within a hairsbreadth of dying. You deserve a few weeks to recuperate."

"Dad, I told you. I'm not rushing back on account of Leslie." A steel vise fastened itself around David's head. "It has nothing to do with Leslie," he repeated irritably.

"Well then, I fail to see any reason why you can't stay on. I'm all alone here, as you very well know, and—"

"You've got Mike. He's right across the river."

"Michael's a doctor, David. Peoples' lives depend on him. You can't expect him to drop his work and come running over here all the time."

David winced, rose abruptly from his chair. He crossed the room to his father, put a hand on his shoulder. "Dad, I'm sorry. I've really got to—"

"Why, in God's name? What's the urgent business that you have to rush back for?"

"There's— there's someone I need to see."

"Someone— You just told me—"

"Not Leslie. Someone— someone I'm fond of." The band of pain tightened around his head. He closed his eyes, pressed his hands to his lids. Zach's face swam up in front of him. *Dear God, let him be waiting for me. Don't let him have found someone else. Please God.* He opened his eyes. His father was beaming at him.

"You might have said so! That's wonderful, David. The best news you could have brought me! After all this time. I resigned myself years ago to the fact of your being a bachelor. And now— When will you be married? Don't put it off, I beg you. God willing, I'll live long enough to see a son of yours."

Christ! Why in hell had he opened his mouth? David cut into his father's happy babbling. "Dad. Please, Dad, I'm not getting married."

"You're not— But you just said—"

"I didn't say a word about getting married. Dad, I've got to go now. I'll—"

His father's hand shot out, seized his wrist with surprising strength. "Don't run off on me, David! What kind of affair are you having, that you aren't planning— Is she a colored woman? Is that it? No? Well then— Son. You're not having a liaison with a married woman!"

"Dad, for God's sake—"

Dr. Carter tightened his grip on David's wrist, overrode his words. "Have you taken leave of your senses? Leaving aside the question of morality, do you realize the danger you're courting? The chance of being called out to a duel? Or worse yet, shot down on the street with no warning at all? Can you tell me this woman is worth—"

"It's not a woman!" David jerked loose from his father's grasp, stared with annoyance at the pained bewilderment on the old man's face. "Dad, just leave it alone, will you? It's not important."

"Important enough for you to desert your father and go charging off to New York with an unhealed head wound! David, I demand—"

"It's a man. It's important that I see him."

"I don't understand you, David. What is it you have to see this man about?"

"Damn it, Dad, it's none of your—" David broke off, tried to choke back the anger welling up in him. "He's a friend. A good friend of mine. Zachary Walker. You've met him."

"Just a friend and yet you have to—"

His father's reproach was drowned out by drumbeats of anger pulsing through him now, coming in violent bursts, pounding against his temples more fiercely than the throbbing headache, anger that seemed to have been a part of him as far back as he could remember. David trembled, fought desperately for control. *Stop it, stop it for Christ's sake! Tell him anything, a business deal, a—* "Not just a friend. I love him. I love him, do you hear!"

The room was filled with the silence that follows the accidental shattering of some favorite heirloom.

"David, what—"

"I love him," he repeated deliberately. "I have a— an unnatural lust for him."

"What in God's name—" his father demanded. But his face was already filling with unwilling comprehension. "David, no! You're overwrought! You don't know what you're saying!"

"I know, goddammit! I'm a nance. A sodomite."

"I've read of such— such *abominations,*" his father whispered. "But I couldn't bring myself to believe— No!" He rose, grabbed David's shoulders, shook him like a small boy. "It's a sin! You're committing a mortal sin, don't you understand that, you and that, that filthy son of a bitch!"

"Shut up, dammit!" David wrenched himself loose from his father's grasp, trembling, his eyes filling with tears of rage. "Just shut up about him, dammit!"

"David, I forbid you! Do you hear me? You're not to go back to him! It's a sin, do you hear me, a mortal sin!"

"Who the hell are you to talk about sin, Dad?"

"David! Don't you dare—"

"Who the hell are you to talk about sin, damn it! Are you so goddamn free of sin? At least we're not bringing any little nigger bastards into the world!" Through his tears he saw his father wince with pain as if he'd struck him. He bolted through the front door and ran blindly down the street.

Chapter 25 - 1864

D<small>AVID LAID HIS ARM ALONG THE BACK OF THE TRAIN SEAT</small>, rested his cheek on it, trying to cushion his head from the rocking of the car. The doors at either end crashed open and shut, admitting the conductor, newsboys, urchins offering gum drops, tobacco and cakes. He ignored their cries, struggled to fix words in his mind to say to Zach, words to mend the rift between them. He'd been so certain Zach would still care. But suppose— He could see Zach's face when he'd left him, cold with anger, as he stalked from his room with bitter finality.

He shuddered, gazed blankly at the passing houses, where lamplight began to show in windows, one by one. The sky darkened, the overhead lanterns spilled their dim light through the train car, turning the passing landscape to wavering reflections. He stared at his face, tried to picture Zach's warm, loving smile. Instead his father's image formed before him, welcoming him home with anxious concern, fumbling bravely through his seldom-used medical kit.

The doctor's concerned frown vanished, his face turned gray with shock, sagged into deeper lines of age. Christ, he's almost eighty years old! How the hell could I have screamed at him like that? My God, at his age anything could happen. His heart— I could've killed him! The train slowed for Baltimore. David got to his feet, nearly fell down the high steps in his haste and raced across to the south-bound platform of the station.

The trip back home occupied seeming endless hours, waiting for the Washington-bound train, searching frantically for a cab to cross the city, the checkpoints at the Long Bridge. His watch showed nearly midnight as he stumbled through the cobblestone streets of his hometown.

The house was dark. David pushed the door open, stood a moment in the front hall. By the light of the streetlamp outside the parlor window he saw his father's figure, upright and still in the wing chair. "Dad?" Silence answered him. David held his breath till he made out the rise and fall of his father's chest, his sudden startled exhalation.

He ran across the room, knelt down by his chair. "Dad? Oh God, Dad, I'm sorry."

Dr. Carter turned slowly. "I prayed you'd return. I thank God you've come to your senses," he said heavily.

"I'm sorry. I had no right to judge you. I know I don't deserve your forgiveness, but—"

"Stop playing the fool, David. Get off your knees to me. It's God's forgiveness you need to ask." David fumbled behind him, sat down on the edge of the ottoman. "I will. I mean, I do. I didn't mean what I said about Mike. I don't know why—"

"It's a bit late for you to reproach me for my sins, David. I've paid for my weakness with Hetty."

"I know. I know you have, Dad." David twined his fingers together, stared down at them. "You and Hetty. I don't even think anymore— If you sinned, it was a different sin," he said, speaking almost to himself. "Denying Mike, selling him—"

"David!" Dr. Carter's fingers dug into his shoulder. "My behavior is not at issue here! I'm talking about that— *that abomination* you confessed to me this evening! Or— No! I can't believe— It isn't true! Some kind of sick fancy— You've a head injury, you're not yourself." He gripped David tighter, his face wild with hope.

"Christ, why would I say—" *For God's sake, tell him what he wants to hear!* He couldn't. Nor could he understand why he was unable to grasp the retreat his father offered. "It's the truth, Dad. I'm sorry. I wish I could tell you otherwise. I— I've never been able to love a woman. I've been attracted to men—to Zach—for years, but I was never able to come to terms with it till now." He reached out suddenly, laid a hand tentatively over his father's.

Dr. Carter took his hand from David's shoulder, gently covered their clasped hands. "Thank God you've come to your senses before it's too late! When you ran out of here I was so frightened for you. And all I could do was pray. I knew it was the weight of your guilt made you lash out at me like that. But you'll be able to rid yourself of that burden now. God forgives the repentant sinner."

"Oh God. I— Dad, I came back to ask your forgiveness for the way I spoke to you. Not to— I still care for Zach, very much so. I mean to spend the rest of my life with him if he's still—"

"No! My God, no!" The old man's face crumpled in pain again. He lowered his head into his hands, shaking with sobs.

"Dad. Dad, please." David watched helplessly as his father wept, finally put an arm hesitantly around his shoulders. Dr. Carter sat upright, threw off David's hand. "You're committing a mortal sin, don't you understand that?"

David looked at his father, started to reach out a hand to him again, drew it back. "If I am, then I'll have to answer for it when my time comes."

"Son, I forbid you to return to this man! Do you hear me?"

"Christ, Dad. If you knew how I've wrestled— If I have to answer for it, then I will. But not to you. I've got to live according to my own lights now. I'm a grown man." For a moment, absurdly, it seemed the first time he'd realized it.

Dr. Carter drew in his breath in a broken sob, a sound heavy with defeat, then gazed at David in a silence marred only by the separate rhythms of their breathing, the ticking of the mantel clock. A slow stream of tears trickled unchecked down the wrinkled hollows of his cheeks. David rose, gently brushed the wetness from his father's face with his fingers, touched his arm. "Dad, it's late. Let me help you up to bed. We can talk in the morning."

"Take your hands off me, David." The old doctor grasped the chair arms, pushed himself stiffly to his feet, eyes still blurry with tears. "If you leave here to persist in that abomination, then don't come back to this house again."

"Dad! Wait, please! You don't—" His father turned, placed a hand on the bannister, began to haul himself slowly up the stairs. "I don't know where I'll be living," David said to his back. "If you change— If you want to contact me for anything, I guess you can write in care of *Leslie's*." He waited through another long moment of silence, opened the door and walked out of his father's house.

Now that he'd finally come to the end of the day-long ride in the packed train, the ferry across the Hudson, the frantic rush through the crowded New York streets, his fears of the evening before returned with paralyzing abruptness. He'd cut himself off from his father's love. If Zach turned him away— David stood rooted to the sidewalk in front of Mrs. Chapman's, oblivious to the clatter of carriage wheels on the cobblestones, the throng of Saturday night revelers hurrying toward restaurants and theaters.

Hell, he'd spent the whole endless trip thinking and rethinking his words to Zach. He couldn't turn back now. He yanked the doorknob from the hand of an exiting boarder, burst inside. Two elderly men were making their way from the dining room. They gave David a look of surprise, nodded uncertainly. He brushed past them, ran upstairs, turned down the hall toward Zach's room. The door opposite Zach's opened. Elliot stepped out, giving a final pat to his cravat, smoothing his mustache. He gave David a puzzled glance. "Can I help you?"

David winced, recalling Elliot's incredulous stare that night he'd found them out, felt himself flush. "Is Zach here, Elliot?"

"David? Jeez, I didn't recognize you with that beard. Chrissake, you look like something the cat dragged in. Where the hell you been? Leslie's been on pins and needles waiting to hear from you. Did you bring your sketches of the mine crater? Ed sent word that—"

"Never mind that now. I'm looking for Zach. Is he here?"

"Jesus." A smirk spread across Elliot's face. "So you really are nothing but a nance. You've come running back to him, is that it?"

Hell, how could he face him? How could he even face him? David took a deep breath, forced himself to look Elliot square in the eyes. "Yes, that's right. If he'll still have me, that is."

"Well, Holy Mother of God!" Elliot's smirk wavered, was chased across his face by shock, bewilderment, a reluctant flicker of respect, then newly expectant scorn as he glanced from David to a point just behind him. "For chrissake! I might've looked for that from Zach there, but—"

David spun around. Zach stood in his open doorway, his face working. David took a step toward him, Elliot dismissed from his mind. He swallowed, his mouth going dry, unable to give voice to any of the loving phrases, the apologies he'd rehearsed over and over. He took another step toward Zach, his hands held out in wordless appeal.

For a seeming eternity of heartbeats David waited, Zach's face hidden from him now by a curtain of stinging tears. Then Zach's hands closed warmly over his, pressed with loving fierceness as he drew him into his room.